STAR RIDERS
OF REN

Also by the author

Guardians of the Singreale. Volume I in the Singreale Chronicles

STAR RIDERS
OF REN

Volume II in the Singreale Chronicles

Calvin Miller

1817

Harper & Row, Publishers, San Francisco

Cambridge, Hagerstown, New York, Philadelphia
London, Mexico City, São Paulo, Sydney

FIRST EDITION

Designer: Jim Mennick

Illustrations by Daniel San Souci

Library of Congress Cataloging in Publication Data

Miller, Calvin.
  STAR RIDERS OF REN.

  (The Singreale chronicles; v. 2)
  Sequel to: Guardians of the Singreale.
  I. Title. II. Series.
PS3563.I376S53 1983 vol. 2   813'.54   82-48408
ISBN 0-06-250576-9

---

86 87 10 9 8 7 6 5 4 3 2

Contents

I.   In the Shadow of the Tower Altar   *1*

II.   The Changelings   *17*

III.   The Knights of Ren   *35*

IV.   Festival of Light   *57*

V.   The Nativity   *73*

VI.   Rengraaden   *91*

VII.   Grendelynden   *105*

VIII.   The Deception   *121*

IX.   The Miserians   *141*

X.   The Descent   *161*

XI.   The Edge of War   *179*

XII.   The Siege of the Six Bridges   *193*

XIII.   Smeade   *213*

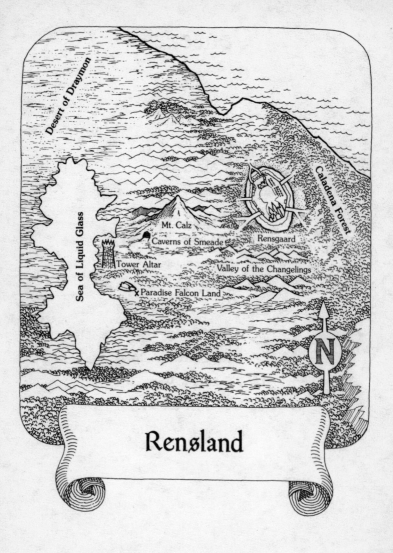

Desert of Draymon

Sea of Liquid Glass

Mt. Calz

Caverns of Smeade

Tower Altar

× Paradise Falcon Land

Rensgaard

Valley of the Changelings

Caladena Forest

N

Rensland

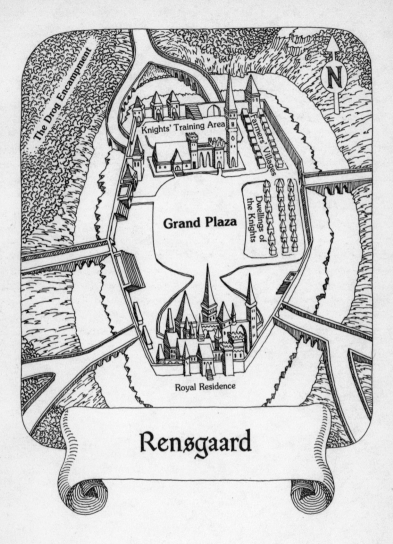

The Drog Encampment

Knights' Training Area

Farmers' Villages

Grand Plaza

Dwellings of the Knights

Royal Residence

Rensgaard

From star to star the conflicts flee
To mock each nation's heraldry.
Some battle cry splits every sky!
Red bootprints trek the galaxy.

CHAPTER I
In the Shadow of
the Tower Altar

REXEL, THE FALCON, rode uneasily on Raccoman's shoulder and peered into the final darkness of the long night. Already morning gently touched the night with fingers of silver. The bright stars at the bottom of the sky riveted the uncertain horizon to the inky sea.

The void through which Raccoman sailed with his wife, Velissa, was warm. He smiled. The starlight glinted on his white teeth.

Velissa smiled back into the shaggy face of her inventor husband, whose face was ringed with gray fur, except for the top of his sun-bronzed head. Neither of them spoke. Both were afraid that the slightest whisper would shatter the enchantment of the night sky that now enveloped them. They sailed on a porcelain dream through a splendor as fragile as a ceramic globe. Their eyes conversed in an eloquent and lively dialogue. The world was diamond-lit. It was an uncharted cosmos, as magic as their marriage and the golden glider on which they surfed the high, night winds.

The craft on which they were seated was a dark, sleek blur by night. The day would wash it with braggy colors and leave it a flamboyant yellow in the sun. The windfoils of which it was built had been welded faultlessly together by the ingenious Graygill who now piloted them through the glittering void.

Piloting was a sophisticated word for the Paradise Falcon—for that was the name of the wondrous plane. The mechanism had no motor, and the only resistance to direction the ship could offer was that which an aeleron rod and primitive rudder could make. Raccoman steered by stomping the rods and nudging the rudder shaft. Thus, playing with the eddies and drafts of stratospheric winds, the air did all that he commanded and lifted them to scrape the underside of stars.

Raccoman and Velissa Dakktare had not always known of these upper winds. Their craft had been hurled upward by the volleys of the tilt winds. It was from these tilt winds that they had first learned the skill of sky-surfing. From this cold, winter sport, they had learned the art of free flight. Now their little science proclaimed itself from the broad, curved deck of the Paradise Falcon.

They had no idea where they were going and, thus, no way of

telling when they should arrive. They flew in pursuit of a land that none of their less daring friends believed in. Through a telescope, they had seen a moving starfield. The moving stars had been invisible to the naked eyes of the other Graygills who once shared their valley. Now the lofty elevation of this flight had matured the vision of these two Graygills. In the windswept stratosphere, the roving stars had become mounted riders, mysteriously opaque and lit from within.

They had no sense of the altitude at which they flew. They did know they must fly as high as they could to travel beyond the red beaches of their own island continent. Somewhere beyond the uncrossed sea, there were other lands that the Star Riders called home.

The trip had already been long and would be longer.

The Paradise Falcon dawdled along in the sluggish upper winds, never moving any faster than the zephyrs that drove it through the night. Raccoman and his wife had not been able to keep pace with the Star Riders, whose swift mounts could speed like blazing comets and leave them snarled in glittering trails of light. The mounted riders they pursued seemed to pass a tangled, glistening net about them and then close them into empty darkness.

So they had found themselves in the starry company the second night of their lonely flight. They never saw the flying knights again. They knew their own craft soared in the same direction that they had last seen the mounted Titans sail. Still, they had no idea how long it would take them to find the distant land from which the riders had come.

On the second day of their journey, Raccoman and Velissa left the snowfields of their own land. Now nothing looked familiar. The world below them tangled itself in knotted forests and then in bald terrain.

On the third day of their flight, they passed above the red beaches of their own continent. Below them, the green ocean churned, yet the sky met the sea in friendship. The vast expanse of water made them uneasy. Like other Graygills, they had never learned the art of swimming. They knew that the Paradise Falcon could never survive an ocean landing and that neither of them would be able to survive in the waters over which they soared. It was now the twentieth day of their odyssey. Raccoman's bride was growing impatient.

Velissa had looked forward to the morning, for they had agreed to take only a small sip of water each morning and night in order that they might survive what they expected would be a long trip. Raccoman had brought only water and a little food.

As the first rays of sunlight began to appear, Raccoman quietly took the water jar from the box he had welded to the upper deck of his craft. He took a drink and handed the jar to Velissa, who also took a sip and passed the jar back to her husband.

As he started to replace the jar in its box, he heard a gurgling, cooing sound from the throat of Rexel, who was still sitting immobile on his left shoulder.

"All right, old friend," Raccoman said grudgingly to the falcon, "but try to make this last all day!" He poured a little water into Velissa's free hand. Rexel walked down the sleeve of Raccoman Dakktare's mackinaw and placed his heavy beak into the water. He took a beakful, then tilted his head back and swallowed noisily as was his custom. The short, light feathers around his golden eyes fluttered in the breeze that had grown with the coming of light.

"Perhaps today," said Rexel when he had finished drinking.

The phrase was not at all cryptic to the pilot and his wife, for each new day, as Rexel took his morning flight, their one hope was that the falcon would return with the report of land somewhere in the watery plain.

"Now?" asked Rexel.

"Now," agreed Velissa.

Rexel stretched his giant wings and craned his neck awkwardly from his night of sleep. Velissa, feeling cramped from the long journey, now mimicked the falcon, stretching her arms high over her head. When her arms seemed nearly to become disjointed, she ceased her effort, relaxed, and yawned. "It's going to be a lovely day," she said with a smile. Her husband seemed overserious, and she playfully pulled his gray sidelocks. She liked him even if he was eight hundred years her senior. He responded to her teasing by scratching one of his pointed ears that jutted through the narrow fringe of hair that fell from his bald head.

Rexel ignored Velissa's romantic adulation of her husband, pulled his wings in close to his body, and bolted into the sky in an explosion of feathers that soon carried him far from the ship.

"Oh, Raccoman, if only we could fly like Rexel! How do you know we will still be able to walk when the trip is over? My legs feel paralyzed."

"You'll walk," he said with a grin.

He grabbed her sidelocks and pulled her face to his—their kiss in the cold, thin air was now a custom. "Velissa Dakktare, you're the high-flying half of a marvelous pair." Raccoman, his usual non-modest self, was the marvelous other half, of course.

When they could no longer see Rexel, Velissa slipped her mitten from her hand and thrust her hand into the neck of Raccoman's tunic that was under his mackinaw. He smiled warmly and let his arm sweep the wind before them.

"There's a land out there! We wait till then . . .
A time and place for us again."

He kissed her in a way that expressed a certain unwillingness to wait. She was prettiest of all in the dawn light. He suddenly shuttered in grim foreboding that he had brought her with him on what might be a perilous adventure.

When the sun had risen high above the horizon, they enjoyed its warming rays. Both of them had noticed that the air had grown warmer every day as they sailed south and east. The green sea now began to blaze turquoise in the full light of day.

To relieve the boredom of the passing days, Raccoman had composed a half-dozen ballads. Absentmindedly, Velissa now began to sing one of them. It was a madrigal sort of tune where Velissa's part in the treble voice raced ahead of Raccoman's basso three syllables to one.

"A welder married a Graygill lass
    And carried her upward into night
He scanned the stones of Demmerron Pass
    And kissed his bride in the course of flight.
So few have flown in the high, thin air.
    and none dared this footless height.
But we have flown where the falcons dare,
    and touched in the upper golden light."

Raccoman joined in, his the counter melody:

"The zephyrs fear
What the listening ear
Of those who brave
The void can hear.
Our voices sing
Where harmonies

Through earless voids
May dare to ring."

They embraced awkwardly. They did not dare abandon the fiber straps of their side-by-side seats. Raccoman brushed Velissa's cheek with the soft back of his mittened hand as she began again:

"There's a land ahead in the night-bound sea
Where the winds are tamed in tranquility
And the stars rise bright in the inky night
Till the waves are silver filigree.
From the continent that's our intent,
The Titans soar as fields of stars.
Our journey's bent till the winds are spent
And the zephyrs name our destiny."

Raccoman's melody died with hers, and they sat silently staring into the endless void before them.

In the distance, they saw Rexel approaching them at a very fast speed. In his beak, he carried a lavender twig bearing reddish, transparent leaves.

"By tomorrow you will be at the shore of the new land," said Rexel after he had landed on the stabilizer bar and placed the twig into Raccoman's outstretched hand. "The water's pure, and the forest is thick!" the falcon added as an afterthought.

"Were there any people?" Velissa asked as soon as the great bird had folded his wings and was comfortably settled.

"I am sure of it," said Rexel, "for I saw huge structures rising from the forest floor—still, I saw no people."

"None of the Titan Riders?" asked Raccoman, with a touch of disappointment in his voice.

Rexel's silence was reply enough to the question.

Raccoman and Velissa were amazed at both the twig and Rexel's swift return. They knew Rexel never lied, but they felt that he knew more than he spoke. The bird had journeyed to the new land as if he knew the way perfectly. Already once or twice in the course of flight, he had suggested a better heading than Raccoman had taken.

Their conversation did not die, but it thinned as they floated forward. To all appearance, the breeze that pushed them completely stopped. The sky and sea were void of any marks by which they might presume to measure their progress. Occasionally, the upper winds would gust upon them at a speed greater than their craft traveled. At such moments, Velissa's sidelocks would flutter in the draft.

Both Raccoman and Velissa thought hard upon the world they approached. The day seemed to bear some new foreboding. They had flown to escape the land of the Graygills, torn by a desperate conflict that left only widows to defend it. The new land that had seemed a refuge to them at the beginning of flight now suddenly left them unsure.

They both hated the war they had fled as much as they loved the home they had lost. The war had cost them everything. Velissa had buried her best friend, the serpent Doldeen. Her father was missing, and Raccoman's Moonrhyme uncle she had last seen face-down in a snowfield. The refugees of Canby, all widows from the Battle of Demmerron Pass, were now beginning the exodus. Theirs was a perilous winter migration to the cliffs of the Moonrhymes and a hope for asylum. The power-mad Parsky now ruled the troubled valley from his seat of tyranny, Maldoon, the once-proud castle of light.

"Good riddance—we are free of the valley of terror!" exclaimed Velissa, suddenly letting her thoughts be spoken. To call the red forests of her former home a "valley of terror" seemed strange. But it was true.

"Raccoman," Velissa said, "my father's home was in ashes and by now, perhaps, the Iron Destroyer has . . ." She faltered and could not go on.

"Destroyed our home as well," Raccoman said, finishing her statement. He patted her arm, then said to comfort her, "But it wasn't much of a home."

There was a wistfulness in his voice that denied what he had just said. His thoughts stole his words as they floated through the morning that soon rode the afternoon into evening. They talked as the darkness came on again, and ate more of the food they had brought and drank a little more of their daily reserves of water.

After midnight, they fell asleep and began the mutual hum customary to Graygills' slumber, proving to the earless void that they were, indeed, asleep. Raccoman, too, had shut his eyes and ears against the silent stars and the humming void. They were dozing as best they could while still belted upright in their seats by the fiber straps.

Their craft experienced a sudden jolt.

Both woke up instantly.

Now there was a breeze blowing directly in their faces.

"Oh, no!" cried Velissa. "The wind has changed. We'll be blown off course."

"Worse than that!" exclaimed her husband, "There is no wind!"

Raccoman had expected this to happen, but now that it had, he felt insecure. Throughout their flight, they had been propelled forward by the upper winds. Now they dropped from the upper layer of winds into the calmer undersky. In the immobile air, their craft appeared to lurch forward at a fast speed. Yet, as Raccoman knew and Velissa would soon discover, this was an illusion.

Daylight came after an eternity or two, and the ocean appeared much closer than it had in the early days of their flight. In violent suddenness, it rose toward the underside of the Paradise Falcon.

Rexel took to the air just as Raccoman and Velissa caught sight of the distant beaches that ringed the new continent in white sands and green seas, for he realized that his added weight would speed the descent of the plane.

Already it seemed to be plunging seaward at an alarming rate. Moments later, the travelers saw that they had sailed over the shoreline, but still they plummeted ever downward toward an uncertain terrain.

A green mist rose about the brown and purple foilage of rain forests much thicker than those of their own land.

Now that the Graygills had left the upper air and realized the climate was becoming warmer, Raccoman unbuttoned his heavy mackinaw. Velissa, who had been sitting on her cape for the extra warmth it provided, now pulled the garment away from her so that it fluttered behind her in the wind like a flag—trailing the yellow ship.

They hurtled over naked beaches that rose abruptly into purple, forested hills. To the southeast, Raccoman could see a gleaming set of white spires and a smaller break of the square domes and glistening architecture that stuck through the roof of the forest. He depressed the stabilizer with his foot. The rudder bar groaned, but the glider rose only a little. There was simply not enough wind to turn the ship. To the right of the ship rose a snow-capped mountain that cut off the Graygill's view of the alabaster city, and they turned and settled in at an odd angle.

In the forest just ahead of them, a large, black structure rose to a great height as it jutted through the trees. Its form was an elongated pyramid, with what seemed to be thousands of steps running from the base up the steep sides to a flattened place at the top. Raccoman wondered whether it was a dwelling or some sort of shrine or altar.

Velissa's eyes swept the purple forest before them. The angle that her eyes followed measured the swift uprising of the forest.

"Raccoman, we're going to crash in the trees!" she cried in panic.

"Cover your face!" he yelled into the onrush of air.

Velissa grasped her blue cape, which fluttered and snapped in the brisk path of their descent. Awkwardly, she pulled the heavy cape forward over her shoulders and covered her head and face. Raccoman braced his arm across his face and stamped both feet on the rudder rods. The nose of the sail plane rose abruptly and the back dropped.

The seconds seemed an eternity. At last, they heard a brushing sound.

The bottom of their craft dragged on the leafy upper arms of the forest.

The sail plane skipped a couple of times on the treetops, then stopped suddenly as the aeleron rod was snared by a stiff, unbending limb. The craft, hanging from the tree limb, nosed downward, and the Graygills were sent hurtling into the fiber straps. But the straps held firm.

Raccoman and his wife were stunned by their sudden stop, but neither of them was injured. When Velissa drew back the blue cape, she could see that they were still a long way from the ground and hanging precariously. She looked anxiously at Raccoman.

"What do we do now?" she asked.

Before Raccoman could answer, Rexel fluttered in between them and the ground.

The limb that held the aeleron rod snapped. The craft took another dive and was snagged again on the tree's lower branches. This second plunge jolted the Graygills face downward, and the uprushing mist still obscured the ground, but it looked for a moment to them as though the mist would swallow them up and be their final view of life. Once more they found themselves hanging by the straps, but this time only a few feet off the ground.

Rexel had been surprised by the second plunge and had leapt to the air barely in time to save himself.

Raccoman decided on a course of action. He undid the fiber

strap that bound him to the Paradise Falcon and lurched forward, swinging down onto the bright yellow surface of his now inglorious flying marvel. He slid down the surface as far as the fiber strap would allow and jolted to a stop when he came to the end of it.

He released the strap and slid out of Velissa's sight into the green mist.

"Ha-hoo, I'm alive!" he called upward, after he thumped noisily to the ground. Velissa heard his voice, but could not see him.

Though she could not see him, she decided to commit herself to the same course of action that he had taken. With effort, she too undid her strap and slid violently forward on the shiny windfoils until she jolted and dangled like a pendulum swinging gently across the yellow surface. The green vapor was almost at her boots. She was afraid to let go.

"Where are you, Raccoman?" she asked the cloud of green beneath her.

"Just out of your way, I hope," he laughed. "Unbuckle and slide on down."

"I have unbuckled; I'm hanging on the strap."

"Well, let go then!" he cried.

She did and hurtled into the green cloud, striking Dakktare full in the chest and knocking both of them to the ground at once.

They heard a familiar flutter as Rexel broke through the low ceiling of mist and settled on a log.

"We are here—alive and free
How false the common falsity
That taught
Estermann—one continent—one sea."

It was a foolish proverb that all of his former friends had quoted. "We have proved the cliché wrong," laughed Velissa. "There was another land, and we're standing on it—yes, standing on it!" She stomped her feet, glad to feel the firm soil once again.

"It's a great ship," said Raccoman, looking upward where the green ceiling of mist was pierced by the yellow point of the sail plane.

The green mist seemed to lay thicker in some places than in others, though everywhere it was impossible to see through it.

Raccoman hadn't used his legs for many days and now he felt unsure of them. The same sensation came over Velissa as well. She, too, felt awkward to be standing after sitting for so long.

They embraced.

Suddenly Rexel croaked one word, "Beware!" and bolted through the green ceiling. The Graygills heard him fluttering out of sight above them. Then they heard his wingbeats stop as though he had found a limb again in the upper sunlight.

Velissa trembled. In the ominous silence of the jungle, some portent awaited them.

Raccoman led the way, and Velissa followed him, to a thick-set group of shrubs. They heard the cracking of limbs and twigs in the thick forest they faced.

"Ughum Hunga!" exclaimed a deep and breathy voice. "Hun, Hun, hunga!" It said, and yet it was more like a choked laughter than speech. The speaker was tall enough to rap the yellow nose of the sail plane, which protruded through the forest mist.

The creature with the breathy voice emerged from behind a brownish-purple tree trunk. In the midst of the grove, a being that was twice the size of the Graygills emerged.

Velissa cowered and shrank down. The evil form before her wore a cracked and leathery face—the head was sparsely bristled with short, stiff hair and otherwise completely bald. The huge eyes were bulged half-spheres of pale white that swam under thick mucous shields. The thin-lipped mouth smiled above heavy, rigid underjaws. The creature's arms and legs were large and ended in three digits. Several more of the hulks, all wearing crossed straps across their naked, leathery chests, soon emerged.

Another of them discovered the point of the Paradise Falcon and tapped it with a claw. "Gukka, Kalanka Hund, Thrane!" he said to the first and tallest of his fellow beast-warriors.

Velissa moved too rapidly in her panic and broke a small twig with her shoulder. She fell to her knees and her breath stopped. The snap had sounded like a clap of thunder. Instantly, the ugly warriors advanced. Raccoman pulled Velissa to her feet, and together they ran through the thicket. A fallen tree barred their way. Raccoman pulled Velissa to the top of the barrier and they jumped down on the opposite side and continued running.

They ran as fast as their stiff legs, unused to exercise, would carry them. Raccoman hurdled a series of small shrubs, dragging Velissa clumsily behind. Near the end of his breath and stamina, he collided into a huge pair of legs and fell backward from the impact. In the terror of their flight from the monsters, the Graygills had run into a second kind of being. Behind them were the monsters, and before them were six huge men, as tall as their evil predators, blond, and clad only in light mail and in tunics that were pale blue in contrast to Velissa's bright blue clothing. The one who seemed to be the leader of these blue-clad warriors had a strong brow that rested handsomely on his wide cheeks. His face was devoid of any mustache or beard. Had his commanding air not been obvious in his very presence, the large white falcon on his breast would have marked him as the leader of the other five.

Raccoman realized that these tall men were the Star Riders he had pursued through the magic skies above his distant homeland, for their identity proclaimed itself from an ethereal banner one of them carried. And now Raccoman knew that they did not always fly, for here in the forest they had no mounts, and their very earth-bound defenses left the Graygills very much afraid.

"Hunga! Crangddammo!" exclaimed the creature with the cracked face who had pursued the Graygills and now emerged through the forest mist.

"Halt!" cried the Titan with the Falcon on his broad chest. All of the Star Riders stopped, standing rigidly in the path of the Graygills' pursuers.

"Gukka! Hallidan!" replied one of the beast-warriors. At the name of Hallidan, the beast-warriors all appeared to draw swords—and yet they didn't.

"Yes, Thrane, it is I," said the leader of the handsome warriors.

"Hughum! Mugrunga bandaggmo, Singreale!" said the leader of the monsters, extending an ugly claw toward Velissa. Velissa turned to Raccoman in terror.

"No, Drog. My master, Ren, intends to have it. We will take the treasure to our Lord," said the blue Titan.

"Singreale! Condungra! Gukka Hunga!" croaked the Drog. He lurched toward Velissa, and the tall knight stepped deliberately between the terrified Graygills and the monster. The fiend's eyes bulged in evil intention.

"I will have it for my master," said the handsome Hallidan. The five other fair-skinned Titan knights moved out of the green shrubs of the purple forest.

Velissa clutched the pouch at her bosom. She was dumbfounded that the two quarreling claimants seemed to have been waiting for her husband and herself. How could they have known? Yet, they knew, and their knowledge caused her to quail at a future as dark as the leathery monsters who demanded her treasure.

"It's as if they had expected us," said Velissa much too loudly to Raccoman.

"Ughum! Mugrunga Singreale!" grunted the beast-warrior. "Bandagmo! Gukka!" His ugly face hissed the venom of his words. Velissa felt that at any moment he would advance and take with force the diamond she wore in the pouch at her neck.

She retreated from the creature and drew nearer to Hallidan.

Hallidan drew his sword. It was a magnificent weapon—a flaming spine of rigid glass. The fire-glass blazed as it left the sheath. "Leave them alone," said the blue knight firmly. The knights behind Hallidan also drew their swords and raised their fiery blades toward the green mist ceiling.

"Gukka, Hunga!" rasped one of the ugly monsters.

From behind one of the black-caped Drogs stepped a small Graygill.

Velissa started, momentarily forgetting the two camps of rivals who now faced each other ready for battle.

"Father!" she cried, "I thought you were dead!"

"No, my child. You can see, I am not."

He came toward her.

"This is not your father," said Hallidan. "It is a Drog dressed in an image he draws from your mind. Look at him through the clear prisms of Singreale, and you will see." Velissa drew forth the diamond and held it to her eye.

"Give me the diamond, my dearest daughter!" demanded her father. Velissa gasped. Through the prismed facets of Singreale, she saw a dozen identical images, each a horrible fiend.

"It's true!" she cried. "You are not my father!" When the Drog who had appeared to be her father was only a few feet from Velissa, Hallidan nodded to one of his knights. The Titan advanced from the line and swung his fire-glass into the old man's side.

Velissa gasped as her father's severed body fell in two halves. Then before she could even turn her head, the corpse was transformed into an ugly monster burning in sulfur smoke. Velissa grasped Raccoman's arm and, with her free hand, slipped Singreale into the pouch beneath her tunic. The Drogs laughed at their nearly successful deception.

Thrane's horrible laugh ended in a leer that cut an evil path through the thick forest. Without speaking, he held his bladeless sword aloft and swung it in a wide arc. There was no blade, and yet the sword seemed to defoliate the brush wherever the blade would have passed if there had been one.

Velissa and Raccoman hid behind the Titan knights and quailed in the thunder of the footfalls of the knights and Drogs as they moved into battle. Rexel flew to a safe perch in the upper branches of a caladena tree well above the green mist.

"Velissa, do you remember the palisades of Maldoon?" asked Raccoman all at once.

Velissa cried in joy, "I do!"

"Would it work again?" he asked. Before she could answer, he looked upward and called into the green fog, "Rexel!" Once more Velissa took the diamond from its pouch and gave its fiery substance to the falcon, who seized the gem in his talons and flew above the misty ceiling of the forest. Then she cried:

> "Singreale!
> Let evil face
> the palisades."

At her word, the diamond in the talons of the falcon elongated into a fiery shaft that split itself into screaming flames that fell in hot, upright bolts of fire around the Drogs. The red spears sliced through the green mist in an uncanny exposition of flame and fog.

When the last shaft of fire had fallen, the palisades of flame formed a complete circle around the imprisoned Drogs. They feared the flame so much that they would not move to the perimeter of fiery shafts that encircled them, but drew together in a tiny knot of life, a trembling cluster in the middle.

Rexel settled back beneath the mist, and the glowing diamond cooled as Velissa stuck it back in the pouch at her neck. Through the glowing bars, she saw the ugly, amber faces of Thrane and the other beast-warriors. She took the hand of Raccoman as if to quiet her fears.

"Come," said Hallidan, and he turned on his heel and led the Graygills away into the forest.

"The palisades will burn out quickly, so we must try to reach the upper slopes of Mt. Calz before the Drogs overtake us. They are stealthy in the forest and could slip upon us in a surprise attack. Their evil Lord will stop at nothing to have the prize you wear at your neck," he said to Velissa. "Night will soon come upon us, and we must achieve the Caverns of Smeade. There we can sleep dry and fight enemies on only one side of us."

The Titans walked fast, and the Graygills had to run at times to keep pace. By late afternoon, they all reached the higher plateau.

On the plateau, the mist was clearing, but Raccoman's hopes for the land dissipated as the day's light dulled to twilight darkness. "We have not escaped war," lamented the Graygill. "Perhaps there is no escape from war."

Velissa saw that Raccoman had suffered greatly during their first few hours in this new land. The hope he had held in the upper winds was dashed. Whoever Hallidan was, whoever Thrane was, their hatred of one another was evidence enough that this new land to which they had come was as troubled as the old one they had left.

Raccoman and Velissa were tired in body and mind. Their legs had been too long bound uselessly to the decks of their glider, and their minds were experiencing the kind of fatigue that camps in cold, damp grottoes of hopelessness.

It was not clear to them how either the handsome Titans or the monstrous Drogs had known of Singreale, but it was clear that they both knew. And it was also clear that the Graygills' hope of survival now lay in following peacefully their attractive captors. For while Raccoman and Velissa had no reason to assume that the blue-dressed warriors had their real interest at heart, still they knew that it is easier to trust a beautiful Messiah than an ugly one.

The travelers' dull fatigue was interrupted by a mute gesture from one of their captors.

One of the knights had raised his hand and was pointing to the lofty plateau before them. "There are the Caverns of Smeade," he said brightly. But his happiness was short lived. Before the open cave burned a black fire around which were clustered several more of the large, dark creatures they had sought to evade.

"An angel or a devil Thou shalt be."
His bony finger pointed down at me.
Oh, that some guide would here decide
What is my destiny.

CHAPTER II

The Changelings

$\mathcal{T}$HE CAVERNS OF SMEADE opened to the south, and directly east of the orifice towered the summit of Mt. Calz. The cavern opening looked as though it had been designed as an inner tunnel to the unexplored bowels of the mountain behind it.

Hallidan and the other five Star Riders were unsure of which course they should take.

"We cannot cross the Valley of the Changelings at night," said Hallidan.

"What is this Valley of the Changelings?" asked Raccoman.

Hallidan looked upward to the dark, unmoving figures gathered about the black fire. It seemed safe to answer the Graygill's question. He beckoned Raccoman and Velissa into a shadowy section of the trail, and after they had sat down, he began to speak.

"A thousand years ago, there were no beast-warriors. Ren ruled from Rensgaard, and Rensland was at peace. Then Thanevial, our best knight, asked Ren to build for him another city west of Mt. Calz. The king refused this request. Nothing happened immediately, but a new and brooding vengeance began to grow in Thanevial's heart. There will be other times to tell you all about his betrayal of Ren, but when he finally left the citadel, he came to the red fluid pits northwest of Rensgaard and stopped to bathe in them. It was then that he became a monstrous creature like the one that you met this afternoon.

"The red fluid pits?" Velissa asked

"The fluid pits have always existed," he explained. "They were there in the time when the earliest forest dwellers were living their simple existence. These pits somehow represented the freedom of our people to choose. Grotesque tales were told of hapless animals who accidentally fell into them and were altered completely.

"In my years, I have twice seen four-legged beasts that had fallen into the fluid pits. Some said they were kamdrammels before their struggles in the pits." Hallidan stopped. He could see by the puzzled looks on the Graygills' faces that he needed to say more. "Kamdrammels are slender-legged and gentle beasts that are but half our size. They graze the lower, grassy slopes of Mt. Calz or the marshy meadows that separate the caladena groves.

"But half our size or not, these altered creatures became fierce, boldly entered Rensgaard, our citadel, and gored a number of knights before they were subdued. And their fierce natures were no worse than their dread forms that terrified the brave who were forced to destroy them for the sake of keeping the peace.

"What caused the handsome Thanevial to bathe in the red fluid was the intrigue of not knowing the full taste of his evil alter-ego. He seemed to hunger for power, and the red pits, which soon became known as the forming pits, lured him into the fierce possibilities of all he later became.

"Those knights who first saw the hideous monster, Thanevial, realized that he had once been a man like ourselves."

Velissa gasped, "Do you mean the Drogs were once men of your stature and appearance?"

Hallidan nodded. "Thanevial lured other knights to his same foul estate. He took the black stones from the desert floor and built his Tower Altar. He stood on it to curse Rensgaard and blaspheme the king. He dreamed that on the pinnacle of the altar would one day rest Singreale, the lost treasure of Maldoon. All power would then be his, and Estermann would be controlled from the glossy surface of his black altar."

"Then you knew where the Singreale was?" asked Velissa.

"We knew," said Hallidan, "but Thanevial did not. Thanevial at first lured only a few knights who defected to join him, but in these latter centuries more and more have done so. The battles have been fierce each time our knights encountered his Drogs. A great many have died on both sides.

"Thanevial was the first Drog. Like those he lured away from their allegiance to Ren, he was the first to see his handsome form become grievous and his face and body become scaly and grotesque. His decision to leave Rensgaard disturbed his powers but did not destroy them. His body showed the consequences of his rebellion. Talons replaced his hands and feet, his fair skin cracked and broke, his facial structure grew grotesque as his hair fell out, and his eyes softened into shapeless spheres of milk-white horror.

"It was the scope of his influence that Ren had not regarded. Thanevial had been a popular courtier, and in time more than three-fourths of Ren's best knights left the castle to join the arch rebel. Thanevial's revolution was costly, and each knight knew he had to pay the price of the ordeal of change to remain in the favor

of the Drog lord. So, one by one, they waded into the red pits.
Their own likeness to the king became defiled. The Valley of the
Changelings is that evil valley where. . . ."

Hallidan stopped. The Graygills listened for any sinister foot
treads in the forest. The five other Star Riders listened, too.

There was movement on the ledge before the yawning orifice of
the Caverns of Smeade. The Drogs were stirring. Hallidan saw two
of them slip away from the black fire. He knew they were leaving
the others to probe the dark woods.

Hallidan promised Raccoman and Velissa that he would finish
the story once they had reached safety, if, indeed, they did. There
were no more than eight Drogs on the ledge before the Caverns of
Smeade. He decided to take the two Graygills directly to the site of
the Drog encampment since he would feel safer in the heights than
in the lowlands. Somewhere he knew they must face the Drogs,
and the cavern ledge would be the safest place.

"Come," he said. The five Titans and the Graygills arose at the
single word. They moved quietly without talking. Steadily the dark
terrain rose. The fatigue of climbing was grueling. The gloom of
darkness brought a fear of the unknown to Raccoman which left
him aching in apprehension. Velissa also could bring no peace to
her trembling thoughts.

In the midst of the dark grove near the lip of the cavern ledge,
Velissa screamed. Her scream was muffled by a dark, rough-scaled
claw. Her free hand clutched the diamond at her bosom, tore it
from the bag, and tossed it to the ground in the very center of
Hallidan's knights. Light exploded. Hallidan blinked through the
sudden incandescence and started upward. Velissa had been seized
by a beast-warrior! For a moment, she seemed small against his
ugly, dark, and leathery chest. But when the Drog saw that she
had thrown the great diamond a small distance away, he pushed
her aside and bolted into the midst of the knights to retrieve the
treasure, now gleaming on the ground. Hallidan drew his fire-glass
sword and raised it just a the Drog was lifting the diamond in triumph. The beast threw back his head and laughed, but his laugh
ended in a wail. Hallidan's sword sang through the still air, severing
the Drog's hand from his forearm. Both his claw and the diamond
fell once again to the ground.

The stunned Drog then screamed in terror and held his severed
forearm, doubled over in the pain of his injury. Sulfuric smoke
poured out of the empty stub as the sword of Hallidan cut a second

swath through the Drog's leathery neck. The shrieking stopped instantly. The headless Drog fell in flames that in an instant became a shriveled and black heap.

Velissa grabbed at Singreale but could not free it from the smouldering remains of the claw that had stolen it. Hallidan took the point of his fire-glass rapier and sliced the evil claw from the gem. The brightness of Singreale appeared again as the rapier cut away the hand that held it. Velissa begged Hallidan to carry the Singreale. He declined as though he were afraid of Velissa's treasure.

Reluctantly Velissa placed Singreale back in the pouch at her neck, and the grove became dark. But the Drogs on the cavern ledge had seen the explosion of light and were alerted to the presence of Hallidan's party. They knew that Hallidan would not traverse the Valley of the Changelings by night.

Velissa and Raccoman tried to stay close to the Titan knights and, at the same time, keep out of the way as they moved on toward higher ground.

"Raccoman, call Rexel," Velissa said.

"But will we not let the Drogs know our position if I do?"

"Still," said Velissa, "as long as the falcon has the treasure, it will be safe."

"And," said Hallidan in a moment of insight, "Singreale will illuminate the trail so the Drogs cannot set upon us in the dark."

His logic was sound.

"Rexel!" called Raccoman.

The great bird had been moving silently through the trees and now dropped into the dark circle, landing squarely on Raccoman's wrist. Velissa placed Singreale in the strong talons of the falcon, who rose again into the air. Light flooded the trail. Hallidan and the others moved upward and on to the plateau where the Drogs had so lately been.

The Caverns of Smeade yawned like a grinning, open mouth directly behind them.

Hallidan took a small map from his belt and unfolded it. He was in the process of laying it out on the ground to study it when, from a distance, came a strange, whirring sound. The largest and nearest of the evening stars appeared to be moving toward them, growing in size and intensity as it approached.

Once, in another world, Raccoman had been intrigued by moving fields of stars. Now the growing light seemed to hold a nearer wonder that mixed with doubt all that the Graygills had endured. As the light finally became a huge flying beast whose long and powerful wings roared above the columns of air, the Titan soldiers fell to their knees.

"It is the king!" they cried in one voice. "On the condorg Galanta!"

The beast landed and drew in its magnificent wings that had seemed to stretch clear across the level mesa. The condorg was leather-winged, but had an equine body. Its thorax and upper neck resembled that of a broad-chested stag. Its regal head had deep-set eyes that sat low on the sides of its angular and tapered head that was most beautiful when the great mount stretched out its beautiful body in flight.

Galanta had settled quickly so as not to stir the dust beneath its wide span of wings. The beast's huge wings nestled almost flat against its heaving sides and it was obvious from the labored breathing of the animal that the king had forced it in a hard flight.

"Long live Ren!" shouted the knights, still on their knees.

The tall and handsome monarch did not acknowledge their salute. Instead, he dismounted and laid the silver reigns across the front of the gold saddle.

Velissa had thought that Hallidan was the most handsome being that she had ever seen, but the sight of this king standing by his great condorg changed her mind. His regal head was encircled by a single gold strand that held his locks securely about his face. His chin was as rugged as his brow was proud, and his eyes were blue and full of light. His short cape fell only past the small of his back, and his loose blouse was tucked beneath a fiber belt that held a long scabbard. His boots were an iridescent silver, and the few steps he took to stand before his beast made Velissa know that he walked like a king.

"Hallidan!" called the king.

"Ren of Rensgaard!" answered the knight, kneeling with his companions.

"Come. . . ," said the king as though he did not quite have the words to finish the command. Hallidan rose and approached him.

"Have you the Singreale?" asked Ren, wasting no time.

"It is there," Hallidan answered, pointing to the sky above them. "In the talons of Rexel, the falcon." The statement seemed unnecessary, as the cascading light still illuminated all the ground around them.

"I must take it with me," said the monarch firmly.

"It is yours, Ren," replied the knight. Then, looking into the sky, he called, "Come, Rexel."

The falcon made no move to descend. Hallidan cleared his throat in frustration and looked over to the Graygills, who crouched in the light and seemed to shrink in bewilderment at the top of their shadows, which fell away from them toward the dark forest beyond. Raccoman looked at Velissa. She seemed to question for a moment before she raised her chin slightly and nodded to him. Then he spoke the same two words that Hallidan had spoken, but with greater results. "Come, Rexel!" he called, and the bird obeyed his command.

Raccoman took the glowing treasure from Rexel and delivered it to Velissa, who advanced haltingly toward the king. With some reluctance, she handed the gem to the towering monarch. He nodded his approval. She stooped to curtsy, but he reached down to prevent her.

"No need of that," he said, "I should bow to you."

She said nothing, and he went on.

"You have come with the stone in time." He turned to Hallidan, "Hallidan, I go on a mission from which I am sure to return. But until I do, watch over my queen."

Hallidan did not question the cryptic statement. He stepped back from the king, and Velissa returned to her place beside Raccoman, who was so dazzled by the king and the condorg, Galanta, that he said nothing.

In the silence that reigned, both Raccoman and Velissa expected that the king would remount and take the Singreale with him into the night sky. But the king did not remount. With resolve, he drove his fire-glass sword vertically into the ground. He took the Singreale and laid it on the horizontal haft-guard of the blazing sword. The white light of the Singreale sat like a silver star above the red glow of the fire-glass blade, and the sword seemed a fiery pillar of hope set against the gathering darkness of the forest.

By the broad light of Singreale, the king unassumingly removed his cape, rolled it, and inserted it in Galanta's golden saddle bag. Then he removed his belt and blouse and, finally, his breeches and boots. Each garment in turn was removed and placed in the saddle pouch until the king stood naked before his knights and the two Graygills.

It was clear that he was worthy of the name of king. His body glistened with a power that challenged the nature all about him to bow down and cry out his excellence. Velissa, as she watched this disrobing with the other knights, felt no embarrassment, for it seemed to her that the king was acting in concert with an unfolding drama that knew no indecency and had to happen just the way it did.

Last of all, the king sheathed the fiery sword and tied it to the saddlehorn.

He held the Singreale in his hand for only a moment. Then he laid it briefly on the saddle of his great mount while he removed the condorg's bridle and bound it to the rear of the saddle so that the proud beast was free.

He lifted again the Singreale, and standing next to his great beast, he shouted, "Home to Rensgaard, Galanta!" He slapped the mount on its rump, and the giant wings unfolded. The great span of leather and heaving muscles drew columns of air, and then the condorg bolted into the sky, leaving the naked king still holding the Singreale.

The king turned away from his astounded observers and walked into the yawning orifice of Smeade. At the black opening, he looked back at Hallidan, the other knights, and the Graygills and said clearly, "I act to save our people. I must go away and take the Singreale with me, and here in the lightless night, I shall be born again." Then he walked into the cave and the light died. Gloom glued the night to the black ledge.

The illogical and yet deliberate pageant had left the party unable to move. However, all were plunged into a deep fear of their circumstances. Now the king and the condorg, Galanta, were gone, and their defenses were most vulnerable in the gathering darkness. Whatever the strange proceedings had meant, Hallidan knew they must not long ponder the event. He quickly ordered the others to gather wood, and a fire was soon set to blazing on the ledge before the cave's yawning mouth. It was now a gaping and awesome, perhaps even menacing, hole whose blackness exceeded the darkness of the night that bordered the deep forest beyond their camp.

"Are the Drogs still there?" Velissa asked timidly.

"They are there, all right," Hallidan replied firmly.

"Where are they?" asked Raccoman.

"In the forest . . . out there," said Hallidan, gesturing in the direction of the forest.

They waited in silence for half an hour. The woods were ominously quiet. The green fog had begun again to filter through the trees and nothing sounded but the jinnidrinnins, four-legged crustaceans that made a dreadful and eerie noise when the mist threaded its ribbons through the caladena groves.

"What's to do?" asked Raccoman.

"Wait till the forest is light, and then we'll travel through the Valley of the Changelings."

Rexel was as bewildered as the Graygills and the knights. He sat for a while in the amber flickerings of the night fire, then took his silent leave to study the dark forest from a lofty caladena tree. Yet the falcon did not seem to greet the strange happening with any sense of alarm. There was a wisdom settled about the great bird, but if he knew anything or understood anything beyond those around him, he kept that knowledge hidden behind his bright eyes.

Hallidan's men kept the fire blazing in the center of the camp. They spent the early part of the night keeping watch and resting in the circle of light that gathered about the brave fire. Hallidan, in imitation of the king Ren, drove the point of his glass-fire sword into the ground and left it gleaming upright. Above the level haftguard, he studied the dark forest in silence.

Two of the knights had brought some dembret nuts in a little sack, and these they shared with the entire party. Dembret nuts were a gray-violet fruit that hung in clusters beneath the broad leaves of the dembret vines. When each of the party had eaten, they all settled down around the glowing sword with little conversation. Their eyes never left the dark fringes of the forest where the night glared back in blind evil.

"Hallidan, how did you know that we were coming to Rensland and that the Singreale was in my possession?" asked Velissa.

She had barely gotten the question out when she heard a fluttering of wings and saw the dark bulk of the falcon settling in the circle of light around the fire.

"May I, Hallidan?" interrupted Rexel. The falcon fluttered to a rock near the standing sword, folded his wings, and then offered this explanation: "I have lived for centuries in Rensgaard—since the night Lord Parskon broke through the walls of Maldoon. My brother, the white falcon, came to take Singreale to Rensgaard. Unfortunately, he was killed in the siege by Blackgills. Back then, I was unused to long-distance flight, and I knew I would be unable to stay in the air during the entire long journey that the two of you completed yesterday. I knew I could not carry both the serpent guardian Doldeen and the Singreale, too, across the wide ocean to a safe place in Rensgaard. So I took them a much shorter distance to the valley of the Graygills, past the western ridges to your grandfather, Velissa. He was once a favored knight in the employ of King Singreale of Maldoon, after whom the stone was named.

"With nothing in my talons, I was able to fly to this continent. And here I remained until only a few months ago when I flew the long, long journey to the land of the Graygills, where I came directly to your old barn south of Canby. When you and Velissa were finally settled on the glide plane, I chose to meet the Star Riders in the skies east of the granite parapet and to inform them that the gem was safe and on its way to Rensgaard. The Star Riders of Ren relayed the message that you were bringing the treasure of Maldoon to Rensgaard once again."

"Word spread throughout the city that you and Singreale were on the way. Two knights who were defecting to join the rebellion took the word to the camp of Thanevial. Unfortunately, your craft went too far, passing over the Valley of the Changelings and landing almost in the shadow of the Tower Altar. Knowing the wind drift tides around Mt. Calz, the king sent Hallidan and some other knights to wait near the Black Tower in case your landing occurred near Thanevial's altar. It has proved itself a wise precaution.

Rexel had finished his speech. The dark orifice of the cavern gapped behind the knights and Graygills. Velissa had never understood why Rexel had come to them in the first place or why he had been such a devoted servant to them. Now she knew that Rexel had more than a simple interest in them. He, along with Doldeen and the white falcon, had been a trinity of guardians from the past, charged with the safekeeping of the treasure. Now, two of the three were dead. The white falcon had been dead for a millennium and Doldeen for only a few months. Remembering Doldeen set Velissa to wondering about the fate of the widows of Canby, and as Raccoman snuggled close, she began to sing softly the song she had last heard sung by Orkkan and the refugees:

"We shall sing in the shade of the ginjon tree
For Canby's fields are the fields of the free
And beasts and men here are timeless friends
In the ageless land of Estermann."

The knights listened to the doleful refrain but could not understand the spell its melancholy words and haunting tune had cast upon the Graygills.

Raccoman thought of the Paradise Falcon still hanging nose downward in the caladena groves near the sinister Tower Altar. He grieved to think of it. He wondered if he would ever be able to conceive of a way to rescue it. There were no tilt winds in this new land. Rensgaard seemed to offer them no fresh hope of lifting the once-proud glider to the upper zephyrs that stirred the ethers of the thin air of outer atmosphere.

"Raccoman," Velissa asked, "is there war on every star in every corner of the sky that holds a planet?"

It was a question that none could answer. Raccoman didn't try.

"Do you think that the white castle of Ren
Is a place for beginning again?"

she asked in wistful rhyme.

Raccoman remained silent.

He looked past the fire-glass blade of Hallidan's sword to the darkness beyond. Whatever images his mind held, they were pleasant ones. The Graygill metalworker smiled and looked fixedly at images one continent and one year away.

In his mind, he saw himself sky-surfing again on giant ginjon leaves. He was turning and rolling and diving. On the ground below, there were congrels and ganzingerfowls. There were parties filled with lively singing and dancing in a land without fear. But the jinnidrinnins grew suddenly quiet, and the dark beyond the light that had been Raccoman's mental playground became at once as still as death.

Death, thought Raccoman—what an obscurity that was, the hideous demon of war. He had rarely seen death before Parsky came to the valley of the Graygills. Now he had seen his Moonrhyme uncle die, all of the men of Canby were gone, and this very afternoon he had seen two sulfuric smoke-filled beast warriors die in the fumes of the inner smouldering life that was their foul existence.

"Why are the jinnidrinnins so quiet?" he heard Velissa ask. "Raccoman," she insisted, "why are the jinnidrinnins so quiet?"

At the edge of the circle of light, one of Hallidan's party stood silently surveying the edges of the clearing beyond the furthest reaches of the amber soft influences of the fire-glass. Velissa studied the back of the Titan guard and waited for her husband to answer her question.

"Velissa, tomorrow we will see Rensgaard and then we will . . ." Raccoman's voice stopped suddenly in mid-sentence.

Velissa took her eyes from the back of the guard to look at her husband. As she saw him slump forward, she felt a sharp pain in her head, and all light died to her awareness as she, too, slumped into unconsciousness.

The Titan guard turned to the wide, black opening of the Caverns of Smeade, only to see the two Graygills being dragged from the brink of the council light into the cave.

"Stand ho!" cried the guard, running forward and grabbing the handle of the ready sword. At his outcry, Hallidan and the others were instantly on their feet. Hallidan shook his regal head to clear the slowness of sleep from his mind.

"Raccoman and Velissa have been knocked unconscious and dragged into the cave," shouted the watchman. Rexel remained nearby in the upper branches of a dead tree and watched. With only the red light from their glass blades to illuminate their way, the Titans walked into the cave.

"How many were there?" asked Hallidan.

"I saw only two."

The warriors ran into the cave for some distance until the small shaft through which they had entered widened into a domed vault. Several tunnels opened into the cave, and they could not be sure which one to pursue. Their fire-glass blades glowed as they focused down a passageway to the right. Instantly, they turned in that direction. In their rapid sprint down the stone tube, it was only an instant before they saw the beastly, hideous faces at the end of the tunnel.

Hallidan ordered the Drogs to drop the two Graygills. This the beasts did, then bolted over the unconscious couple and drew their own swords. The swift arm of Hallidan swung the fire-glass blade in a dreadful arc that passed through the low stone ceiling of the cave and dislodged an avalanche of soft stone before it cut in two the body of the taller Drog. The tunnel reeked with the foul acrid smoke that issued from the body of the beast warrior as he collapsed.

The second Drog raised his sword to strike, but Hallidan's fire-glass blade again sliced through the side of the tunnel and sprayed the Drog with rocks. A chunk of rock struck in the mucous surface of his ugly eye. As he dropped his sword, the sword of another Titan knight sailed as a missile through the air and penetrated the leathery chest of the beast-warrior. Fumes of smoke poured out into the confining passageway.

The odor of the dead Drogs was as much as the knights could

stand. Two of the Star Riders squeezed by Hallidan and picked the unconscious Graygills off the floor. Another knight, still brandishing his sword, raced back through the stone corridor to the vaulted room. The Titans reached the center of the room before they noticed that the larger tunnel that led to the north of the Caverns of Smeade was blocked by four more Drogs.

"Ughum Hunga! Condungra!" cried one.

An unusually large Drog moved to obey. Swiftly he ran to the knight with the raised sword and swung the blade of his invisible sword through the knight's body. But the Drog's victory was short-lived. He, in turn, was cut down by the blade of a knight to the right of Hallidan.

One of the three remaining Drogs rushed forward to engage Hallidan in battle, then stopped short. He cautiously backed away when he saw Hallidan raise the blade of his fiery weapon and begin to advance.

"Come, monster," taunted Hallidan, holding his bright blade out to the Drog. The Drog looked at him and again advanced with drawn sword as if he would destroy his courageous foe. But when he saw Hallidan's eyes narrow in determination, once more he backed away.

"Monganka! Hunga!" cried another Drog who seemed to be issuing an order to the retreating Drog. "Condungra! Monganka! Monganka! Gukka Crangdammo, Hallidan!"

At this command, the monster advanced toward Hallidan. Hallidan extended his open hand to the creature.

"Come closer, Drog. When you are close enough to touch my open hand, I'll fold you into sulphur fumes, and the black fire which warms your evil soul will spill upon the floor."

The combatants circled, facing each other, and etched the floor with bootprints and claw-scratches intermingled.

"Come, Drog. Wouldn't you like to feel the smooth, swift death of my fire-glass? Or are you afraid?"

The Drog stepped back from Hallidan. He turned to face the Drog commander.

"Hunga! Crangdammo Monganka!" the commander screamed at him, before he swung his own sword through the thick neck of the cowardly monster. The severed head rolled to Hallidan's feet, and the headless torso lurched forward and shuddered. With his sword point, Hallidan rolled the Drog's head back to the feet of the arch Drog himself.

"Order your other cowards forward!" cried Hallidan. The words were barely out of his mouth when the other evil Drogs dashed out of the tunnel into the darkness.

"Well, Drog, it looks like it's you and I. Come and let the fire-glass warm your evil soul even as it silences it."

Hallidan taunted the Drog to come within sword range. A small light of the same intense quality as the lost Singreale appeared down one of the other tunnels. Along with the new light, a musical, almost nonsensical voice called out to the Changeling who faced Hallidan. Both the Star Rider and the Drog seemed puzzled by the strange illumination. Around the new light issued an intriguing melody:

"Commen commen Droggynoggen
Chonnie chonnie hie!
Hon! Hon! chonnie chon!
Droggynoggen die!"

The light blinked off. The Drog turned from Hallidan and ran into the dark tunnel to face the strange, new light. He was gone only an instant when the Titans heard a loud scream, then eerie silence.

In the red glow of their fire-glass swords, the knights cautiously crept along the tunnel where the strange voice and the light had appeared. Soon they found the smouldering body of the Drog. Something or someone had torn its throat away. Its ugly, leathery head with the milk-white, bulging eyes was nearly torn off.

Whoever or whatever had killed the Drog could not be found. The knights were puzzled, yet dared not tarry long in the dark cavern.

They turned once more to go outside. The other knights soon came out of the cave carrying the unconscious Graygills.

"To the glory of Ren and the citadel!" cried Hallidan with a rapid thrust of his glass-fire that seared and split the night air.

Hallidan's remaining knights cheered briefly. Then one of the Titans said gravely, "The Knight Lanadin is dead. Bring him out of the cavern." Lanadin's passing left only five knights to do battle against the terror still waiting in the darkness.

The knight known as Rendemar carried Lanadin out of the cave. The others made a litter for him out of poles hewn from trees and out of the black capes of two of the dead Drogs. They carried him into the forest and then buried him in a shallow depression of earth made a little deeper by their fire-glass swords.

When they all had been outside for a while, the cool night air began to revive Velissa. Shortly after, Raccoman began to stir.

"Where are we?" asked Velissa.

"Where we camped during the night," said her husband.

"What happened . . . Oh, my head!" she cried, feeling the bump where the Drog had struck her to steal her consciousness.

Raccoman moved to Velissa's side. He, too, was unsteady, but he held her for a moment.

"It will be light before long," consoled one of the knights, "and in the light, we will move on through the Valley of the Changelings and at last to the borders of safety."

The party waited till the jinnidrinnins grew silent again. The first rays of the morning sun trimmed the purple from the night sky. It was going to be a beautiful day. Nearly all of the green mist had dissipated in the clear air of Rensland.

For two more days, five Riders and two Graygills traveled without encountering any Drogs. On the third day, the single file of knights pulled closer together and locked their positions to watch the thicket areas beside the trail. They were near the Valley of the Changelings, and the new Changelings were unpredictable. They were usually ready to fight and eager to kill. Some merely wanted to hurry on to the Tower Altar to receive their orders from Thanevial himself, but most were eager for the fight.

When they had reached the center of the valley, they found themselves in a large, red, grassy area. Someone was approaching from the Rensgaard side of the valley.

"Congaard!" cried Hallidan.

The Titan knight did not acknowledge Hallidan, but walked straight down the path through the center of the field. As he passed, Hallidan saw his face closely and cried, "No! Congaard, no!"

Hallidan shook his head. It was too late for Congaard to return. His eyes were already dilated and beginning to swell out on his face. His hands were becoming scaly and his fingers were webbing and changing into claws.

Never swerving from his purpose, the decomposing knight turned at last from the path and found a shallow pool of dark red fluid. He removed his coat of armor and mail, and laid them next to his fire-glass sword. When he was completely naked, he lay down in the deep red spring. Velissa and Raccoman watched in horror as the red liquid of the spring boiled over his white body. The stained skin grew dark in the inky fountains as the scarlet hues turned to venomous black and bubbled around the changing form.

"These are the forming pits where knights become monsters," said Hallidan.

Velissa turned from the horror before her. Then she saw other forms lying in other dark pools, each in a various stage of transformation.

"Will all of these creatures end as Drogs?" asked Velissa.

"It is their choice," replied the knight Rendemar. "Ren will hold no knight against his will. Here is the dark volition of the forces of light."

"Why do you not kill them where they lie?" asked Raccoman Dakktare.

"It is forbidden by Ren. Here is the valley where they decide, and they must be free to decide for themselves. Here we may not kill—but we may be killed by Changelings newly come from these forming pits," said Rendemar.

Raccoman watched Congaard's transformation. The same foul odor or smoke that had filled the air when the Changelings were killed now possessed the air in the valley. The sulphur stench was overwhelming.

"Move on," said Hallidan, motioning to his group of knights. Rendemar led the way down the trail.

In a few moments, the Titans and the Graygills had passed through the worst part of the stench, and within an hour, they all stood on the clean high slopes of Mt. Calz.

"In another day, we will be home," said Hallidan. As they neared the summit of the ledge, Raccoman and Velissa caught sight of Rensgaard, the capital city of Rensland. The white spires of Rensgaard dominated the forestscape before them.

As they stood looking at the gleaming city, each of the knights fell to one knee, and in the genuflecting position, their clear voices rang out in a song that Raccoman and Velissa would soon join in singing:

"This the land where honor reigns,
This is the land where truth is king.

Here is the kingdom void of change
Where men live free forever!"

The knights stood. Hallidan gestured to the alabaster citadel, and turning to Raccoman and Velissa, he said, "Welcome to the land of Ren."

There are castles of light in canyons of glass,
In glittering empires that dreamers achieve.
There's a king—I've been told—on a dais of gold,
Whose treasures are given to those who believe.

CHAPTER III

The Knights of Ren

T HE ESTERMANN SUNLIGHT brushed the scant clouds aside and fell in splendor upon the facets of the alabaster city. The square towers stood like opaque prisms that gathered the golden light of day and tossed it downward, upward, and outward, all at the same time.

"It's beautiful!" said Velissa Dakktare.

"Beautiful! Splendid!" agreed her husband.

The entire city looked like a huge castle driven down into the rock of the mountaintop plateau east of Mt. Calz. Its walls, towers and inner dwellings were built from crudely quarried stones that reached upward and, in some instances, became towers that flew the banners of this proud state.

Raccoman could tell by looking at the intricate architecture that the Titans were better than the Canbies at building cities. Perhaps their race was older or simply had more experience in building.

The knights studied the city before and after singing the Matin. They rose to their feet and prepared to enter one of the high portals that connected the main gates with the land around the castle. The way that the city thrust upward into the sun produced a natural canyon-moat whose precipice sides swept upward in a steep column of stone that was level on top.

Hallidan suddenly realized that Raccoman and Velissa were viewing his gleaming city for the first time. The Graygills gazed in rapture at what the Riders were so accustomed to seeing that they rarely stopped to behold it. The knight smiled at their fascination. "We'll take the west bridge into the city," he said. "You can see the great square from there."

"Look!" cried Raccoman, pointing nervously at a condorg that had just appeared above them. As the creature circled, the whir of its great wings churned the air noisily.

"Rengraaden!" cried Hallidan.

The rider of the condorg heard his name, wheeled his mount in midair, and settled suddenly at the promontory of land on which they had been standing. Rengraaden was also a Star Rider, and seemed to possess an unassuming preeminence over all who gazed upon him.

Velissa and Raccoman moved back quickly. Like all the Star Riders they had seen, Rengraaden was exceedingly handsome. His flying steed was almost as large as Galanta, and on the back of its peerless head, where one might have expected to see a mane, was a ridge of soft bone that ran to the crown of his head and then stopped. This feature Raccoman had overlooked on the king's condorg, but he was soon to discover it was a common feature of all the great animals.

"Ho, lay-ho!" cried Rengraaden. "How goes the king?"

"Ho, lay-ho!" answered Hallidan. "The king is gone!"

"Ren is *dead*?" asked the Star Rider in disbelief as he dismounted.

"Not dead, gone!" insisted Hallidan.

In a moment, Rengraaden was standing face to face with Hallidan. The two men walked to a shaded area beside the high trail that overlooked the city and squatted in the dust to talk. Hallidan related in detail the story of the rescue of the Graygills and, more astonishing, the king's unusual disappearance. Rengraaden pressed his friend to disclose the place where the king had disappeared, but Hallidan refused.

Hallidan had enjoined the party never to reveal either the place or the strange circumstances of the king's disappearance. He feared that one of the defecting knights might inform Thanevial of the location of the king's departure, and then the Caverns of Smeade would be overrun with Changelings, swarming like ants through the labyrinthine passageways, searching for the Singreale.

By the third day of their journey, Velissa and Raccoman knew that they must also keep the great secret of the king's strange midnight ritual before the death-black opening of the terrifying caverns. If the beast warriors found either the king or the great diamond, the war could go ill for the Star Riders. If the Drogs found both the king and the treasure, all hope might vanish.

"Not a word of this!" Hallidan had commanded the knights, "for Ren's life may hang now in our trust—and wherever he is, he has only the Singreale and nothing else to defend himself."

"The secret is safe," Rendemar had said, and all had agreed.

Rengraaden's steed snorted and threw back his head. His gleaming flesh glistened in the lather of what must have been a hard flight. Rengraaden turned to look in the direction of the Graygills.

"I see you have the Graygills. Is the treasure safe?" asked Rengraaden.

"It is . . . or was," said Hallidan. "The last we saw of it, the king bore it away. Soon afterwards, we had to fight the Drogs. Lanadin was killed. Rensgaard will grieve the loss." Hallidan paused for a moment to remember the lost knight. At length he said, "Your condorg is lathered in the effort of his own flight."

"I flew west of the Tower Altar. The Desert of Draymon is smouldering in the heat of the liquid sand. The molten seas are bubbling, seething fire—for this is the time of their surging. The glass seas are furiously caught in the sun tides. The edge of Thanevial's forest may be caving in. The liquid sand is lapping now at the very edge of the Caladena Forests. If the tides continue, Thanevial may be forced to move his whole kingdom east before the year is out."

Hallidan frowned and remained silent.

"If the Drogs move east, it could hasten the inevitable war," Rengraaden said.

The crease in Hallidan's brows deepened, and his disconsolate jaw opened barely wide enough to reply, "Today begins the last Festival of Light we shall see before the blood flows."

The statement captured the attention of all present. None of Hallidan's Star Warriors spoke. Velissa and Raccoman studied the faces of the Titan knights and found them handsome and proud, but silent and serious as though they could not speak before the horrible portent that Rengraaden had suggested. Hallidan spoke at last.

"How was the queen when you left the city?"

"She is well . . . ," Rengraaden began and then stopped, realizing it would fall on him to report the king's disappearance to the queen.

"Come, Rengraaden," said Hallidan, "and meet the Graygills." Rengraaden approached Raccoman and Velissa. He reached his hand downward and Raccoman reached his upward to the knight who was a little more than twice his size. With his stubby fingers, Raccoman tried to grasp Rengraaden's elbow in the characteristic greeting of the Titans. Rengraaden tried not to smile at the small hand that reached for his own. Raccoman had seen them go through their ritual of greeting only a time or two, but he knew how it was to be done. Still, it was fruitless for him to try to reach very far up the Titan's forearm. Rengraaden smiled broadly at Raccoman's lost attempt and grasped his elbow with ease.

"You have come to Rensgaard on a glad day," said Rengraaden. "It is the Festival of Light."

"I am only sorry that they have come in a time of unrest," said Hallidan.

"Unrest is universal," said Raccoman. "The land we have left was troubled by a terrible war. Velissa, my bride!" said Raccoman, presenting his small wife to the knight.

Velissa stepped forward, and Rengraaden dropped to one knee and bowed his head before the beautiful woman who stood beside her Graygill husband. Even on one knee, he was taller than Velissa.

"I am delighted to know you," said Rengraaden. "You are welcome to Rensgaard."

Velissa, not quite knowing what to say to the Star Rider, smiled and bowed her head.

Presently Rengraaden stood and turned on the heel of his gold boot. "I'll join you at the festival, Hallidan," he said, then walked to his condorg and mounted it. The winged steed wheeled as the knight drew on the reins. The giant wings unfolded as the steed took three running steps and vaulted into the sky.

"Ho, lay-ho!" shouted Rengraaden.

"Ho, lay-ho!" shouted Hallidan.

In a moment, the steed and rider became a black and irregular spot against the bright sky. Velissa watched, entranced, until her eyes stung.

"In less than four hours down this trail we shall come to the towered bridge across the west chasm," Hallidan told the Graygills.

Velissa seemed not to hear. Her mind was on something else.

"Hallidan, tell me of the queen of Rensgaard."

"The queen?" Hallidan looked puzzled. Then he remembered the question he had asked Rensgraaden. "The queen . . . oh, yes, the queen! She is Ren's wife, and she is with child. It is the first child ever to be born to the house of Ren."

"And you—are you married?" asked Velissa. Raccoman eyed her, surprised by Velissa's impertinence.

Hallidan laughed out loud, suddenly realizing Velissa's concern. Since the Graygills had happened upon this continent, the queen was the only woman Velissa had spoken of. Hallidan was amused by her naiveté. "Not married," he finally said. "I never married in better times, and now the days seem too desperate."

"There *are* other women, then—besides the queen?" ventured Velissa hopefully.

"Lots of them," said Hallidan. "But they seldom leave the citadel. The Changelings would steal them and carry them west to the Tower Altar."

"The Drogs, of course, have no women?" Velissa asked.

Hallidan laughed again and then felt ashamed that he had put Velissa ill at ease. "I'm sorry, Velissa. It's just that all Drogs were once knights."

"I see," she said. "And this is why the women fear them."

"They have from time to time captured some poor woman who ventured beyond the safety of the citadel."

"But why?" Velissa asked, then wished that she had not.

Hallidan's silence was answer enough.

One of the other knights reminded Hallidan that they all would miss the opening of the Festival of Light if they tarried much longer.

Hallidan led the way and each of them followed. Velissa and Raccoman walked in the middle of the file of tall men. Rexel, who had been circling overhead, suddenly descended to Raccoman's shoulder and said, "Raccoman, tell Hallidan that we are being pursued by a party of several Drogs." Raccoman quickly passed the word to Hallidan. Hallidan passed the word and the knights walked faster. Their long strides fairly forced Raccoman and Velissa to run to maintain their position in the middle of the file. Just as the towered bridge was fully in view, Rexel bolted into the air. Hallidan's party had not gone fifty paces further when the knight in front of Raccoman and Velissa fell. His shoulder was covered with blood. He tried to raise himself from the ground, but he could not.

Fifty Drogs came out of the trees on either side of the trail and formed a circle around the knights. "Mugrunga Graygills!" croaked one of them. "Bandagmo. Hunga! Gukka!" Hallidan realized that the monsters would be willing to trade the Graygills for the freedom of the rest.

"Scum!" replied Hallidan.

Another of the knights clutched his stomach and lurched forward. Velissa was terrified to see the knight's hands covered with blood as he fell. Both knights had been struck by invisible spears.

"Ughum! Condungra Singreale," said the same Drog who had just spoken. "Singreale, Graygills, Malakunga!"

Hallidan motioned for the Graygills to move behind him. "The Graygills stay with us!" he said, waving his sword gently as he spoke. He thought to confess that they did not have the Singreale, but then realized that their ignorance now might better serve the cause of Rensland in the future.

Hallidan stepped forward, confused as to what he should do

next. His quandary was brief. In a moment, the ugly beast-warriors began to scatter, and the sky grew dark with the huge winged shadows of condorgs.

Ren's out-numbered knights greeted the advance Star Warriors as a bulky rain of joy. Two Drogs swung their unseen blades into the bodies of the condorgs, whose blue-light blood infuriated the beasts. The condorgs wheeled and smashed the ugly faces of their assassins with their clublike feet. The Star Riders dismounted, and the searing arcs of burning fire-glass met the empty but deadly hiss of the invisible weapons of the Changelings.

Three of the Star Riders, arriving late, brought their mounts down on the ugly Changelings and trampled them into the dirt. A dozen more condorgs arrived. The flying knights dropped like hail upon the Changelings, swinging their long fire-glass blades. Ugly heads rolled from scaly necks, and sulphur smoke rose from the headless torsos of a score of dying monsters. When Hallidan saw that the Star Riders had things well under control, he hastily led Raccoman and Velissa across the tower bridge.

"You'll be safe here," he said and turned again to the fray.

Back he ran across the triple-arched bridge that towered above the canyon below. Velissa and Raccoman watched the knights finish their slaughter of most of the Drogs. The rest were soon set to flight. Hallidan and the others gathered the two wounded Riders and carried them across the towered bridge.

No sooner were all the condorgs back in the sky and the bright warrior knights in the city than the last section of the tower bridge was raised, leaving the triple-arched span ending in thin air so that none could cross over without risking sudden death on the precipitous slopes below that broadened at the base of the stone walls.

Hallidan stripped off his mail and then removed the garments of the two wounded knights. He worked feverishly to revive the Rider with the wound in his abdomen. But it was to no avail. Now two of the six had been killed in the rescue of the Graygills. Only four were left. The mission had been costly.

The other wounded Star Warrior had received only a surface wound in the shoulder and soon was able to stand and embrace Hallidan. One of the other knights was commissioned to carry word of the outcome of the mission to the queen. The Graygills were safe in Rensgaard, but two knights were dead and another was wounded, and the king himself had disappeared.

This latter word would be the hardest of all to bear. Not only had Galanta returned riderless to the citadel, but all of the king's clothes and belongings had been found. The worst had been supposed by the city. No king would send back his condorg and his clothes of his own free will. Izonden, his queen, could only assume that her husband had fallen into the worst possible circumstances.

The return of the king's condorg had filled the women of the city with fear, but it had steeled the Star Warriors with a new resolve. In the brief day that had lapsed, the city had prepared for all-out war. The Riders had taken to the sky, circling Mt. Calz and flying to every possible reach of the country.

Their activity, though fervent, was pointless because it was without direction. They knew neither where to go nor what to do. Rengraaden was on a mission of surveillance to the Tower Altar to discover the extent of the latest eruption of the glass seas. Hallidan was on a mission of rescue to the forced landing of the Paradise Falcon, and the king, who never left the city, suddenly flew away on a mission that he had shared with no one.

"The king—have you seen him?" asked a Star Rider as Hallidan commissioned one of the knights to bring specific word to Izonden.

"We have seen him, and while the tale is difficult to relate . . ." Hallidan paused a moment, trying to decide how much of the strange tale he should reveal at once. "While the tale is difficult to relate," he repeated, "we believe that he is safe, at least for the time being." Hallidan dismissed the knights, but not before they had exclaimed a spontaneous salute in which they had never been more of one voice: "LONG LIVE REN OF RENSGAARD!"

Hallidan could see that the city needed, more than anything else, the word of hope that he had supplied. It was perhaps the force of his gesture that caused them to disperse, but none of them asked about the Singreale. Perhaps they knew that the great diamond could not be more valuable than the king himself, and while the king was out of the city, there was nothing that could offer them any greater security.

Having witnessed the death of Lanadin at the Caverns of Smeade, Hallidan walked tenderly to the Star Warrior who had been killed in the ambush just beyond the West Gate. He lay silently in the sun. The breezes blew through his hair and touseled his blond locks. The great knight knelt above the sleeping soldier. He kissed the silent head of the dead Rider. The sight stole into Velissa's soul. She remembered that she had seen her father alive so many months before in another world. Yet here was a pathos she could measure. It was a soldier's goodbye, and she felt a tearing in her bosom as the living giant kissed the sleeping giant in the warm sun.

Hallidan was shaken by remorse.

He stood and ordered the remaining men of his command to carry the fallen Rider to the custom of the final ceremony that would take place when his widow was present. Though the Star Riders never held elaborate ceremonies of death, they rarely interred their fallen until the widows were present.

The morning had been long. The two days past had seemed a year.

Velissa and Raccoman wondered what they would do now that they had reached the sanctuary. A tall, beautiful woman approached.

"I am Raenna, the wife of Rengraaden," the woman said, nodding slightly to Raccoman and Velissa. Her eyes were a clear and penetrating green that looked through things rather than at them. Her hair was blonde and fell like a wash of gold across her naked shoulders. Her gossamer garment was a translucent white that hung across one shoulder and fell beneath a gold cord that lightly encircled her waist.

"I am Velissa and this is my husband Raccoman," said the wife of the Graygill. At that precise moment, Rexel descended out of the sky and landed on Raccoman's shoulder. To Raenna's surprise, Rexel introduced himself, though he did not need to.

"We know you!" laughed Raenna.

"And so you should," replied the falcon. Raenna reached up and stroked the bird's head.

Rexel told her briefly of the rigors of the Graygills' long flight and of their skirmishes with the Changelings. Raenna seemed to feel an unseen hurt at their unhospitable reception in Rensland. Velissa reached up and touched Raenna's downcast face.

"We are glad to be in your city," Velissa told the regal woman before her.

The momentary silence that followed soon ended as Raenna said to the Graygills, "You are to stay with Rengraaden and me."

She turned and began to walk in the direction from which she had originally approached. She gestured for them to follow and they did.

"You are to meet the queen tonight—after you have rested, of course," said Raenna.

Velissa was ill at ease with the idea of meeting the queen and yet, at the same time, she welcomed it. She followed Raenna across a wide plaza that appeared to be a parade area. Then they turned down a narrower street that was lined on either side with sun-washed dwellings. At length they came to a wide, single door. Raenna lifted the latch and admitted the Graygills, following them inside.

The room in which they stood was clean and simply furnished. For the moment, Raccoman had forgotten that Rexel was on his shoulder. When he did remember, he nervously cleared his throat. Raenna smiled back, and said, "Of course, the falcon is welcome, too."

They then talked for a while about the flight of the Paradise Falcon and of their rescue by the party of Hallidan. Raenna explained that Hallidan and his knights had flown part of the way, but had decided to go on foot the rest of the way to Thanevial's altar territory so that they might escape notice. Velissa noted that the plan had evidently worked, since the knights had not run into the Drogs until after the Paradise Falcon had nosed into the caladena grove. The knights had correctly anticipated the glider's path of flight and followed them.

Raenna explained that she would have to leave them for a while. She had been asked by Hallidan to tell Lanadin's wife of her husband's death in the Caverns of Smeade. Raenna told the Graygills to sleep if they could. The idea sounded wonderful to both Velissa and Raccoman. The bed where Rengraaden and Raenna usually slept was twice as long as it needed to be to accommodate the Graygills. Rexel perched on the back of a large chair to rest, and Raccoman and Velissa soon fell to the unconscious hum that marked their wholehearted participation in slumber.

They had not slept long when they were suddenly awakened by the abrupt entrance of Rengraaden.

"Ho, lay-ho, my friends!" Rengraaden greeted them with somewhat of an apologetic cheer, sorry that he had awakened them.

"Ho lay-ho!" answered Raccoman sleepily.

"It will soon be time for the Festival of Light to begin," explained handsome Rengraaden.

"How will the city be able to enjoy the holiday with the Drogs so near the walls?" asked Raccoman, still trying to collect his leaden thoughts.

"The bridges of all six gates are drawn. The city is sealed. We are safe, and the queen insists that the festival proceed with laughter and dancing." The tall knight removed his boots and sat down on a couch in the corner of the room.

"What about Lanadin's widow and the widow of the knight killed at the approach to the towered bridge?" asked Velissa, who had finally shrugged off her drowsiness enough to join the conversation.

"It will be a heavy holiday for them, indeed," agreed Rengraaden, "but we cannot call Lanadin back to life. At least he died nobly in defense of the crown. Congaard's widow is another matter."

Velissa shuddered when she remembered the Valley of the Changelings. She would not forget the sight of Congaard stepping willingly into the horrible red forming pit.

Rexel cocked his head, but said nothing. Rengraaden continued, "Yes, Congaard's widow doubtless loves the king and will feel nothing but shame at the treachery of her husband. Now that he has joined the Drogs, he will likely try to call her to Thanevial's altar."

"Would he call his own widow to the horror of Thanevial's camp?" asked Velissa, horrified by such an idea.

"If he catches her outside the city, he would try to drag his own wife to the abuse of his evil lord. She would be chained to the Tower Altar for atrocities so degrading they cannot be spoken of in Ren's city. Many women have been captured by Changelings. Those who die quickly are the lucky ones."

Velissa grimaced and turned away, touching Raccoman's arm as if she needed to reassure herself of his presence even to bear the thought of all that she imagined for the doomed widows of Rensgaard.

"Yes, indeed," said Rengraaden. "Last year one of the Changelings finally caught his own wife and dragged her into a party of the beast-warriors. The horror of her cries was heard by a party of our knights. They tried to rescue her, but when the Drogs were finally drawn away and slain, the poor woman had cut her wrists on a Changeling's blade and was dead."

"Poor soul," said Velissa, her voice trailing off.

"How . . . ," asked Raccoman, faltering, "how could a man take his own wife to this desecration?"

"He could not have considered such an atrocity before his defection to the camp. But once such traitors pass the valley, their natures and desires, even all their allegiances, change. They will do anything their evil lord suggests. Yes, my friends, Congaard's widow is in danger, if she ever leaves the city without an escort of knights."

It was grim conversation, and Rengraaden realized it.

"The times are serious. The war must come," he said simply. Then his face brightened and he went on, "But not today. Today I shall dance with Raenna, and tonight we will join the city's festival and celebrate the coming of Ren. There will be food and laughter and wine. Should I die this next year in the conflict with Thanevial, at least I will die with the memories—the warm memories—of this glorious festival."

Velissa smiled weakly, Raccoman more broadly.

Just then the door swung open. It was Raenna.

"Ho, lay-ho, Raenna, my love!" exclaimed Rengraaden, leaping to his feet. He grabbed his wife. It was clear that her time with Lanadin's widow had not been easy. Her cheeks still glistened with the ardor of her task.

"Ho, lay-ho," she said with mock cheer. "Oh, Rengraaden, how hard it is for these women to learn of the death of their men!"

"Now, now, it's the holiday!" said Rengraaden.

"I could barely stand to see her with so crushed a spirit," she went on, ignoring her husband's consolation. "Each time you leave the citadel, I am uneasy that one of the wives will come to me exactly as I have just gone to her and . . . oh, Rengraaden . . . oh, oh."

Raenna collapsed against him and folded herself close and delighted in the strength of his arms.

Raccoman pulled Velissa a little closer while they observed the Titan couple.

"Now, Raenna, my love," said the knight, "it is time to stop this mood. It's the Holiday of Light, and while we have the moment, let us call up the cheer."

By late afternoon, the Graygills and the knight and his wife left Rexel alone in the house and stole quietly into the purple street. They could already see the green mists stealing up the distant slopes of Mt. Calz. The street men were lighting the flambeaus that guarded the night. It was not really dark enough for the torches, but there was a spirit of expectancy in the air as the city prepared for the festival to begin.

Raccoman and Velissa shared the story of their joyous voyage with Rengraaden and Raenna. Raenna had never left the continent of Ren and was fascinated by the events and sights that composed the Graygills' narration. While they related the story of their flight, the square before the white stone facade of the royal residence filled with people. There was a sense of expectancy to the crowd that now began to press into every empty space of the plaza. From every outlying quarter of the citadel they came. Never had Raccoman and Velissa seen such tall and handsome men or such elegant and stately women.

Now and then there were introductions of the Graygills by Rengraaden and Raenna. Soon they found themselves in the presence of Hallidan as well. As the night deepened and the stars bled through the deep-blue sky, a gong sounded before the castle, and the knights all fell to one knee. Every eye was fixed upon the stone balustrade that ran the width of the castle facade. Everyone knew the king was gone, but the festival would begin here, if it was to begin at all. A trim figure in white appeared high above them.

It was Izonden, the queen.

She walked to the rim of the stone balustrade that separated her from the waiting throng below her. It was clear to those who awaited her word that this Festival of Light would not be bringing as much joy to the queen as it would to her subjects. She seemed reluctant to speak, but at last she did.

"My dearest subjects. As you know, the king will not be here for this Festival of Light. With great joy did Hallidan and the Star Warriors make known that His Courage, the king, is still alive. . . ."

She hadn't meant to stop at this point, but her words, though already common knowledge, still stirred such excitement among her subjects that they all broke into applause. The applause continued long, and the strength the queen received from it seemed to enable her to continue once it subsided.

"A little more than an hour ago, I searched through the contents of the silver pouch that the condorg, Galanta, returned to the citadel. I found a letter addressed, not to myself, but to you, the beloved subjects of His Courage, the king. While the letter is yours and concerns both the Festival of Light and the safety of your beloved but endangered city, I have found it the greatest possible comfort to myself. Ren's love for you, his people, moved him to fly from the festival and enter upon an undisclosed plan which he believes will help to save this city. Ren's love is parent to his sacrifice and we must trust his wisdom and believe that he is a monarch who lays aside the dignity of his office in the heavy burden of his concern for all our welfare."

(47)

No one stirred. Their silence before their exquisite queen was witness to both her anxiety and the weight of the occasion. At length she began to read:

Here, my subjects, is the Desire of Ren:

To those my subjects, my life, my crown, the proud men and the valiant women of the gleaming city of Rensgaard,

Singreale, the treasure of Maldoon, has come back to us. Although we are outnumbered many times over by our brothers, at last there is hope. I now believe that we can win against the dark forces of Thanevial. The best part of my plan is too strategic to disclose, for it can only be successful if I act in complete isolation. I do not shrink before the challenge. Rather, I revel that I may lay aside the ensign of my office . . . yes, even the security of my office, and do the very thing that I have always demanded of each of you—to act, if necessary, to give up life itself in the defense and honor of this citadel.

I call upon you for that which is highest in all relationships: trust! What may be reported of me will seem itself a great lie. But I shall come back to you when the time is right, and when that time comes, all of the reasons that I have acted in the manner I now choose will become as apparent as the joy of the citadel set free.

For this Festival of Light, I, your king, command you now in my absence as I would in my presence: dance and sing for seven days. Singreale has come and the Festival of Light shall celebrate the hope with great joy. Let your joy be as complete as mine, even though we are separated by our cause. My task is to celebrate alone the power of Singreale, who, while you dance and sing, begins a lonely vigil that Rensgaard may see a thousand festivals to come.

> I command you to trust,
> And if you trust,
> I command you to celebrate the Light!
>
> Your Monarch,
> Ren

The letter was finished. It was clear that the king would tolerate no sadness, and none believed that he was dead. Wherever he had gone, whenever he would return, they knew they had two commands. The first was to trust, and the second was to celebrate.

Izonden spoke one final time: "The defense of the citadel shall belong to all of us! Rengraaden, Hallidan, and myself—we three will commit ourselves first to the trusting and then to the celebration, and always to the preservation of Rensgaard. Let us sing and dance: I command you all to Evensong!"

Just as though the king himself had commanded it, the knights dropped to one knee and faced their lofty queen.

Velissa was deeply stirred, and she watched to see if the ladies remained standing. Raccoman dropped awkwardly to one knee beside Rengraaden and Hallidan. Gradually he was adjusting to this new way of life in the citadel. All around him, knights drew their swords and their bright red fire-glass blades stabbed the cool night air above their heads.

Evensong began. It was a lusty melody full of a throaty allegiance:

"Rensgaard stands in towering stone—
  White in the center of the mountain peaks—
And the Riders dwell in the citadel
  Where the firestorms rage and the thunder speaks!
Ren is King! Ren is Courage! Ren is Hope!
  Ren is truth and ageless splendor, washed in light!
Come to the glorious land of Ren.
  Behold the star that rules the night.
Ren is King! Ren is Courage! Ren is Hope!"

Evensong died away, and the knights stood. They listened for the beginning strains of the music. The tall men and tall ladies formed two doubled columns and then a high arch of searing fire-glass saber blades. The fiery swords were beautiful whether set against the alabaster facade or the white-blue stars. The knights, with flare and showy precision, sheathed their swords and moved to the stately music. They led their ladies through what appeared to be a high march tune. The stepping became lively and so elegant were the dancers that Raccoman whispered to Velissa that never had he seen such dancing in the land of the Graygills. It was an exaggeration, for Raccoman was himself the best dancer from either world. But the tall people before him did possess a stately grace not given to Graygills.

Hallidan, not having his own lady, sat quietly by the wide stone plaza with the Graygills.

"You must try the next one," said Hallidan to Raccoman and

Velissa. "You have told us that your people were the best of the dancers and singers in the land from which you've come."

"Perhaps," said Raccoman. "Perhaps!" he said a second time as if he needed to convince himself that he had a place among these tall and stately people.

The second number was a spritelier tune, and Raccoman listened long enough to be sure that this was more to his liking and ability. He found himself dropping back into the rhyme that had been so characteristic of him until the pursuing Drogs had stolen all of his courage and most of his presence of mind. He had hardly begun to step to the bright music when he felt his old self-confidence begin to return. Raccoman never felt really good until he felt sure of himself, and egotism was the side of himself that he most enjoyed.

"The dancing has come—let no one be glum,
Velissa Dakktare, we're a marvelous pair.
We shall dance till our legs and feet have gone numb
And we've left all of Rensgaard—amazed and struck dumb!"

He stopped his rhyme only long enough to catch his breath.

"Come dance with me!" he said to his wife with a broad grin and too much flair.

"I shall, indeed," she laughed.

Raccoman's yellow attire and Velissa's blue garments seemed to dazzle the Titans like a bright, two-colored spinner. Indeed, the Graygills so took to their high stepping that in a moment the knights and their ladies had stopped to watch and soon took to clapping their hands in time with the bright chords that Raccoman and Velissa stamped into the paving stones. The horror of the previous days fell away in the merriment, and bright diamonds of light returned to Velissa's large eyes.

At last the music stopped. The knights laughed and cheered the fatigue of Raccoman's short legs. "More, more!" they cried. Hallidan called them back to the side of the plaza area. Several women were standing near him. Hallidan was unmarried, and so attracted both single women and the widows of those knights already killed in the Drog battles. He also attracted the women called the Miserians—those women whose husbands were not dead but had become traitors and monsters, having baptized themselves in the forming pits of the Valley of the Changelings. The Miserians had lost their husbands and yet never could have husbands again. They were stately and lamentable women—disconsolate over the defection of their men. Yet they, too, came to the Festival. And like the others, they begged Raccoman and Velissa to go on dancing.

"Tell them . . . whew . . . tell them, Hallidan, we cannot do more now," said Raccoman.

"Then give them one of your ballads," Velissa said.

"Would you?" cried one of the Miserians who had been completely captivated by the fiery rhythm that had so recently sent the little couple spinning among the knights and their ladies.

"The musicians could never handle the Claxton or the Lindon," objected Raccoman as Velissa dragged him to his feet.

"All right, then, make up a ballad and dance to the melody we have just finished," suggested Velissa.

> "All right, my dear, I will let them see,
> The bright stepping prowess of Raccoman D.,
> Who may be the best that they'll ever see,"

he said, forgetting any semblance of modesty. But Raccoman knew that modesty and great dancing never keep company. It was better to dance well than to let any false humility dampen his style.

Velissa was glad to see once more the abundant self-confidence that had been stolen from her husband in the dembret jungle and caladena groves.

"My dear, you're the standard all men should be," she exclaimed. And the knights laughed at Velissa's appraisal as Raccoman quickly agreed that he was, indeed, "The heartbeat and key, the idol deserving of idolatry."

> "Give us an old tune that ripples the flutes
> And as sure as maroon caladenas have roots,
> I'll stamp you a ballad in bright yellow boots."

The music began once again, and after the passing of a half-dozen chords on instruments like none the Graygills had ever seen before, the ballad began. As Raccoman had learned in a thousand years of merriment on the continent of his birth, he did justice to the old reputation he had held among his people before the war of the beasts had begun.

> "We have come from the land where tall men stand
>   Half-a-man less than men stand here.
> And it must be told that our ship of gold

> *Tracked the footless void of the atmosphere.*
> *We have sailed from the land of the grumblebeaks*
> > *And the jagged skies of mountain peaks*
> *To the purple trees and the green mist woods*
> > *And the jinnidrinnins' song is good.*
> *Ho, lay-hie, see the condorgs fly*
> > *And the fire-glass sword is the light that speaks."*

His song was as animated as it could possibly be. It was filled with his own impression of jinnidrinnins and grumblebeak, whose clumsy flight he tunefully animated. The Knights of Ren, never having seen one, could neither fully understand nor appreciate the excellence of his illustration. However, when it came to illustrating the grand condorgs in flight, his stubby frame provided only a comic parody of the grandeur of the winged steeds. Feeling that he must do better on the second verse, he first danced a short while to the quick rhythm of the piece and then began again.

> *"We felt insane when our yellow plane*
> > *Snagged on a caladena tree.*
> *Through the green mist fog came the handsome Drog*
> > *To welcome us with his Changelings three.*
> *How cheerful the cracked-faced warrior-beasts*
> > *Welcomed us to their Drog-lord feasts,*
> *And we almost entered Thanevial's trust*
> > *Till we found that the feast he planned was us.*
> *Ho, lay-hen, to the Titan men*
> > *Who came to us from the court of Ren.*

Again, his antics were splendid. His imitation of the Drog lord was superb. Never missing a step of his cadence, he hunched his back and dragged his yellow cuffs on the stone floor, while bulging his eyes. The knights doubled over in laughter.

> *"We have quailed in the terror of the Drog lord's greed*
> > *Singing ho, lay-ho in the forest air.*
> *We have fought and won in the Caves of Smeade*
> > *Where the fire-glass blazed and the Titans dared.*
> *In the purple groves where the great trees rise*
> > *And the woods are filled with a thousand eyes,*
> *Where eyes see not, and ears can't hear*
> > *And the dread unseen is the dread you fear,*
> *We have walked the heart of the evil glen,*
> > *And raised the tribute unto Ren."*

The chorus was finished, and the musicians kept the tune picking its way from star to star as Raccoman's dance finally wearied, and he ended the sinister march of the Changelings. To be sure, not every verse was as funny as the middle verse had been, but nonetheless, he was such a compelling entertainer that the knights could but offer him wholehearted applause when he finished.

Raccoman had become all the more a symbol for the day. If he, a half-Titan by reason of his stature, could survive, surely there was hope. If he could still believe and sing in such a time, then the men of the citadel should hope. What reason had any of the Titan knights to be morose when smaller souls could dance?

After the knights and their ladies had enjoyed several more songs and dances, the mood of the evening became one of expectancy. It was not long before the gong sounded again. Izonden, the queen, came alone to survey her people.

As she advanced through the holiday throng, each man fell to one knee and each woman bowed her head. Raccoman and Velissa watched her approach. It was clear that the queen was with child, but her dignity was not compromised by her obvious impending motherhood. She walked directly toward Raccoman and Velissa.

Raccoman, mimicking the knights, fell to one knee, and Velissa bowed her head as the queen approached. With kindness, Queen Izonden lifted Velissa's chin and, stooping quite a distance, raised Raccoman to his feet.

"You are welcome to Rensgaard," the queen said.

Like Velissa, Raccoman was drawn to the queen of the white citadel. Like Velissa, he was intimidated into silence by the regal deportment of the queen. Suddenly the sky above them was interrupted by the fluttering of wings. Raccoman looked up.

"Rexel, no!" he exclaimed, for it seemed to him that the queen was about to be attacked by the falcon. An instant later, however, his fears vanished as the beautiful bird dropped onto his own small forearm. The golden feathers around the bird's neck glistened.

"Rexel, you have done your job well," said the queen, reaching out to stroke the head of the falcon. Then Raccoman's inner vision cleared. Rexel had been the key. The falcon had served as the vital link between the two worlds. He had served the Desire of Ren by leading the unsuspecting Graygills to the continent where he had numbered the centuries in the service of Ren and Izonden.

Velissa's eyes filled with tears, for now she knew that their flight from one land of war to another land of war held a meaning that was more than they could have reasoned. She was struck dumb by the insight that one's life and fate can sometimes be held a world away from home.Though not everything about their circumstances was completely clear to her, Velissa found that she was no longer afraid. She looked at the queen and smiled. Izonden's golden crown seemed to sweep the stars. As Velissa beheld the towering dignity of this woman before her, she could not help but love her. Nor could she erase from her mind the image of the naked king who had taken the treasure of two worlds and entered the desolate darkness of Smeade.

Velissa barely whispered to the queen of the Star Warriors, "Izonden, you are woman of great courage!"

The queen could only disagree, for somewhere in the lonely jungles around Mt. Calz, the naked king, for reasons of his own, kept the Festival of Light in utter darkness.

"No," said the queen resolutely, "Ren is king, Ren is courage, Ren is hope." Izonden had answered with the last line of Evensong, and her love for her husband compelled Velissa to agree.

"Yes. Ren is courage."

In this life, watchfulness can't keep
  The dreaded demons from our sleep.
We fear that dreams may come to be
  Dread hauntings of arch treachery.
The friend who begs us stay the night
  May prove a fiend in lesser light.

CHAPTER IV

Festival of Light

$\mathcal{T}$HE FESTIVAL OF LIGHT lasted for seven days. Compared to the terror that they had undergone in their rescue, the Graygills now found life tranquil. Yet Velissa woke twice in the middle of the night during her first week in the citadel. Hers was, indeed, a troubled sleep. In the darkness of her room, the lingering Changelings seemed to be leering at her, and their leathery and loathsome appearance haunted her shallow dreams.

On their third day in the home of Raenna and Rengraaden, the Graygills' handsome host arrived home at an early hour of the afternoon. Hallidan and Raccoman were at the parade ground near the royal residence. Raenna was shopping in the farmers' area of the city. Only Velissa had stayed behind.

She felt very much alone. She knew no one in the citadel, except those she had lately met. With Raccoman away, she tried to pass the hours first by napping and then by walking before the dwelling on the sunny street. When she had grown bored with walking, she re-entered the apartment and brewed herself a cup of the herb tea that Raenna had taught her to prepare. In the midst of her boredom, the fire, small though it was, seemed to heat the house to an unbearable warmth.

Suddenly the door opened. Velissa turned and saw it was Rengraaden.

"Are you alone?" he asked.

"I'm afraid so. Raccoman and Hallidan are gone to the parade ground, and Raenna to market."

"Velissa . . . ," The handsome knight moved slowly and then chose his words one at time. He took a chair near her and drew it even nearer. "I am glad you are staying with us. I would like you to come with me tomorrow. At this Festival of Light, I would like to present a special gift to Raenna. There is a star-stone mine—old and abandoned—near the northwest slopes of Mt. Calz. I would like for you, since you are a woman, it is natural that you would know what my Raenna would like. . . ."

The Star Rider faltered badly.

He reached his hand and touched her arm.

His fingers felt warm and she recoiled, then stood up and walked to the door.

"Velissa!" he said forcefully, getting to his feet and moving between her and the open doorway.

Velissa had never quite realized how tall the Star Riders really were until now, when she was being menaced by one and she felt in awe of the towering Rengraaden.

Hearing her name spoken so emphatically, she became afraid. She tried to squeeze between the Titan hulk and the door frame. "Velissa, I want you to ride with me. You must understand, Velissa; I must have your consent. I need Singreale." He caught her shoulder with his huge hand.

"Please, Rengraaden, you're hurting me!"

"Velissa, look at me. Do you understand? The great diamond, what did you do with it?" Velissa decided at once that she would not reveal the king's landing at the Caverns of Smeade, but Rengraaden's strong fingers curled into her thin shoulder, and she found the pain excruciating.

"You will tell me. Do you understand? I *will* have Singreale!"

Velissa dropped to one knee, trying to pull free from Rengraaden's grasp but it was useless.

Then, in a moment of insight, she took hold of the hilt of his sword and raised it a few inches out of its scabbard. Only a few inches of the fire-glass glowed, but they would be sufficient. She jammed the hilt toward the knight's body. The fire-glass seared a burning hole in his tunic, and when the fiery blade touched his side, he screamed and released Velissa. She darted out through the door as he was left doubled over in pain.

Velissa ran down the lane between the long apartments and turned between two dwellings towards the parade ground.

She ran full into Raenna.

"Whatever is the matter?" asked Raenna. "You look terrified."

"Oh, Raenna," exclaimed Velissa, embracing her. "Rengraaden. . . ."

"Rengraaden?" asked Raenna in surprise.

"Rengraaden—" For a moment Velissa could not make herself go on. Then she said, "Rengraaden came into the room—he came in too suddenly and he frightened me—I guess it's his size. I'm not used to such Titan men as those in the king's guard."

Velissa did not lie very well, and while Raenna gave the appearance of believing her story, the terror in the Graygill's eyes told her there was more to it. She realized that Velissa was either protecting herself or protecting Rengraaden. She invited Velissa to go back with her to their dwelling, but Velissa vigorously declined.

"No, please, not now," she pleaded, and then added, "I must go look for Raccoman."

"Very well," said Raenna, "but come along when you find him and we'll share a meal before Evensong. We can attend the night's festivities together."

The two women separated. Raenna went on to her home somehow afraid to face her husband, though she had not the slightest idea why. But the meeting never materialized. Rengraaden had slipped out of their cubicle and left the lane the other way. Nor did they meet the entire night.

By the time that Velissa found Raccoman and Hallidan, her emotions were more settled. Hallidan noticed nothing amiss in her demeanor. Raccoman was immediately aware of some inner turmoil. On their way back to Rengraaden's dwelling, Velissa related the entire story to her husband and begged him not to leave her again. Raccoman promised to do all that he could to persuade Hallidan to ask the queen to give them a place of lodging all their own. They both agreed to keep the whole matter secret, since Rengraaden was Ren's nephew. They realized that no one would believe Velissa's tale anyway, and the telling of it would only weaken the credibility of the newly arrived Graygills.

The days that followed were spent in activities that sustained the joy of the citadel. Those who tended the fields still brought their produce on crude hand-drawn carts into the city. The fields east of the citadel were open to the ravine, and thus, their produce could be grown without threat. Beyond the fields, there was a ridge of mountains that fell away sharply to the sea beyond. The fields that were farmed lay in the upper mesas at an elevation as high as the mountain on which the citadel stood. The Drogs rarely circled the citadel to trouble these mountaintop farmlands.

The Drogs were carnivorous and would have shown more interest in the field-tenders than in their produce. When the Drogs could kill a beast or bird, they feasted on them. Their members had already killed so much of the game in the forests that, as they increased in number, they began to turn to cannibalism. Although the war had not yet grown to such a scale that their ranks had been thinned by combat, the survivors of each siege often retrieved their fallen companions for their own foul nourishment.

The field-tenders feared the Drogs. Ren had declared that all farmers should always come back into the city before nightfall, but the order was unnecessary. The fear that the Changelings would come upon them made the farmers cautious. The idea of being devoured was a horrible incentive to precaution.

The dwellings of the field-tenders stood at the lower end of the citadel by the east-chasm bridge. This bridge was the one that crossed the deepest part of the gorge that surrounded Rensgaard, and therefore, the farmers were safe. The field-tenders and their wives were welcome in the celebrations and festivals of the citadel, and they enjoyed the protection of the knights as the knights enjoyed the food produced by the farmers.

There was no difference in either size or intelligence between the knights and the farmers. And in the days before Thanevial's treachery, there had been no difference in their status. Like the Graygills, the Titans had metal-workers, stone-workers, and those who worked with wood. But, unlike the Graygills, the Titans also had those who worked with glass. The boiling sand pits in the Desert of Draymon provided a liquid source of hot glass that could be drawn and cooled and shaped. The glass was used in many ways: for eating utensils and vessels, for panes for the small windows in the outer-upper walls of the citadel, and most importantly, for the blades of the knights' fire-glass swords. It was a hard and unbreakable glass that remained liquid at its core and cooled slowly after years of use. The fire-glass swords were not only unbreakable and very sharp, but they were searing hot and had to be carried in fiber scabbards to keep them from burning the legs of the Titans who wielded them—as Velissa had taught Rengraaden.

During the mornings, the knights continued their training for the all-out war they knew must come. Hallidan was the leader of the instructors of the new knights, who were largely drawn from the young field-tenders who had decided to leave the occupation they had inherited from the parents. Other young knights were drawn to the defense of Rensgaard because they were the children of Titans already in service of Ren. The young knights-to-be who had come from the fields, of course, needed the most instruction, while the offspring of the warriors had viewed their calling from the center of their family life for years and thus had an easier time during training. Most of them were already familiar with how the fire-glass must be handled. This was well, for the glowing liquid center of each sword made it a difficult weapon to master. The liquid movement inside the fire-red blade had a gravitational momentum of its own in combat.

Raccoman agreed to sword training, and shortly discovered it was a more difficult task than he supposed. The Graygill was present to watch the glass-workers on the third morning of the festival. He was a little weary from all the dancing of the night before, but completely fascinated as he watched the glass-workers set upon a large pot of molten glass which had been brought that very morning from the Desert of Draymon by a group of six knights on condorgs.

The tall craftsmen were perspiring in the heat of their occupation. They cracked the thin scum at the top of the cauldron and drew upward, with special finesse, a thin stream of the bright red liquid. In but a moment, it had hardened into a minute, invisible ribbon that gleamed in the red light of the dark room where they worked. No sooner was the ribbon formed than the huge glass-worker gently lowered it again into the cauldron. The molten glass received it in a shower of furiously hot sparks that flew upward around the bright ruddy face and hands of the glass-worker. In the course of these repeated dippings, he began to shape the blade by turning it on a treadle wheel. Within two hours, the blade, a short one, was formed and fastened to a fiber belt and at last it was placed in a scabbard of special fibers, impervious to its fire.

The craftsman then handed the small sword to Raccoman, who in the simple act of taking it in his hand, seemed to give the weapon additional length—for once the Titan surrendered it, the blade was just the right size for the Graygill. Raccoman tied the fiber sheath to his belt and thanked the glass-worker more than was really necessary. The tall craftsman smiled with a face reddened by the glow of the cauldron before him.

As they left the glass foundry, Raccoman unconsciously strutted. It was the first time the Graygill metal-worker had seen a glass-worker in the creation of his art. Besides, this sword was his very own.

"Remember," counseled Hallidan, "the fire-glass is hot. Never touch the blade with your bare hand, and be sure that your wife or little ones never touch it—I'm sorry."

Hallidan was clearly embarrassed by his slip of tongue. Raccoman had no children, and Hallidan, having no wife, was neither as observant nor as considerate as he might have been. Raccoman ignored the comment seeing that Hallidan seemed a bit overwrought by his mistake. Clumsily, Raccoman tried to ask further as they strolled toward the training ground, "Why are there so few young children in the city?" Raccoman and Velissa had already noticed, and in private, had discussed the fact that there were almost none.

"The certainty of war has caused my people to be cautious in bringing children into such uncertain times," answered Hallidan.

"Is it for the same reason that you have not taken a wife?"

The question was brash, but Raccoman seemed not to notice his own impertinence. Hallidan smiled. There was something that he should not say and yet he did. "If I could have a prize like the woman who keeps Rengraaden's cubicle, I would marry in spite of this accursed war," he replied. "Raenna is Rengraaden's and none of the others appeal to me."

Raccoman saw that Raenna was some sort of standard for Hallidan, and so he said to him:

> *"A home should be shared*
> *And even in war it is better to be*
> *Grieved by a lass who has just lost her lad*
> *Than to battle uncared for—disconsolate.*
> *When you've battled the Drogs*
> *And the land is at rest*
> *You may wish for someone*
> *To warm your own nest."*

"Now, now," laughed Hallidan, a good sport, "I'm a bachelor. It seems to fit me. I must admit life gets a little lonely sometimes. You wouldn't understand that, I guess!"

"I offer you a thousand years of empathy," replied the Graygill, looking up into the broad, handsome face of his tall friend. "I thought I would never marry, but, I finally found a Graygill lass who likes older men as well as one who likes to sing and dance."

"Well, you've got to be the best at that," agreed Hallidan.

> *"I'm the best you ever will see*
> *The model, the standard*
> *The hope and the key."*

Hallidan could now adjust to Raccoman's little stature packed so tightly with his own self-importance.

They continued talking until they arrived at the training ground. There they saw a couple of hundred young knights receiving various kinds of instruction from two hundred instructors. Raccoman was eager for his own training. He was quickly assigned by Hallidan to a very blond Titan knight named Sandalin.

"It's his first time with fire-glass," Hallidan cautioned Sandalin.

Sandalin smiled and then looked very serious. "Never touch your weapon with your body," he said.

Raccoman, who had only been used to the metal swords of the Canbies, was afraid of his weapon and confessed this to Sandalin.

"Fear is good—the more fear, the better, till you have learned to handle the glass. I have seen a young knight lose a part of his hand or lay the deadly blade against his body and severely wound himself. The Drogs fear the glass-fire and well are they afraid."

Raccoman set himself to parrying with his deadly blade against the mentor Sandalin. Both of them wore special metal armor that protected them from the razorlike edges of the searing weapons that they were using.

Raccoman found it difficult to handle the sharp liquid core of his weapon. No matter how much force he exerted on the hilt, the weapon seemed to have a mind of its own. It took him a week before he finally learned to let the weapon wield its own destructive path.

The Graygill felt the strong disadvantage of his size. His every parry that might connect had to be aimed upward and extended to the full length of his stubby arm. For an entire morning, he struggled with his disadvantaged size to learn the best ploys and stances of the battles he expected to fight someday.

It was on the morning of the fifth day that he began to consider the question of what advantage his short height might give him in his own style of combat. All of a sudden in his parrying with Sandalin, he pictured his own move, and he swung low, no longer trying for an awkward, upward thrust. The blow fell across the metal plates above Sandalin's ankle with a force sufficient to slice the plate and leather of his mentor's boot. Sandalin cried out in pain.

Raccoman, in embarrassment and fear, felt instant shame, and he laid the sword aside carelessly, brushing it with his hand. He instantly howled in the agony of severely burning himself. Carefully then, he sheathed the fire-glass and turned to Sandalin, who had ripped off the metal plates that protected his leg and just as quickly tore off his boot. He was relieved to see that the boot and steel had taken the greatest extent of the abuse and that his burn was only superficial. With great concern, Sandalin also inspected the burn on Raccomna's hand and was greatly relieved to discover that it, too, was but a surface wound.

They both laughed, and Raccoman learned two lessons he would never forget. Short warriors may not decapitate an enemy, but, as Sandalin put it, he may "defootilate" a foe. The other lesson that Raccoman learned from the terrific pain in his hand was never to touch fire-glass with his naked hand.

By the afternoon of the fifth day, Raenna had helped Velissa learn how to treat a wound. Velissa knew that the wives of the knights considered it their obligation to care for their husbands should they return from the fighting with wounds.

"The weapons of the Drogs leave torn and bloody wounds. Unlike fire-glass, which sears its victim with bloodless wounds, their swords bring a terrible loss of blood," said the beautiful wife of Rengraaden. "There's a blend of several herbs that will stop a lesser flow. But if a wound is deep enough or any body part should be destroyed, the best way to stop bleeding instantly is to apply the knight's own sword to the injury."

Then Raenna stopped for she could see that Velissa was troubled by the idea of her small husband being severely wounded by his large foes. Velissa fought the burning at the corners of her eyes and the lump in her throat. What was to come in the war she could not guess, but she borrowed enough from Raenna's composure to ask, "If Raccoman should return with a great wound or a limb missing. . . ." She faltered at this point, paralyzed by the vision her mind contained. But calmed by Raenna's courage, she began again and asked, "Would I have to sear the wounds?"

"Not usually. If the knight is conscious and has strength enough for the task, he will sear his own wounds."

Velissa knew that Titans were great of courage, and yet she found it impossible to believe that they could bear the pain of such a self-inflicted treatment. She wondered if Raccoman could find the courage for such a treatment. She turned from the thought and locked her mind against all such considerations.

From the time of their parting on the third day of the festival, Rengraaden and Raenna were to remain separated for another three days. Where Rengraaden had spent the time, Raenna could not guess. She knew that he had taken his condorg and left the city. It was most unusual for any knight to stay out of the city overnight. Except for surveillance of the other continent, the Star Riders were almost never gone for the night.

When Rengraaden did return near dusk on the sixth day of the festival, Raenna could tell her husband had come back preoccupied with something far away.

(65)

"Rengraaden, you've returned, but your heart and thoughts are still away."

The handsome Star Rider only grumbled. Raenna went to him, put her arms around him, and drew him close. Yet as she pulled him near, he tore her hand from his side as his face drew up in pain.

"You're hurt!" she cried, looking at the ugly burn on his side just above the hilt of his sword.

"It's nothing," he said as he walked away from her.

"How did it happen?" Raenna knew better than to probe, but she had never seen her warrior so gloomy and remote.

"I burned it with my sword accidentally," he complained. Inwardly, he was surprised that Velissa had not yet reported their private matter to his wife.

Raenna knew he was lying, yet she brushed that possibility from her mind. Rengraaden was her warrior, and she would not permit herself to doubt a man who had never in their five hundred years of marriage given her the slightest reason to doubt.

She went to him again and sat down on his lap. "Don't tell me that, after a thousand years of handling fire-glass, you suddenly forgot its power?" she said and laughed.

"Stop it, Raenna!" he demanded. "Get away from me!"

His words were biting. She obeyed, walking first to the open window and staring disconsolately away over the purple caladena groves in the distance. The day was beautiful. Rengraaden needed solitude, she understood, and she needed to give it to him. She moved to the doorway and walked outside.

There she found Velissa sitting in the shade of the eastern wall and studying the same distant caladena groves. Velissa could tell that Raenna was carrying someone else's mood, but she didn't know it was Rengraaden's.

"Velissa," she said, "do you mind if I enter your private world?"

"I am too much in yours," said Velissa. "Maybe Raccoman and I will soon have our own apartment."

"Please don't feel as though you are in my way" Raenna paused a moment and then abruptly changed the subject, "Velissa, Rengraaden is back."

Velissa shifted uncomfortably and said nothing.

"Is there something between the two of you?" Raenna asked.

"Nothing," said Velissa, "Raccoman and I are in the way at your house. Surely we will soon have our own apartment."

Raenna turned the conversation.

"Rengraaden burned his side," said the tall woman. "I'll need to prepare some herbs to give him release from the pain. I'm afraid the pain has left him out of sorts. I've never seen him as gloomy and distant as he is today."

Raenna could tell that, besides the pain of war, her husband was carrying some new and unspoken grief or appetite that he found hard to speak about. She further knew that Velissa's refusal to come into the apartment with her until Raccoman returned was further evidence that something had gone wrong.

On the sixth night of the festival, as they retired for the evening, Raenna heard Rengraaden talking in his sleep. "Singreale, Singreale, Singreale—mine!" he moaned between labored breaths. At last, he shouted the word with such fury that he woke himself.

"Are you all right?" Raenna asked.

"Fine," he answered. "Raenna, I must have Singreale, and I believe the Graygills know where it is. You must persuade Velissa to take me to it."

"But why? They have already said the king has it. Surely it will be safe with Ren."

"I believe Ren is dead and Velissa is lying."

"What? That idea is preposterous." Raenna was firm. "Izonden has called us to trust."

"Izonden is cunning. She and Velissa know where the diamond is. And I intend to find out."

"How—no, not how, why?" Raenna pressed, asking and unasking the same question. "Why do you want it? It will only spoil you and perhaps us. Why?"

"Raenna, I want to rule. You could be my queen."

"But I don't want to be queen—not at the price of accusing Izonden of treachery and turning my back on Velissa with vile accusations."

Raenna was suddenly and terribly afraid.

Rengraaden turned his face in anger to the wall.

On the seventh and last morning of the Festival of Light, an incident occurred that was to mark the festival with doubt. Velissa and Raenna were with their husbands at the Matin. Just as the Matin began, Rengraaden dropped to one knee and raised the fireglass. Raccoman was learning. He faced the king's facade, and assumed the posture, and strained to follow the deep-throated anthem with his own higher voice.

Raccoman was so intent on getting the words of the anthem correct, he did not see what Raenna and Velissa could not fail to mark. As Rengraaden sang, he faced the king's residence. Yet from time to time, Rengraaden's gaze fell into melancholy that turned in some inner longing past the snowcapped peak of Mt. Calz.

> "This is the land where honor reigns,
> This is the land where truth is king,
> Here is the kingdom voice of change,
> Where men live free forever."

The last line of the Matin Raccoman sang alone. Only then did he notice that the Star Rider did not sing with him.

On the last night of the festival, the singing and dancing went on for an unusually long time. The Graygills had at last mastered the dance steps of the knights and ladies, but with their own short stature, they still failed at their best attempts to achieve the gliding, almost floating grace of the Titans.

It was the quick dance which the Graygills did well. The knights were so enchanted by the welder and his wife that they were compelled to stand and clap the furious beat to which Raccoman's yellow boots stomped the white pavement. Velissa's blue skirt swirled tight against her body, then loosened and twisted tight again in the opposite direction as the pair made the music time.

Each night the company had clapped until Raccoman composed a song and danced his words into rhythms. On the last night, the innovative musicians played their unusual stringed instruments in such quick plucking of the strings that Raccoman felt at home at last to sing the forest rhyme he had sung so often throughout his long life.

When he finished singing, Raccoman saw that Velissa's face was touched by a sadness he could only observe with pain. They both were already homesick for a world they knew was set across the ocean and a world that had died in the days they had lived through and now were gone. The knights, sensing the Graygills' pain, kept silent. Then Velissa began to sing in her low and beautiful voice the words she knew were an allegiance she was determined never to forget. The threat of Rengraaden faded as she sang:

> "Let us sing at the base of the ginjon tree
> For Canby's fields are the fields of the free,

May the sun long rise and the morning skies
Herald the anthem of liberty.
Heigh-ho! Heigh-ho! Our children may roam
Through the friendly fields of Castledome.
For beasts and men are timeless friends.
In the ageless land of Estermann."

Half-way through, Velissa could not go on. Her images of the past choked her, and she fell silent. Raccoman, sharing her pain, stepped to her and took up the melody until her own voice was strong enough to join in again.

When the song was finished, the Titans realized a new appreciation for the Graygills who had fled their own war-torn land in the quest for a land of peace and whose wistful hopes had been dashed by Thanevial's rebellion. Slowly, they offered a volley of applause, not so much for Velissa's performance, as an affirmation of her disconsolate spirit. Only one knight did not join in the applause. Rengraaden uncannily curled his lip in disdain while he looked far away past Mt. Calz once again—this time more fixedly than before.

In a moment, Rengraaden's hard and focused reverie was called back to the scene at hand by Hallidan, who cried, "Ren is forever!" He followed it with a second cry, "To the Friend that begs the Light!"

It was the custom of the last day of the festival that Ren would come to the royal facade and ignite the ceremonial fire. But Ren was gone. No sooner had Hallidan voiced the historic cry than the queen emerged from the castle, having come directly from the palace behind it. She was carrying the ceremonial torch which she plunged into the huge pile of dry caladena twigs. The flames leapt upward, orange against the blue-white light of the stars. The knights, with one sweeping motion, lifted their brilliant red fire-glass blades to the sky and cried, with the amber flickerings of the fire full on their faces, "Ren is forever!"

Again Raccoman and Velissa knew neither the words nor the sequence of the dramatic liturgy, and they did not try to participate. The ritual ended with the knights singing their anthem to the death of fire and the coming of Ren, the Light King. At the end of the ballad, each knight took his cape and smothered the fire until only white smoke was left. The smoking caladena branches caused Velissa's eyes to burn.

Then came the king's part of the liturgy. The queen walked with dignity to the center of the balustrade. She lifted her slender arms exactly as the king would have done. All eyes turned in her direction.

"To Singreale!" she cried. Light from the hungry fire filtered in swordlike rays through the smoke whose heavy streams were now laced by red swords, white stars, and the lofty image of the queen standing with arms uplifted above the crowded plaza.

With the utmost dignity, Izonden descended the long cascade of steps. Though she was great with child, her image was a striking one that served the festival well in the absence of the king.

At last the music began again, and the Graygills fell to conversation with Hallidan about their ocean crossing. In recounting his last days in the valley of the Graygills, Raccoman told Hallidan of the death of his Moonrhyme uncle, Krepel. The mention of the word *Moonrhyme* made Hallidan stop short.

"Your uncle—a Moonrhyme!" he blurted out and then followed his outburst with a question, "Are you a Moonrhyme, too?"

"Only half," Raccoman admitted. "My mother was a Canby, but my father was the brother of Krepel and a full-blooded Moonrhyme."

"His name?" asked Hallidan, rather insistently.

"Garrod," Raccoman answered.

"Garrod!" exploded Hallidan. His face was alight, and he dragged Raccoman to the center of the plaza in great excitement. Raccoman had not the slightest inkling of what Hallidan's strange outburst could mean.

In the center of the camp, Hallidan drew his fire-glass blade and cut loops of red light against the starry sky to call the attention of the crowd.

"Men of Rensgaard! Ren is Forever! I give you Raccoman, Son of Garrod the Moonrhyme!"

The knights appeared transfixed. Silence, born of a sudden and unexpected source that left Raccoman bewildered, fell like an unseen net across the plaza. The men dropped to their knees and lowered their heads. On the face of one knight near the front of the crowd was a smile, and Raccoman saw his lips form the name of his Moonrhyme father: "Garrod!"

Some men once were serpents,
　Some serpents once men.
Too freely they changed,
　Then changed back again.
But those who change much
　Find their memories are cursed
And lost to recall
　Which form they held first.

CHAPTER V

The Nativity

iT WAS A CUSTOM after the last
night of the gala festival to bar the city and spend a day in rest and
thankfulness for the peace of Ren. War was in the wind, and the
security of the Rensgaard had to be preserved with deep moats
and sentries. The six drawbridges of the city's gates were to remain
drawn. All commerce was banned during the day following the festival. Those who tended the fields were forbidden to leave the city
as were the knights of Ren.

The openings in the high towers were sealed by the upright
bridges that left the canyon moats deep ravines of fear. The
knights and their ladies lingered after the festive final evening was
concluded. They sat beneath the stars to enjoy the last night of the
holiday, their future as uncertain as the crumbling edges of the
molten seas in the Desert of Draymon. An unnamed sense of desperation pervaded the air. It caused the inhabitants of the citadel
to hang on to the sunny moments of every day and the silver-
purple nights. Days and nights seemed in short supply to those for
whom a future might not come.

The revel was over, and in the lateness of the hour the conversation soon began to lag. One by one, the Titans began to disperse.
They left the torchlit starscape and retired for the day of rest that
would follow the festivites. The first to leave the square were the
widows. Next, the Miserians, the wives of the infamous defectors,
retired. The Miserians knew that those who had been their husbands were now Changelings. The Drogs who were once their men
now plotted against the existence of the very city in which their
disconsolate wives still lived.

Raccoman and Velissa had been astonished over the reverence
that gathered about the two of them at the mere mention of Raccoman's father. They were amazed that the ancient name meant anything in the land of the knights. Hallidan began to unfold the tale of
the Moonrhyme named Garrod. It was a saga of fascination for the
Graygills. Unhurried, Hallidan sat long with the Graygills while the
festival square gradually emptied of its citizens, and he explained
why Rensland held the name of Raccoman's father in worship. The

knight told them that Garrod had arrived in Rensgaard shortly after the defection of Lord Thanevial.

"But arrived how?" protested the Graygill.

"I cannot say how. I cannot even say why," answered Hallidan. The amber torchlight flickered on the handsome face of the Titan as he continued. "All I can say is that we discovered him just after the unthinkable act of Thanevial's defection and the atrocity that split the kingdom into shredded horror."

Raccoman could not believe that Hallidan was old enough to remember events that had happened almost a thousand years ago when Raccoman himself was but a boy. Something in Raccoman's heart wanted to be a child again in the faraway land where he had been raised. He remembered what he had been told of his father. After his service in the distinguished army of King Singreale, Raccoman's father left the valley of the Canbies. He passed then into the land where he had been born five hundred years before his son, Raccoman. The Grand Cavern of the Moonrhymes was the place where Garrod came to know life. The cavern was in the Moonrhyme cliff dwellings north of the stone sentinels of Demmerron Pass. Raccoman told Hallidan of how, according to those who had last seen Garrod, the Moonrhyme was inspecting a baffling set of labyrinths inside the interlaced tunnels of the dwellings and was lost underground. Though a rescue party was sent after him, his remains were never discovered.

"Why do you say remains?" Hallidan asked the Graygill.

"Because," Raccoman spoke slowly as he looked across the walls of the citadel into the stars that seemed to know more of the riddle of Garrod than did Garrod's own son.

"Because," Raccoman said, "the inner caverns of the Moonrhymes had a great many unexplored tunnels that ended in deep pits walled with watery shafts and foul-smelling slime."

"After months of looking for him, it seemed futile to search any longer for Raccoman's father. He could have been lost anywhere in the cavernous depths," Velissa said, interrupting Raccoman's tale because she sensed he had grown too emotional in the telling of it.

"It was the system itself that the Moonrhymes most cherished," Raccoman said, finally able to go on. "Some said he had gone blind while roving these black tunnels, perilous as they were. The Moonrhymes had managed to survive the ills that had eradicated all life in the lower valleys of Canby, and my father . . ."

"What ills?" Hallidan broke in.

"Who know what ills?" replied Raccoman, looking away.

"The ills—whatever they were," said Velissa, taking over during her husband's melancholy trance once again, "were referred to as 'the cataclysm.' It happened long ago, before the people built villages in the lower valleys. They told of a white fire that laced the valleys and scathed the mountains in an embrace of death. Whatever the cataclysm was, it destroyed all life on the lower plains, and only the Moonrhymes in their mountain burrows and blind tunnels managed to survive the fire storms."

"Most people," continued Raccoman, "believed it was not the precipice cliffs that saved the Moonrhymes. It was not even the surface caverns, for they were not deep enough. Some believed that there must have been an inner set of tunnels and chambers that protected them during the height of the fire storms. Most suspected that my father became lost while trying to find that system of inner caverns."

"But how did he get here?" asked Hallidan, probing for some answer to the riddle.

"And what made him such a hero in Rensgaard?" asked the Graygill metal-worker, heaping riddle upon riddle. Raccoman had no answer to Hallidan's question. But Hallidan could answer the Graygill.

"When Thanevial was a courtier at the citadel," Hallidan explained, "Ren and his queen were younger then and their hopes for a child were not so haunted by fears. Still, the king and his brother were the last two members of a royal house that stretched for thousands and thousands of years into the past. It was important that one of them provide an heir to the throne of the citadel. As you know, Titans never have more than one or two children."

It seemed pointless to Raccoman for Hallidan to make the statement. Raccoman and Velissa had, indeed, noticed that most of the couples here were either childless or had only one or two children. On the fifth day of the festival, Velissa had seen a woman with two children and remarked how unusual the woman had appeared with a child on either side of her as she made her way across the plaza area of the city.

The Titans did live to be incredibly old and never seemed to grow infirm with the millenia that marked the boundaries of their lives. No one knew how many years Ren had lived. He was old— quite old. Still, he appeared as virile as a youth of only two or three millenia. Raccoman knew that Hallidan, even as he told the story, had to be at least a thousand years old to speak of the events he now discussed as though they were only yesterday. The Graygill smiled inwardly to realize that this indeed was likely how the knight viewed them. Raccoman watched the handsome, yet studied, face as the Hallidan continued. To the Graygill, the Titan's blue eyes beneath the ruthless shock of blond hair seemed especially intent as he recounted the next part of his tale.

"It was Rey, the king's brother, and his wife who were the first to offer the hope of a heritage for the gleaming citadel. They had a son. At long last, there was an heir. The king named the boy after his uncle, the king."

Light flooded Raccoman's mind. He rushed to the name before Hallidan could speak it. "Rengraaden!" he exclaimed.

"Yes," said the knight.

"His father is the king's brother?" asked Velissa, dumbfounded.

"Was," replied Hallidan.

"Was?" asked the Graygill.

"He was murdered.

"Murdered?" said Velissa in disbelief. "By a knight?"

Hallidan, wearied with the interruptions of the Graygills, only nodded and waited a few moments before he went on.

"On the night of the child's weaning festivities, less than a thousand years ago, the citadel suffered its first unthinkable defection. Until that time, the knights and their ladies had lived in the citadel in a grand unity that never questioned its allegiance to the king. Thanevial had been, for centuries, a beloved courtier. Envy was unknown in this realm. Perhaps had we Titans experienced jealousy ourselves, we might have seen him growing jealous. It began when Rey's baby was born.

"It was natural that the king would exalt the status of his brother, Rey, and his son. Ren walked with his nephew in his arms and seemed as proud of the child as if it had been born into his own home. As he continued to exalt the infant and his father, Thanevial became more and more remote. At last, he no longer came to the festivals, and he always seemed troubled and angry.

"A few days before the weaning festival of Rengraaden, the king reprimanded Thanevial because he had knocked Rey to the ground in a dispute between two of the farmers who supplied the royal houses, as well as Thanevial's own house with food. Thanevial felt that the farmers supplied the best of their produce to the royalty and brought only inferior food to lesser knights. Thanevial complained that his larder contained spoiled fruit. In the argument that erupted, Thanevial struck the farmers, and when Rey interrupted the fight, he was struck to the ground.

"It is unfortunate that Thanevial had allowed his jealously to consume him so. But it is also forbidden for knights to show violence toward anyone in the citadel. The king had no choice but to reprimand Thanevial. And Thanevial did not take the reprimand easily.

"Thanevial glared at the king and stomped from the court in a violent hatred of his lord. It was the first time that I had ever seen such hatred. I, like the others present, was possessed of a new chill that settled down upon the royal city.

"The days between the incident and Rengraaden's weaning festival were marked by a cold foreboding in the air. It stole into every nook and cranny of the royal city. Some horrible winter of hate was beginning, and the knights knew it. They all felt the evil sting of an ugly emotion that never before had been set loose in the city.

"The weaning festival was a weak attempt to regain the lost joy. We laughed and sang and danced, but there hung a horror over the party that only the brooding Thanevial could explain. His hatred barred him from the party. It was after the party that the atrocity occurred."

"Atrocity?" asked Raccoman.

Hallidan ignored the interruption. "It was not immediately known. Rey's family did not come to the square the next morning, and about noon it was discovered that their home had been violated during the night. The knight and his wife were dead, and the infant prince was missing. And as all suspected, Thanevial had also disappeared. He left the city unseen by night.

"Rensgaard was locked in shock and fear. Fear because—at that time—we had no weapons with which to defend ourselves, and we were confident that the evil Thanevial, having murdered once, would not hesitate to kill again. We had ridden condorgs only for pleasure before those days. Fire-glass blades had been made only for domestic use."

"And the baby?" asked Velissa softly.

The knight acted as though he had not heard Velissa's question. His reverie was undisturbed.

"The infant Rengraaden? Was he just stolen or was his life also under threat?"

"He was presumed dead, though of course we could not know

for certain. After leaving the citadel, Thanevial wandered for several days around Mt. Calz. He carried the baby with him. At the end of the first week, when the king and his wife were drowning in despair, Thanevial demanded that three knights be surrendered to his own lordship in exchange for the infant prince. Thanevial wanted to begin a new dwelling for himself west of Mt. Calz. Ren refused to grant his demand and sent out several scouting parties of knights to find both the renegade and the child. But it was impossible to find the baby, for Thanevial was holding him in one of the passageways of the Caverns of Smeade."

Raccoman shuddered when he thought about that dark place and the Changelings with which they struggled in the tunnels. Velissa moved closer, and Hallidan continued his tale.

"But Thanevial's hiding place had been found by the newcomer, Garrod, whose presence on our continent had not yet been detected. Thanevial did not realize that the cautious Graygill had discovered him, and he was most unaware of the Moonrhyme's presence in the purple forests near the green mist environs of Mt. Calz."

"Why was my father so cautious?" asked Raccoman.

"That, too, is a mystery that will never by unraveled," replied Hallidan. "Why he never disclosed his presence to Thanevial cannot be known. Perhaps the gargantuan size of the defecting knight frightened him. Or perhaps he felt some inherent evil in the stealth and bearing of the first Changeling. Thanevial's eroding appearance and monstrous foreboding may have kept Garrod from approaching him. But we do know this: Garrod watched and followed the Drog lord until he realized that Thanevial was not only a fugitive but an evil one as well. At the same time, Garrod also kept well away from the Titan parties that were searching for the hapless infant. He never made himself known to them either.

"According to his own story, Thanevial left the infant in the hollow caverns and started out on a trek west to the misty Caladena Forests that stretched all the way to the perilous Deserts of Draymon. According to Garrod, Thanevial had developed a habit of thinking aloud, perhaps because he despised the silence of his aloneness. But in his audible mental meanderings, he mumbled that he was leaving Mt. Calz for a trip that would require a few weeks.

"He left the baby to die, delighted that Rensgaard would no longer have an heir. No sooner had he gone than Garrod rescued the infant and he took him for the first time into the warm sunlight. Garrod moved through the shadowy forests like an unseen phantom, bringing the prince to Rensgaard. With the baby in his arms, he came at last to the citadel.

"There Garrod's short frame and unusual face were so unique that all he met in the streets of Rensgaard fell back from him. The knights had never seen a Moonrhyme before. When Garrod stopped at the towering gate house and begged for food for the child, one knight saw the royal seal of Ren on the child's gown and brought them both to the king.

"Your father became the hero of the citadel. He was heralded by the jubilant king as the saviour of Rengraaden. He grew in popularity in the court of the Riders. The knights and ladies loved his simple wisdom. Like yourself, his stature was but half theirs, and if you will pardon my saying this, his gills and pointed ears and side-locks gave him so special an appearance that everyone wanted to meet him and know about the place from which he came."

"So that is how you learned about the land of the Canbies?" asked Raccoman.

"And about the death of the king, Singreale, and the disappearance of the splendid diamond that bore his imprimatur and signaled his power."

"But Rexel," said Velissa, suddenly remembering the falcon that had befriended Raccoman and her in their final weeks in the valley of the Graygills. "How did he come to the employ of Ren?"

"Rexel had flown the tortured lands of the Graygills. Once he knew that the diamond and the serpent who guarded it were safely hidden, he soared the upper winds across the green and trackless seas that separate our lands. He circled our alabaster citadel, but like Garrod, he remained cautious and seemed afraid of those of us who dwelt in Rensgaard. It was not until after Garrod had come to the city and knew the kind character of the very large inhabitants of this land that the falcon was assured we were a people of peace. His fear and suspicion of the Titans then vanished. Having found us a kind race, devoid of vengeance, Garrod went to the royal family and begged permission to return to Mt. Calz. He moved along quiet forest trails and the lofty crags of mountains till at last he found the falcon. Having once served at Singreale's throne, he had known well the guardian falcon, and he brought him by swift course to Ren's court.

"Rexel amazed the court with his talk and his sky-born wisdom, and he became, like the Moonrhyme Garrod, the conversation of the citadel. Rexel knew the awesome power of the lost treasure. It was his desire to be its guardian once again. He longed to fly again to the land of the Canbies and join the serpent in the protecting of the gem. Still, he explained to the king that the time was not right. He felt that when the Blackgills ended their migration, they would return to the land of the Canbies determined to find the Singreale.

"It was the falcon's tale that inspired us to think of training the condorgs for long-distance flying and later for war. As you know, the condorgs are lit from within and make night flying an exciting venture that appealed to the knights. The first few who flew at night were called Star Riders by their wives, and the name became accepted. They flew at night in surveillance parties to discover the land, hoping to gain insight into the lost treasure of the dead king.

"Centuries passed. The Riders never landed.

"It was on one of those flights, while we were flying unusually low, that we encountered you in the night sky."

Raccoman remembered the exhilaration of the tilt winds and the warm sensations of the frigid sky. But he was not interested in the history of the Star Rider's surveillance. Only one question now burned in Raccoman's desire.

"What happened to my father?" he blurted out.

"Garrod kept talking of a young son whom he had left in the land of the Graygills," the knight said. "He kept talking of going home. We asked him how he had come, but he would not tell us."

"Maybe he flew on Rexel," said Velissa, remembering how the falcon had once grown so large that he could be ridden.

"But Rexel cannot enlarge himself without the Singreale!" Raccoman objected. "And the Singreale was already then in your grandfather's keeping, one continent away. Besides, Hallidan has already said that my father and the falcon came to Mt. Calz at different times." Raccoman felt impatient with Velissa. "Let him go on," he said, hoping that the knight would soon bring his tale to its completion.

"The son he loved must have been you," said Hallidan. "But he refused to tell us by what method he had come to our continent. He was afraid that the evil Thanevial might use that same mode to travel to the land of the Moonrhymes. He guarded the secret well, for now the arch Drog was a hideous form to look upon. He feared lest his secret revealed would betray his own people to the monster murderer of Rensland.

"At last, Garrod took a knapsack filled with as much bread and fruit as one could carry and set out from the west gate of the city.

He was headed home. He asked us not to follow him or try to discover how he traveled. We agreed. We hated to see him go for we knew that we would miss him much. He never reached the land of the Canbies. In fact, he never even reached the caladena forests west of Mt. Calz. He was killed near the entrance to the Caverns of Smeade by the Drog lord who was angry that Garrod had saved the child, Rengraaden."

"How do you know he was killed?" asked Raccoman.

"A scouting party found his body." Hallidan paused as if to avoid the rest of the tale.

"All of the story, Hallidan—I must know it all," insisted Raccoman.

"I—" Hallidan began slowly, avoiding Raccoman's eyes. "I found his body—it was partly devoured."

"By beasts?" asked the Graygill.

"There are no beasts in these forests who eat meat. Like the knights, the beasts eat other kinds of foods than flesh."

Nothing more needed to be said. Hallidan's reluctance to finish the tale and Raccoman's own experience of watching the Drogs cannibalize each other revealed to him the fate of his father and the horror of Thanevial's depraved nature. Thanevial was the killer, and he was the feeder. His father's life and flesh had suffered from the Drog's evil appetite for meat and the grudge that fed it.

Hallidan's giant frame seemed shaken by the anguish of the last part of his tale. He pulled the metal-worker and his wife close to him. The story had been difficult for Raccoman and for Velissa as well, whose life and fortune were bound up in her husband's welfare. The Graygills looked like children in the massive embrace of the well-muscled and powerful Hallidan. His naked arms and chest looked strong to them in their moment of need.

When they had sat for a long time in silent grieving, the Graygill metal-worker turned to the knight and asked through clean eyes made bright by his tears, "What is the fascination that causes the knights to leave their king and pass through the Valley of the Changelings?"

"What is ever the intrigue of the forbidden?" replied Hallidan. "Perhaps some inner craving for a kind of bloodlust they have never known. Perhaps just the urge to know some kind of power or sensuality they have never tasted in the rigors of their honesty and honor. Perhaps their virtue becomes too routine, their purity too predictable. I cannot say."

"Have you ever considered defecting?" asked Velissa.

Hallidan looked down, then briefly at her, then far away. His eyes glistened.

"Yes," he said, "I love the king and I have seen the hideous things that stomp in blood after their defection. I have seen these malformed Drogs growing in the red gore of the forming pits. Their appearance itself murders decency and joy. Yet in their hideous rejection of our noble king, there is some compelling sense of intrigue that I cannot lay aside. Perhaps it's the horror of all I don't know. . . ." He stopped and looked up like a pleading child and cried, "Oh, Ren, may I never cease to love you! Teach me to fear the intrigue that curses honor and stomps your great love in the bloody fluids of the forming pits!" He shouted his plea and then buried his face in his hands, trembling in fear.

The conversation had stopped. In the quiet that followed, the knight and the Graygills noticed that the square had emptied.

"Well, the festival is over," said the knight, gratefully changing the subject. He stood up and turned toward his dwelling. "Goodnight, my friends," he said. It was a wistful parting.

Velissa took her husband's hand and returned the knight's simple good-night.

"Hallidan," called Raccoman. The Titan looked back. "It's been nine hundred years or so, but I simply have to know. Did you love my father?"

"The Moonrhyme was a giant," replied the knight before he walked away. Raccoman smiled up at the white stars.

The morning came swiftly as the night had been short.

Raccoman was in the streets early and yet not as early as Rengraaden. Rengraaden of late often seemed lost in some remote madness—this was one of those times. But why? wondered Raccoman. The king's namesake had once been in line for the throne. He now realized he no longer was. Soon Queen Izonden would be delivered of the child she carried. Although outwardly Rengraaden rejoiced with other knights over the coming birth, it seemed to most that his pleasure was either vacant or seething. His position as the heir to the throne had been usurped. This seemed to give him a heavy bearing that his stately wife could not ease. Raenna could see that he was not as happy inwardly as he should have been. And she had confided to Velissa, on the Graygills' second day in their home, that she felt her handsome husband was not adjusting easily to the idea that he would never occupy the royal residence as king.

Raccoman had expected that he and Rengraaden would fall into a special friendship as soon as the handsome knight knew that it was Raccoman's father who had been his saviour when he was an infant. But this never happened. In fact, Rengraaden's resentment toward the metal-worker even seemed to grow. During the last half of the festival, the royal prince and heir often looked away with distant longing to the slopes of Mt. Calz.

One day Raccoman saw Rengraaden mount his condorg and asked him innocently,

"Where does the king's heir fly today?
To the nearer field or faraway?"

"Far!" replied the knight in an unpleasant tone of voice that invited no more questions. Raccoman excused himself with a weak smile.

A moment later, he saw the shadow of the Rengraaden cross the plaza paving stones, and he looked up in time to see the knight disappear into the western sky. Raccoman was generally light-hearted and did not give himself up to consideration of the moods of his friends. Their inner beings, like his own, had the right to privacy. Still, there was something in Rengraaden's demeanor that was unfriendly, and something cold in his intention alarmed the Graygill.

Garrod's grace toward the infant knight should have made close friends of the Graygill and Rengraaden, but like Velissa, Raccoman now feared the royal heir. After the fourth day in the citadel, Raccoman and Velissa had moved out of their temporary quarters in the knight's home, and while Raenna and Velissa visited every day, not much had passed between the Titan and the Graygill since they had found another cubicle in the east wall for their residence. Velissa was glad she was no longer Rengraaden's guest.

These days it was never hard to find space in the citadel. So many of the knights had become Drogs that there were plenty of vacant rooms in the once-crowded city. Often the Miserians left behind by their defecting knights would console their loneliness by moving in together. These grieving and lonely ladies could not bear to face the living quarters which for centuries and more had been happy places of togetherness. In better times, the women of Rensgaard had been happy for their handsome men had given complete allegiance to the king. But now their square dwellings were lonely and haunting reminders of the knights' lost allegiance that left their women disconsolate.

Raccoman went to the training ground to continue his lessons with fire-glass. In little more than a week of the long Estermann days, he was becoming skilled. His height and amusing "defootilating," as he referred to it, had become a technique and a tactic of pride. But he had resolved that as soon as the festival was over, he would begin his training on the condorgs. The defecting knights not only left many rooms empty in the apartment system of the walled dwellings, but also provided many extra condorgs.

Most of the knights flew to the Valley of the Changelings on their condorgs. The condorgs always returned to Rensgaard, however, while their masters endured the forming process. There were also a large number of young condorgs. And since they were nearly a year old before they could fly, the containment area contained all sizes of the beasts.

"Which condorg shall I take?" Raccoman asked Hallidan, who had graciously agreed to give him riding lessons. Raccoman was a little nervous. He had been quite a sky-surfer in the lands of the Canbies, but there he had only glided upon the winds. Flying on a condorg was something new. He had never tried to stay astride a beast that had an independent mind and vigorous muscles. He tried to imagine the power contained beneath the saddle, a power that moved swiftly and gladly into the sky. Raccoman now wished that, like Velissa, he had ridden the falcon, Rexel. What good preparation it might have been for the training he was about to undertake.

Hallidan could see that the Graygill was nervous. "Which condorg?" asked the knight, repeating Raccoman's question as they walked through the feeding area where the beasts stayed till it was their time to be ridden. "Let's see . . . which condorg?" Hallidan rubbed his chin and looked over the herd.

Their deliberation was overlong. Condorgs love to be ridden, and many of them had not been touched since their masters had become Drogs, for none of them remained with their masters once the knights became Changelings. The huge beasts were sensitive in nature. They could not bear the sight of the monsters who had been men before they had carried them to the forming pits. The Condorgs bolted skyward when approached by a Changeling. Some of the bewildered creatures had not been ridden for centuries.

One very large condorg pushed through the circle of the others and nudged Raccoman in the back with its head. Raccoman turned and saw that the huge beast seemed anxious. Yet its persistence amused Raccoman. The huge steed stretched its wings out over the circle of friendly animals that had now closed in around the Titan and the little metal-worker.

"Very well," he laughed. "I shall take you," he told the persistent condorg.

"Not him," warned Hallidan.

"But why not?" asked the Graygill.

"He's one of the older ones—hasn't been ridden for nearly as long as you're old."

"I like him," insisted the Graygill, "and he's big."

Raccoman stuck his chin out obstinately.

"This is the one for me" said Raccoman. "What's his name?"

"Merran. But he's old. Pick another," the Titan insisted.

Raccoman was becoming weary with the word games.

"It's not his age, it's something else. What's wrong with Merran?" insisted Raccoman.

"He—he was Thanevial's," the knight replied uncertainly. "There was talk of burning him at first, but we felt sorry for him and let him live. He certainly couldn't help what his master was or became. When other knights began training for the animals, they always refused him."

"Well, not me! I want Merran."

"Very well," Hallidan said reluctantly.

The Titan slipped the bridle he had been carrying around the giant head of the condorg and let it out from among the others. In the nearby rigging room, they found a small saddle and moved the backrest forward until it better fit the Graygill, though none would have said it was a good fit. Step by step, Raccoman watched the rigging procedures. When Hallidan had finished, he stripped the beast, and Raccoman repeated the rigging procedure very well, considering that Merran was so tall. The old mount sensed his difficulties and knelt on it forelegs to help the Graygill hoist the saddle over its shoulders. Raccoman quickly moved the fiber girth behind the pinions of Merran's wings and drew the cinch tight. While the beast still knelt, Raccoman climbed awkwardly to the saddle. Merran stood up, and that alone terrified the Graygill. The condorg was so tall that to Raccoman, it seemed to have already taken to the air.

Raccoman looked down uneasily. His fire-glass sword in its protective sheath swung against his leg and jutted out over the right wing of Merran.

As soon as Hallidan had rigged his own condorg, he drew alongside Raccoman.

"Lock your knees back of the forestrap and lean forward. Don't stand in the footlocks."

"What then?" asked Raccoman.

Hallidan urged his own condorg forward a few steps and cried, "Skie—ho!"

At the command, his beast bolted into the sky. They flew away so fast that Raccoman felt alone. He temporarily froze as he felt his own mount shiver in anticipation of flying with a mounted rider. He couldn't say the word.

Hallidan circled back over Raccoman and Merran, and seeing the Graygill's fears, decided to help him with the words that wouldn't come, "Skie—ho, Merran!"

Merran took three steps and bolted into the sky. Raccoman's left boot slipped from the footlock, and he slipped sideways in the overlarge saddle. It was not a graceful take-off, but he had soon righted his foot position again, and then he looked down. Immediately, he quit looking down and clamped his eyes shut instead. From a distance, he heard Hallidan laughing at his fears.

Gradually, the Graygill adjusted to the speed at which the condorg flew. The other animals, sensing that they were not on any real mission, took to the sky without riders. Raccoman somehow felt secure surrounded by the humming wingbeats of a great riderless herd. He nudged Merran into a higher altitude, turning the great beast upward. The other beasts followed them. He felt as though he were guiding the entire herd of animals.

The sun was warm, and the day was a study in the greens and blues of Rensland. When he was high enough, Raccoman could see the ocean he had crossed only a few weeks earlier. Somewhere beyond it, the land of the Canbies was embroiled in a bitter war of survival. It was hard to believe, in the beautiful sunlight, that anything could really be wrong on Estermann. Yet, the Graygill remembered, with a chill, that everything was wrong on Estermann.

Raccoman looked back on the herd he led and saw a young condorg. The animal was so small that it amused him with its frantic shallow wingbeats as it tried to keep up with the others. Playfully, the colt nipped at a mature condorg that must have been its sire or dam. But however the large beast was related to the little one, it took its large wing and brushed the baby aside in a gesture of annoyance. The little condorg then doubled up into a white ball in the sky and fell like a rock for some distance before it regained its balance and caught hold of the thin air once more with its tiny wings. Raccoman laughed out loud at the antics.

Once the herd had reached an impressive height, the condorgs stretched their long wings in the morning sun and glided as though the upper sky was made of glass. Never had Raccoman felt the exhilaration of the upper skies. Merran finned the obedient air, and his rider relaxed, taking his feet from the footlocks. Hallidan pulled alongside.

"Never take your feet from the footlocks," warned the knight. "A sudden change in the air or anything that frightened your mount could cause him to shy and you would drop from the sky."

At this reprimand, Raccoman once again reinserted his feet in the footlocks. When they were only a few hundred feet above the feeding lot within the citadel and preparing to land, Merran bolted upward and Raccoman was nearly thrown from his saddle. The Graygill was glad then that his feet were secure in the footlocks. The condorg had been startled by Rengraaden and his mount, flying into the landing area at a very steep glide. He had apparently been on a very fast flight for his condorg was soaked in its own fluid.

Velissa was waiting for her husband and Hallidan when they arrived.

As Hallidan and the two Graygills walked in the warmth of the bright sun of noon, the Titan teacher met Rengraaden, who was talking with a group of other knights. The knights were examining a new sword that Rengraaden was showing them. Rengraaden was very proud of it. Hallidan heard him say, "I found it near the sandglass seas of the Desert of Draymon."

"Why are you so excited about a hilt?" asked one of the knights who had not been on a foraging assignment.

"Watch!" cried Rengraaden. He swung the hilt at a stone railing a short distance away. The hilt remained in his hand, but the stone was sliced in two and fell away.

It took the other knights a moment to absorb what had happened. They stood stunned at the miracle. At last, one of them gasped the truth, "An invisible blade!"

"Yes," said Rengraaden with a smile, "an invisible blade."

"And you found this?" asked Hallidan, lifting an eyebrow.

"I did," said Rengraaden.

The challenge was subtle, but it cooled the air between Hallidan and Rengraaden.

"Ooooh," gasped Velissa, staring downward.

A deep red fluid clung to and discolored the heel of the crown prince's golden boot.

Rengraaden turned and walked away.

Hallidan looked pale. Raccoman restrained himself from staring too directly at the knight's discomfort. They both remembered where they had last seen invisible swords and pools of red fluid.

Mere bones sleep shallowly
  And never rest afraid.
But graves are always cold and deep
  Where character is laid.

CHAPTER VI

Rengraaden

VELISSA FEARED the lonely streets. A single demon reared a handsome head above the alabaster ivory stones of Rensgaard. A simple walk to the market area of the white streets filled her mind with terror, for a single image, handsome— yet horrendous—rising in gold boots and caped with the wind and crowned with the sun, menaced all her lonely moments.

She debated with her fears. But her fears always won and pushed her further and further from all confrontation with Rengraaden. She and Raccoman kept the whole story to themselves. Velissa could not even bear to tell Raenna, though she felt sure that Raenna suspected her Titan husband and the Graygill lass were involved in some conflict. Something sinister now lurked in the crown prince. Yet, it was not altogether what he had done, but what he might have done had she not managed to burn him with his own fire-glass. Velissa realized that she would not be able to make that trick work twice, should the Star Warrior find her alone again. Thus she kept her doors closed against the possibility.

The apartment that she and Raccoman had taken on the fourth day following the festival was impossible to lock. None of the apartments in the white city could be bolted, for there were not bolts. Such barricades were unnecessary in a city of honor—at least, that was the reason that was always given for their absence. So Velissa labored hard to shove a bureau against the door after Raccoman left for the training grounds to work with Hallidan and make a warrior of himself, if he could. But she had always been careful to remove the bureau well before her husband returned home. In her own mind, she felt safe from Rengraaden.

Early one afternoon, just a short week after she had begun this procedure, Velissa was awakened from a nap by the sound of the door thumping against the barricade she had placed there. The banging against the tall, heavy chest grew more and more intense until the door was shoved against the bureau with such force that it sounded as though it would splinter into pieces.

Velissa was terrified.

"No, please, Rengraaden. Please, leave me alone—please— please." Her voice softened in a plaintive decrescendo.

"What is this?" Raccoman demanded as he broke through the door and squeezed past the heavy chest.

"Oh, Raccoman, it's you," cried Velissa in strong relief. "I thought. . . ."

"You thought what?" he insisted.

"It isn't what I thought, but who I thought it might be." Velissa realized that she could not turn back now from the confession that was coming in a wash of honesty.

"Who, then?" asked her husband as he pried her fingers from his upper arms, dissovling the intense embrace she had placed upon him. They both sat down.

"Rengraaden!" she exclaimed. Suddenly Raccoman understood that Velissa had been living in constant fear that the king's nephew would force her to leave the city with him. And he knew her fears were justified.

Velissa's upper shoulder was still bruised from her encounter with Rengraaden nearly three weeks earlier. The huge hand of the crown prince had left its mark of savage brutality as clear evidence to the Graygill that his wife had reason to be terrified and to barricade the door.

Velissa looked at her husband and knew that his mind had raced elsewhere to something more serious but related.

"Velissa," he said, "neither of us may be safe. Do not leave our quarters for any reason."

"What are you *not* telling me?" she demanded.

"Velissa, two of the knights in our rescuing party were murdered last night."

"Murdered?"

"Yes," he said, hesitating, "strangled."

"Are there Drogs in the city?"

"Drogs do not murder in this fashion. It must have been done by a knight."

"Ren—Rengraad—Rengraaden." It took Velissa three attempts to complete the name. Raccoman shrugged.

"It has to be. Who else?" Velissa said. "He's tried to make each of them disclose where the king is. Now there are only four of us left who know the whereabouts of the king or Singreale: ourselves, Rendemar, and Hallidan."

"If Rengraaden is responsible for the murders, then neither of us is safe," he said.

Since Rendemar and Hallidan were both unmarried, they decided to share Rendemar's quarters and spend their nights sleeping and watching in turns. The murder of the two Star Riders who had been part of the Graygills' rescue team had set off a reign of terror in the city. By nightfall, Hallidan had ordered a continuous watch for the royal residence. It was the best he could do to allow the queen a night's sleep. Still, Hallidan felt insecure. How could he know that one of those he sent to defend the queen might not be the assassin?

He had immediately supposed that the reason that the Riders were murdered was because they held the special secret they had promised not to disclose. Either they were disposed of because they had refused to tell the whereabouts of the king and the Singreale, or they were the victims of some burning grudge that someone in the citadel bore against them.

When the special night watch had been set near the royal residence, Rendemar and Hallidan entered Rendemar's apartment. The slaying of their brothers was uppermost in both their minds.

"Why?" asked Rendemar.

"Who?" asked Hallidan.

Each answered the other with silence. Rendemar's brow knitted. "Do you suppose that someone here is angry for us bringing the Graygills into the citadel?"

"No, no," Hallidan said firmly. "Someone tried to find out about the king or the stone or both. The Riders were committed to secrecy, and rather than endanger the king, they kept their secret and were . . ."

"Both murdered within a matter of hours."

"Do you think the murderer will try for us now, too?" asked Hallidan. It was pointless for Rendemar to answer his friend's question. The very fact that they were both at Rendemar's quarters was proof enough that they both felt themselves to be in danger.

"It will come, or rather, *he* will come for us. We're the last two alive who know about the king and Singreale.

"Yes," agreed Hallidan. Then suddenly, he jumped up. "No, we are not the last two alive who know—we are only the last two knights!"

"The Graygills!" shouted Rendemar.

Without further discussion, they both buckled on their fire-glass swords and ran out into the street. A few moments later, they arrived at the Graygills' quarters. But they could see through the open window by the torchlight that Raccoman and Velissa were chatting casually and did not appear anxious. Hallidan felt ashamed and decided not to disturb them. The city was alerted to the presence of an assassin within the walls. There would be extra patrols on duty all night. From hour to hour, a Rider sentry would pass beneath the Graygill's window and would check for any trouble in the streets.

"It is better not to alarm our friends," Hallidan told Rendemar as they passed on down the streets. "They will be safe." It was a firm statement. Rendemar agreed that to alarm the Graygills was unnecessary.

"Hallidan, we are both capable. We will not need each other. If we trust our sentries to defend the Graygills, may we not trust them to defend us as well? If we barricade ourselves against the night, we will needlessly add to the tension in the city."

"I know you're right," agreed Hallidan. "The other knights look up to us. If we appear to act in fear, then we will only spread the fear."

Convinced that they must not be alarmists, they both agreed that each should sleep in his own quarters that night. By the time they reached Rendemar's quarters, their minds were resolute and the decision had been made. They agreed to meet on the morrow. Hallidan left.

In the morning, Raccoman and Velissa were awakened by a sharp rapping on their door. One of the Riders who attended Izonden told Velissa that she must come with him immediately to the palace.

"Will it be all right, Raccoman?" she asked.

"I'm afraid you have no choice," said the sentinel.

Raccoman was instantly angry. "Who says she has no choice?" he demanded.

"We all obey the queen when the king is away from the castle," the sentinel explained. "It's the code of Rensgaard."

"I'm coming, too," he said.

"I'll be all right," she said, taking his arm. 'Don't worry. Let me get my cape. The streets are cool until the sun is high." In a moment she had tied the blue cape around her shoulders. She then touched Raccoman on the face and promised, "I'll be back before long."

When she arrived at the palace, she was ushered directly to the main room. It was an arched and vaulted enclosure in which the tall and official furniture seemed in good company.

Velissa gasped to see Rengraaden standing near the queen.

"Hello, Velissa," said Izonden.

"Hello," she replied, then looked at the tall warrior. His lip curled and his face went hard.

"Rengraaden tells me that you may know where my husband is." It was at once a question and a statement.

"Izonden, please!"

The queen could see the fear in her eyes.

"Now, now, there is no reason to be frightened. You are safe in Rensgaard."

"Please, please," begged Velissa, looking again at the stone-faced Rengraaden. "We are sworn together not to disclose the king's whereabouts to anyone."

Izonden stood. "Velissa," she reminded the Graygill, "I am the queen."

"I'm sorry," said Velissa before she fell to silence. She knew that she dare not confess the secret in front of Rengraaden, for even if it was safe for the queen to know, she knew it would not be safe for Rengraaden to have the information the queen now demanded.

The queen felt uneasy. She saw Velissa glancing anxiously at Rengraaden.

"You needn't feel uncomfortable before Rengraaden. He is my nephew. You are free to say anything in his presence. It will be safe with him."

Velissa wanted to cry, but she fought the weakness until finally it passed. She stiffened herself and said firmly to the queen, "Two men have died. They may have died for knowing what I know and for not telling what I now consciously choose not to tell." Velissa was half the size of the queen, but there was no mistaking her resolve. It was clear that she would tell neither the queen nor Rengraaden her secret. For the survivors of the rescue team, the secret had become a covenant of life and death.

"Very well," said Izonden, "tell me this: Do you know if he is alive, Velissa?"

"I know he was, and I believe he still is. And I also believe that his safety depends upon our enemies not knowing his whereabouts. I shall keep the truth even from you, for two of your best knights have already died. Izonden, my queen, may I go?"

"You may," agreed the queen, waving her from the room. Izonden was disappointed, yet pleased that Velissa had called her "my queen."

"And," said Velissa, "could the sentinel accompany me home?"

"Rengraaden, my nephew, will accompany you. He is the best of the Star Riders. You will be safe."

"No!" exclaimed Velissa. Then she caught herself. "No, Izonden. Just send the sentry who accompanied me here. Your nephew need not take the trouble."

Velissa so wanted to tell Izonden what little she knew of Rengraaden, but she knew the queen would have little reason to believe her. Rengraaden was the heir until such time as Izonden's child should be born, and even then he would be second in line for the throne. Moreover, Rengraaden was the most respected of all the Riders, while Velissa was a newcomer. She knew that she must make no attempt to indict the royal warrior.

Still, Izonden saw that Velissa was somehow afraid of Rengraaden. Though she felt the Graygill's fears were entirely groundless, she agreed to send Velissa home with the same sentry who had brought her to the palace.

"Thank you, my queen," said the Graygill. "I know I must appear ill at ease. But I am afraid for your king as I am afraid for both my husband and myself. After all, two Riders have been murdered right in the citadel."

But Velissa was wrong.

Hallidan knocked three times on the door of Rendemar's dwelling. When there was no answer, he decided to walk on in. The door swung inward and he fell back at the horror that greeted him. The room was in complete disarray as though it had been the scene of violence. Rendemar was dead, tied in a chair. He had been dead for most of the night, it appeared. His eyes were only partially open, and there was a seared wound that caved in his chest. He had been run though with a fire-glass blade—perhaps his own.

The sword had been laid, after the murder, on a table nearby and the wood was scorched black from the intense heat of the blade. Hallidan was amazed that the charred table had not burst into flame, but had only continued to smoulder throughout the night.

From the appearance of the room, it seemed to Hallidan that the dead Rider and the assassin must have struggled terribly before Rendemar had been subdued and tied up. It appeared that he might have been tied to the chair for some time before the fire-glass was driven into his chest. But why? Surely, thought Hallidan, the reason must be related to the secret that Rendemar, along with the rest of the Gragill rescue party, had vowed never to share. It was clear he had kept the whereabouts of King Ren and the Singreale secure.

Hallidan was about to turn from the horror before him when he noticed that his friend's hands had been mangled. The dead Star Rider's fingers had been seared off his hands by the blade of the same fire-glass sword that had ended his life once and for all. Hallidan at first thought that perhaps this was an accident that had occurred during Rendemar's final struggle with the assassin. Then he noticed that the fingers on each hand were cut away irregularly. They had not been cut away all at once by a single swing of the searing blade. They had been cut away one at a time.

After Velissa left the queen, she made a very sound decision. Perhaps the safest place to hide from Rengraaden would be in his very cubicle. She made her way through the long shadows of the morning to the very place that she and Raccoman had gone when they first came to Rensgaard. She wanted to go straight to Raccoman, but she knew that Rengraaden would look first for her there.

She brushed shadows with Hallidan and saw that his face was white. His strong legs were carrying him in the direction from which she had come. He stopped for only a few moments.

"Velissa," he said, "do not go home. Rendemar was murdered in his quarters last night."

"Murdered?" asked Velissa.

"Murdered and mutilated," said Hallidan.

"But I must warn Raccoman," said the Graygill.

"I have already done that, and I have told him to walk the sunlit streets to the training grounds. There are many knights there. He will be safe. I'm going there now, and I think both Raccoman and I will be safe if we stay together."

"But where should I go?"

"I don't know, only do not go home!" Hallidan was insistant.

"I was on my way to Raenna's," Velissa admitted.

"Fine, you will be safe at Rengraaden's."

The Titan Rider spoke nothing more but hurried on toward the royal residence. Velissa felt that there was no use in trying to break Hallidan's confidence in the queen's nephew. It was odd, she thought: Hallidan felt that she would be safe there because it was Rengraaden's residence, while she felt that she would be safe there because Rengraaden would not think to look for her at his own home. Hallidan saw Rengraaden as Velissa's protector, but she saw him as a brutish terror.

Now she found herself hoping that Raenna would be home and that Rengraaden would be away. She suspected that Rengraaden and Raenna were drifting apart, for, she surmised, Rengraaden now wore a mask that few in the citadel could see. She desperately hoped that Raenna could see it, but she could not be sure.

She listened at Raenna's window. She heard nothing. She was grateful and raised her hand to knock. When the door flew open, she died a thousand deaths. But it was not Rengraaden.

"Velissa, come in," said Raenna. "You're trembling, exactly as you were that day I met you in the street."

"And for exactly the same reason," said Velissa, as she stepped inside. "Raenna, have you any reason to suspect your husband of treachery against the crown?"

Velissa hated herself for blurting out such words, but she was too frightened and confused to consider the issue of tact. It was a brutal question. Raenna said nothing, but turned her face to the wall. Velissa could see the tall, elegant frame convulsing.

"I tell you, Izonden, Velissa lies!" Rengraaden was saying to the queen. The queen was uncomfortable with his vehemence.

"How do you know, nephew?" she asked.

"Izonden, we found her two weeks ago talking to a group of several Drogs in a grove barely three miles from the west tower of the citadel. There can be no other explanation as to why she is still alive unless she is one of them. They have reasons to release her or they would not have done so. I believe she is Thanevial's accomplice. She is a spy, my queen."

"Then you think she does not know where my husband is?" asked Izonden.

"There's the rub! I believe that she does. She may already have betrayed our king to the Drogs with whom she all too recently held council," Rengraaden said. Rengraaden's lies left his accusation full of loopholes. It was inconsistent to accuse Velissa of being Thanevial's accomplice and yet not disclosing Ren's whereabout's to the evil Drog. Izonden's tortured mind seemed unable to grapple with the inconsistencies.

The queen looked away, saying nothing. She was turning her nephew's accusation over in her mind, not wanting to believe it and yet knowing she must. Her silence continued until Rengraaden at last broke it.

"My sovereign," he said, "Velissa must be made to tell the whereabouts of Ren. Whatever it takes—whatever procedures we must follow—however drastic the measure, the crown of Rensgaard must be spared, and soon!"

The sharp sound of hurried heel clicks on the paving of the royal residence reached Izonden and her nephew, and a moment later, Hallidan interrupted them.

"My queen!" he exclaimed. "Forgive me for this interruption, but Rendemar was murdered in the night."

It was as though he spoke too much, though he blurted it out in but an instant. The queen held her head in her hands, not daring to look at life even through her long fingers.

Her nephew went to her and caressed her as if to take away the pain of the news. "What has gone wrong in the citadel?" asked Izonden.

"Someday the king will return and all will be peace," consoled Rengraaden. "You must believe his last promise."

"But there have been three murders in little more than a day," said the queen. She moved to a chair, led by her nephew. Her swollen frame needed to stabilize itself. To carry both her nearly born child and the weight of these insane circumstances seemed more than she could bear.

"Izonden," said Hallidan when she was seated and had rested for a few moments, "all of those murdered held one thing in common." The queen did not acknowledge his statement but only waited. He continued, "They all knew where the king was last seen."

"Did Velissa Dakktare also witness the king's 'disappearance'?" asked the queen.

"She did," agreed Hallidan.

"Then you were right," said the queen, turning to her nephew.

Rengraaden shifted on his feet. "Madam, may I be excused—to the stable—my condorg needs grooming." Rengraaden waited for her to give him leave, but she had scarcely waved him a slight permission when he turned on the heel of his gold boot and walked briskly from the great room.

"What was he right about?" asked Hallidan.

"He said that he believed Velissa knew the circumstances of my husband's disappearance. Oh, Hallidan, we must make Velissa tell what she knows. We must guarantee my husband's safety."

The queen was upset but determined.

"Izonden, I, too, know the circumstances as well as the place where Ren was last seen. But we are committed to keep the secret. If the word is released in the palace and if any of the knights defect with the secret, then your husband's whereabouts will be announced from the top of Thanevial's Tower Altar. We must not permit that."

"But why does Velissa lie about her allegiance to Thanevial?"

"She has no allegiance to Thanevial," cried Hallidan in unbelief.

"But Rengraaden said that he saw her talking to a group of Drogs not far from the west tower. She must be lying."

"Rengraaden said . . ." Hallidan's face became illuminated. "That has to be the connection—Rengraaden—no, no, no!" he shouted as though Izonden had not been in the room.

"Izonden," he said at last, turning again to the queen, "did he say anything else about Velissa?"

"Yes, he said that she knows where my husband is and that she must be made to tell what she knows, for the king is in danger. He said that we must make her tell the truth, no matter how harsh we have to be to force it out of her. Oh, don't you see, Hallidan. Rengraaden is right. Velissa is Thanevial's spy! We must make her confess. Rengraaden must be heard."

Again Hallidan turned to the wall. "No. I won't believe it."

"What won't you believe?" asked the queen, interrupting his dark thoughts.

When Hallidan turned back to her, his deep-set eyes were glistening with a horrible new inner agony, and he breathed but one word, "Rengraaden!"

That night Hallidan, emboldened by his new realization, took Raccoman to his home. He was determined to wait with the Graygills until the assassin made his next move. And though he believed he knew who the assassin was, his mind was still reluctant to admit the truth. He had no intention of sharing what he knew with Raccoman until he was sure. When they arrived at Raccoman's cubicle, the place was in chaos, with and all of the rustic furniture thrown at odd angles around the room.

"I told Velissa not to come here. It is apparent that she obeyed."

"Do you know where she is?" asked Raccoman, greatly alarmed.

Hallidan said nothing, but turned on the heel of his boot and went out the door. Dutifully, Raccoman followed.

"Do you think Velissa is safe?" Raccoman asked again.

"No one is safe!" Hallidan's words were final.

As they walked, a silence stood between the giantesque Star Rider and the infantesque Graygill. Raccoman used the silence to build up his own courage until the moment when he would see his Velissa safe again. Hallidan's mind vaulted over the sinister moment to the stately Raenna. He shuddered. Was Raenna safe? Did she have any idea of what evil the future held? Hallidan quickened his lengthy strides. Raccoman forced his shorter ones.

"If there was one face, one woman, one touch of dignity I could claim for my own," thought the bachelor knight, "it would all be Raenna, Raenna, Raenna!" He dismissed the thought. Raenna belonged to Rengraaden—the matter was settled. But Rengraaden was not worthy to own the prize that graced his home. "Still," thought Hallidan, "I must not condemn him whom Raenna loves just to hope that her love might be mine." Then, feeling guilty, he turned his mind to Velissa and Raccoman and waded on through the afternoon sun. The white paving stones were so hot that they burned his feet through the soles of his boots.

At last they arrived and were grateful to find that the women were safe.

Velissa and Raenna had already agreed on the horrible issue. In the quiet talk that followed, Hallidan could only nod and wonder in painful silence that the most respected Titan of the forces of Ren was not only a traitor to the king but was also the logical assassin of those who had died. Now just three who knew the whereabouts of Ren were still alive. It was imperative that they remain together and confront the common enemy.

Raenna began to cry. Hallidan went to her and held her while she cried. He felt sick inside, hurting because Raenna hurt. He knew the feelings that he harbored could be explained in no other way than the stirring of a love he had no right to feel. Still, an unseemly part of him gloated that the king's nephew was unfit for the elegant Raenna. His emotions were so mixed in one instant he hated Rengraaden's vile nature and yet was glad the traitor had proven himself an unworthy consort to the very woman whose face had floated in Hallidan's dreams and presided over all his empty moments for a decade.

While the four of them cowered, the darkness was interrupted by a sudden footfall. The door swung open.

"Rengraaden!" cried Raenna.

The evil prince could see that her face was wet with a pain that spilled out of some deep fountain of longing and lostness.

"Traitor to the crown!" cried Hallidan, drawing his bright, red sword. Then he added one further condemnation as he faced the prince, "Murderer!"

Velissa cowered in the shadows. Like his trainer, Raccoman drew his short sword. Rengraaden, on seeing the Graygill's short stature and tiny blade, threw back his head and laughed. His laugh was cut short by the determination in both of the men. Hallidan and Raccoman advanced like a giant and his son.

Rengraaden did not draw his sword.

Instead, he slammed the door shut, and they heard his boots clicking in rapid cadence down the narrow stone canyon. Hallidan ran out into the street in time to see Rengraaden mount his condorg, which waited at the end of the narrow lane.

"Skie-ho!" he cried, and the condorg vaulted into the waiting air.

"He's not coming back is he?" asked Raenna.

"No," said Hallidan simply. "Never."

Riddles may diddle and fiddles may play—
  Nonsense be near-sense and darkness be day.
Truth digs for visions and hears every sound—
  Digs, and yet sifts every spadeful of ground.

CHAPTER VII

Grendelynden

FOUR DROGS CAME upon a little

opening in a dark cliff whose base was completely whiskered with dembret vines. The Changelings had been attracted to the mossy wall of the dark stone precipice by a weird kind of music they had never heard before. Coming from the little orifice of a small, shaded cave was a choppy progression of half-tones. The almost-music issued without accompaniment in what would have been to a good ear a painful sound:

"Chon, chon, em taken, taken en em tree!
Taken en em caladena, taken en em tree!
Ha, ha, chon, chon, broka cutta vine!
Cutta broka caladena en em broka mine."

One of the Drogs peered into the black opening. A single eye deep inside the cave opened, and light from the outside fell upon it. The eye lit up as though it contained an independent light of its own. Then it closed and the lights went out.

"Hunga. Caladranga!" grunted one of the Drogs, drawing his sword. He entered.

The light blinked back on, then off. Then two lights blinked on side by side. The Drogs still outside the cave thought that this tiny intrigue, whatever it was, was most amusing. They fell to laughter when the lights both went out just after the Drog entered the cave opening. It was so dark that the other three could see nothing of the Drog once he entered.

The unpleasant yet cheerful voice began again. The melody flattened. The semi-song, clearly unclear, continued. It was a mono-tone melody, happy for all its madness.

"Hinnamin Droggynoggens—boggen boggen stone!
Ha, ha binnamins Droggynoggens groan."

The light blinked on and off again. The three Drogs grunted in pleasure at the absurdity of the whole sequence. But their humorous confusion meant nothing. Both lights blinked on and off. Still they could see nothing of the Drog that had entered with drawn sword to investigate.

"Binnamins, chon, chon, taken en em tree!
Droggynoggens four em-boggen, Droggynoggens three!"

The unseen Drog stopped. The darkness was intense within the cave. The silence was deathly. Then both lights blinked on. The three Drogs heard their huge, ugly companion swing his blade and shout, "Hunga, Gukka!" His sword made a deafening sound as it cut the air.

There was a high, piercing scream. The absurd song stopped. "Hunga, hun, hun, hun," rasped the three other Drogs in laughter at the thought that the singer of the song had been dispatched. There was only silence for the moment. The three Drogs laughed again and then stopped laughing, unable to make a thing of what they had heard. The milk-white mucous-filled eyes looked at each other, blinking in a search for understanding. They were trying to decide what had happened in the darkness. Surely their fellow Drog had dispatched the singer and would soon emerge, dragging the remains of the riddlesome bard behind him. They laughed once more, but stopped suddenly when the acrid fumes of sulphur rolled out of the dark opening.

One light blinked on as though it was puzzled, then another blinked on beside it.

"Wonken donken meany meen: Ringgem dingem diss!
Uglee Droggynoggens swingem blade.
Swingem uggul-killem, uggul-killem
Uggul Droggynoggen miss."

The words stopped again and both lights blinked off.

Now the sulphur stench was so strong that the three Drogs knew that it was their brother who had been dispatched. A second Drog leapt into the same orifice that had swallowed up his brother. One light blinked on near the top of the dark opening, then blinked off and on several times in rapid succession. It was clearly a bright yellow eye. It disappeared for a moment and reappeared to the right and slightly behind where it had first come on. At last it closed off altogether.

Out of the darkness, the discordant song began. The two remaining Drogs were not so amused this time as they had been earlier. They strained into the utter black to catch any hint of the second Changeling who had gone in to dispatch the creator of the unusual melody.

"Droggynoggens three three—hoonie hoonie hoo—
Swingen uglee-killee, uglee-killee—uglee-killee too!
Chon, chon, caladena, caladena hoo
Kill em halfa Droggynoggens,
Leavem halfa Droggynoggens.
Fora Droggynoggens, soona Droggynoggens too."

There was a second scream. The lights came back on. More acrid fumes poured forth.

The last two Drogs became unsure. They decided to go into the cave at once. They left the sunlight of the dembret woods and moved inward through the orifice.

"Ughum, Gukka. Galanka!" grunted one of the Changelings.

The two lights blinked on before them, then went off again. It was hard for the Drogs to tell how far away the lights really were. One of them decided to talk to the voice.

"Chounga—Ughum Hunga—Ganb!" grunted one of the Drogs.

There was no answer. Out of the darkness, the other Drog spoke, "Hunga—Ganb—Ganb!"

It seemed odd that the ugly Drog in the darkness would call his unseen foe a beast. There was only more silence.

The last Drog to speak grunted in his gravelly voice once again, "Ughum—Galanka hung—bandaggmo!" And the other Drog tried to mimic an entreaty to the unknown thing that sang in the cave.

"Sing em chon, chon . . . Droggynoggy two,
Gona chon, chon cutta light
Hoo boonie hoonie."

It was a poor attempt since the only possible singing worse than that which had come from inside the cave was that which the Changeling tried to do. Indeed, the Drog's mimic of the unseen thing was so bad that as soon as it ended, both lights blinked on just ahead of them in the dark.

The Drogs could hear each other breathing and nothing more. They could tell they were close together, but they could not tell how close they were as they drew their blades. Both Drogs swung. And both screamed at once. A double portion of sulfur smoke billowed out of the opening of the cave. The darkness had become deathly quiet.

It was too bad that there were no Drogs left to see the lights blink on again. This time they stayed on, for there was nothing left to fear. The song began on a gleeful note. The poor melody gradually flattened into a mere recitation that had no hint of melody. It was as though the voice refused to sing if there was no one around to hear. The source of the sound approached the opening of the cave.

"Wherry wherry emmis hairry! Hairry, hairry boggen!
Badden badden gone-em all! Gone-em Droggynoggens."

As this short phrase ended, there stepped out of the cave a creature only half as tall as the Graygills and only a fourth as tall as the Titans. He looked as though he had hatched from wet clay. His skin, that which was visible, was dark brown. Most of his body appeared to be naked, except where it was covered with shaggy hair that fell out over his upper lip and hung from every corner of his angular head. His feet were as regular in shape as those of the Titans, but they were much shorter. From his bare shoulders hung thin arms, and he looked so comical that he would have made anyone laugh, except that no one was around to see him. His eyes were wide-set, round, and bright yellow. His skin tone and hair color so perfectly matched the brown earth and stone that he was scarcely visible in the thatch of dembrets. He wore no sword with which he could have dispatched the Drogs. Yet they were gone, as were the second two.

For whatever reasons were his, he made his way off into the dembret forest in the direction of Mt. Calz. Being so short, it would take him a long time to walk there if, indeed, the mountain was his destination. He no longer sang his off-key, near-sense song. Instead, he talked to himself.

"More-em more-em, hoonie hoonie chon chon hoo,
More-em, more-em Droggynoggens, uggul-killem too!"

A month later, a party of Titans settled their condorgs on the wide open plains before the Caverns of Smeade. They had been to the edge of the desert west of the Tower Altar. It was clear that the liquid sand pits were bubbling in tides of lava larger than they had ever seen. Another portion of the forest had caved in, and now the giant tides were lapping at the thick belt of the Caladena Forests that ran in a wide purple band for several miles around the base of the Tower Altar. It was clear that the Desert of Draymon was growing and encroaching at a fast pace on the liveable area that Thanevial could call his kingdom. It seemed inevitable that the entire Tower Altar would one day be eaten up in tides of molten sand, devoured in hungry boiling seas of glass.

Even if Thanevial had been inclined to preserve the peace, it was clear that he could not preserve it for long. For his kingdom now faced the growing Desert of Draymon and the horrible molten sand that would dissolve the black stones that formed the hideous altar, topped with the chains and bones that symbolized the evil he seemed to desire.

Six knights landed on the same ledge that Hallidan's rescuing party had used when they rescued the Graygills. While the six rested, they were set upon by a party of twelve Drogs. Two of them were killed outright in the surprise attack. Three of them, seeing they were outnumbered, managed to get to their condorgs and escape. But one of the knights fled for security into the Caverns of Smeade. And once inside the large and domed inner cavern, he picked at random one of the many tunnels that fed the vaulted chamber and made his way into the dark passageway to await the arrival of the Drogs. He determined not to draw his sword, since the fire-glass would immediately reveal his whereabouts, making it easy for his pursuers to locate him.

He ran at first down the passageway and then slowed to a walk in the darkness as he felt his way along the walls. He tripped over something he could not see and fell headlong into the further recesses of the cave. After he had stumbled over the soft object in the dark, he sat up and peered back at the little aperture of light through which he had come. He was sure that at any moment the aperture would be sealed to darkness by the ugly black bodies of his Drog pursuers.

As he studied his predicament, trying to imagine what the soft mass was that he had tripped over, he was surprised to see a yellow light blink on before him. Then another beside it. He heard the strange voice that spoke in riddled lines. He felt both afraid and comforted because the voice and the lights were so near. But the lights went off just as the aperture of light behind him was plugged by an advancing monster. The semi-singing began in the darkness, accompanied by intermittent blinking:

"Renling chon, chon, emma-emma-gnee!
Leavem uggul-killem Droggynoggen,
Leavem smokey-nokey Droggynoggen,
Leavem grunties unto me."

If the moment had not been so utterly serious, the knight would have laughed at the strange song.

The sinister and evil form that had blocked the passageway and plunged the scene into utter darkness stopped and laughed when he saw the little light come on and then wink off again. And he bellowed in laughter so loudly that he could not hear the little voice singing its off-hand and off-tune intrigue.

> *"Darkee blackee en-em-chon: gleemy yellow eye!*
> *Gleamy chon emma-Gnee . . . gnee gnee hie!*
> *Groggy chon emma-Gnee, Droggynoggen die!"*

The invisible blade of the Changeling split the dark air between himself and the trembling knight. There was a scream, then a thud, and acrid fumes were set free in the darkness. The knight was bewildered. He could not understand the creature in the dark cavern with him, but it seemed to be on his side. Its lights blinked on in his direction, and he felt reassured by its semi-riddles.

A second form entered the tunnel and plunged it into darkness. The confident Drog laughed at the unseen thing and its odd melody until his own sulfuric fumes filled the black tunnel. The same fate awaited the ten other Changelings.

When it was all over, the grateful Titan left the cave. But first he bowed gratefully to the blinking eyes, whose strange existence clearly hated the evil Drogs as much as he did.

Outside the cave, the Titan found that night was coming on. The knight puzzled over the strange episode he had just survived. His condorg had wandered a little way into the trees, frightened by the Drogs. He went to it, quickly mounted, and together they bolted into the sky, heading back to Rensgaard as swiftly as the condorg could travel.

The knight wondered how he would ever make real to Hallidan what had occurred in the cave. This much he knew: he was grateful that they had an unseen ally in the forest and caves. Whatever was his manner of fighting, he was totally efficient. And he was humorous beyond belief in his onslaught. Only when the knight was flying safely in the darkening sky did he have the presence of mind to laugh out loud.

"Hah, hah, hah!" he laughed heartily, feeling crazy in his own exultation. "Ho, hay, ho! Chon, chon emma-emma-gnee!" It was all of the nonsense he could remember, but he laughed again and again and repeated the crazy syllables half a dozen times in the thin air. His condorg flew furiously, and the knight suddenly felt foolish, unable to believe his own behavior. He was nearly sure that the knights would not believe his tale. But he would tell it anyway, glad to be a "Renling" and not a "Droggynoggen." When he thought seriously about not being a "Droggynoggen," he broke into laughter all over again while his dumbfounded mount flew home.

Hallidan found the knight's tale bizarre, but he believed, and with good reason. He and Raccoman, too, had heard a strange song and seen blinking lights an the Caverns of Smeade.

The dark had beat the knight in arriving at Rensgaard. Several times as he attempted to tell his tale, the knight broke into gales of laughter and repeated the strange near-sense syllables of the creature that he had met in the dark and that had remained in the dark.

Hallidan walked to Raccoman's home, and the two of them agreed that in the morning they would return to the Caverns of Smeade and see if they could find the carnage of the Drogs and locate the Ally. They knew of nothing else to call him except the Ally. The name was more discriptive than actual. It was an appropriate name, however. Anything or any being that could kill a dozen Drogs with nonsense syllables was clearly a formidable ally.

On a particular afternoon when Velissa was alone, there came an urgent knock at her door.

It was Raenna. She was in tears.

"Rengraaden did not come home last night!" she blurted out at once.

"And this morning?" asked Velissa hopefully.

"No, he did not come home this morning." She trembled and softly said, "But his condorg, filled with fear, returned. He was so skittish, and his eyes were wild and terrified as though he had seen his master in another form . . ." Her words trailed off, and she finally no longer fought the tears that came from somewhere deep inside and convulsed her.

Velissa was small compared to Raenna, but as far as her short arms would reach, she stretched them in an effort to hold her aching friend.

"They say his condorg was stained with the red fluid that I twice before have cleaned from his boots!" she cried again. Velissa said nothing for she had feared that this moment would come and yet had desperately hoped it would not. "Oh, Velissa," Raenna said, still weeping, "to think my Rengraaden is one of them . . . those hideous halflings that serve the foul lord of the Tower Altar. Why, why?"

Velissa offered no answer. Raenna knew there were no answers that either of them could understand. "He more than all others knew the treachery of the arch Drog. How could he even desire to honor the assassin who murdered his parents and left him to die in the Caverns of Smeade . . . he, the king's nephew! How?"

Finally, Velissa fixed them a cup of blue herb tea, and after a couple of hours, the disconsolate Raenna left her. Velissa tried to get her mind off Raenna's grief. If only Rengraaden had been killed, his wife would have at least survived him with a sense of honor. Now Raenna could feel only shame at his horrible defection.

By night, the rumor was confirmed by the conversation in the streets. Raenna's husband, the only heir to the throne of Ren, was now a Drog lord. When Raccoman returned, he felt only shame.

For dinner, he and Velissa walked to the house that was now Raenna's alone and shared with the Titan woman a delicious, thick vegetable stew whose recipe had come from their past in the other land. Raccoman pulled up a chair across the table from the two women and exalted a loaf of black bread, repeating words that he had also learned in that other land:

"To the maker of the feast
To the power of loaf and yeast
Till the broth and bread have ceased
Gratefulness is joy."

But he and Velissa ate little, and Raenna ate nothing. She appreciated their attempts to console her, but they were not able to cover the shame that Raenna felt.

"Oh, Raccoman," Raenna cried, "your father rescued him, saved him from a dark death, saved him to be king of this citadel, only to have him come to this!"

Raccoman seemed distracted as the Graygills walked back to their own cubicle on the eastern wall.

"I hope . . ." he said, then paused.

"What?" asked Velissa.

"I hope the war comes soon."

It seemed a blood-thirsty statement, and Velissa was shocked into silence.

"Because of the Ally," he went on, "there is more hope than ever. But the more the war is delayed, the more defections there will become. The Drogs will soon overwhelm the knights of Ren. Now we have some chance."

Raenna's grief gradually eased and became bearable in the ensuing weeks. Her dignity held a kind of sadness that marred her queenly bearing with a load that seemed to blunt her carriage. However, at least there were no new defections, and Raccoman was pleased that the knights were all prepared for the conflict, whenever it came and however it occurred.

The morning was bright.

The knight and the Graygill flew on their huge condorgs near the summit of Mt. Calz. They circled so near the peak that it seemed the cordorg's wings would brush the icy rocks that crowned the upper snows. Raccoman looked at the snow and longed for the valley of the Graygills. This snow was the only snow on the mountain and, indeed, the only snow in the whole of Rensland. The weather at the lower elevations where the knights lived was warm for the Graygills.

Still, all the knights wore heavy clothing for flying at these upper altitudes. Raccoman and Velissa had brought the heaviest of clothes with them for their flight to the continent where Mt. Calz offered the only snow around.

"Ho, lay-ho!" called Hallidan, leaning to the left side of his mount and pointing downward.

Raccoman reigned the giant head of his condorg backward and with his knee in the right side, set the beast in a gliding arc to the landing place far below. In his descent, he saw the yawning orifice of the Caverns of Smeade. The land seemed quiet.

Soon the condorgs landed, taking the few running steps that were their custom before they stopped, and folded their wings. The place was so quiet that it completely belied the tale that the knight had told. The pair dismounted and looked around for any Drogs who might be laying for a second ambush. They saw none.

"Which of the tunnels?" asked Raccoman.

They entered the main chamber and peered down the corridors.

But the question became superfluous. The horrible odor that emanated from one of the tunnels was too pungent to be denied. Raccoman lit the torches they had brought, and they turned into the stench-filled passageway. The amber light fell on the stone walls, and the further they went, the stronger the stench grew. Soon they found the sulfuric erosion of a dozen bodies heaped like a blockade in the tunnels. Whatever or whoever was responsible for the carnage was not around. They looked for winking lights, but found none.

"Look," said Hallidan, putting the toe of his boot under one of the ugly, cracked heads. The mucous eyes had shriveled into black decay.

Raccoman gasped, "And I thought they were dreadful when they were alive."

"Don't look at his eyes—look under his chin!" ordered the knight.

Raccoman looked. Beneath the Drog's chin was a place torn so severely that it appeared that the Drog's head had nearly been severed. This wound had not been inflicted by a sword but by a tearing action.

"What would make a wound like that? A knife or short blade?" asked the Graygill.

"A strong, swift hand, or a set of teeth perhaps, but not a weapon," replied Hallidan.

They checked only two or three other corpses. Each had been dispatched in the same way. In some cases, their throats were merely torn away, while other corpses were nearly decapitated. All had been mortally wounded by a strong set of hands. According to the surviving knight, whoever owned the lethal hands also owned a set of winking lights and sang to its victim in riddles.

They searched the caverns, but did not find the Ally. After a while, the stench grew so unbearable that they knew they could no longer stay. They made their way back through the tunnel and then went outside to mount their condorgs. As they left the cave, both felt better about their chances of surviving the coming war. They knew they had an unseen friend who had his own ways of showing his allegiance to Ren.

Raccoman and Hallidan found the remains of a cold campfire on one of their morning surveillances. They also found a unit of twenty-four Drogs—all dead with their throats torn. Over the next four weeks, other knights came upon the remains of fifteen other Drog units, each of them destroyed by the Ally.

For several weeks following the festival, Raccoman and Velissa found themselves separated by the intense training Raccoman was undergoing in the arts of the certain future war. While Raccoman flew with the knights, his wife tended to the affairs of the citadel.

Velissa busied herself with ordinary tasks, while Raccoman rejoiced over the success of their new, unseen ally.

The weather was always sunny in Rensgaard, unlike the snowy, windy seasons that Raccoman and Velissa had known on the other continent. They did not know what to call that continent, since neither the one they had come from nor the one they had come to had ever been named, and thus they were forced to refer to it as "the other continent." This seemed logical for, as Raccoman had said in his poetic fashion:

> *"It's easy to reason our whereabouts though,*
> *Since Estermann's lands include only two.*
> *With these continents two and never another one,*
> *If this is the one, then that is the other one."*

And so they continued to speak of the land that they had left as "the other continent."

They spoke often of the other continent, wondering about the fate of those Graygill women in Orkkan's exodus. They wondered if they had reached Moonrhyme territory and if they had been granted sanctuary in the caverns. They wondered if Parsky still lived in Maldoon or if he had moved his reign of terror to the debris-choked streets of Canby.

They spoke of these things again at breakfast several weeks after Raccoman first acquired Merran.

"Do you really think the Canbies had a chance on the icy ledges, I mean in the exodus?" asked Velissa.

> *"Who's to say? They have Orkkan,*
> *With Collinvar, if he could stand*
> *At Demmerron and prove a man.*
> *Perhaps there's hope for all we planned*
> *In the other lands of Estermann."*

She said nothing. Their cubicle had a small, cased window that looked out over the eastern forests. She peered through the little enclosure. Raccoman could see by the bright light that came through the window and fell full upon her face that the day was beautiful.

> *"I must go. The knights think they have seen*
> *A thousand Drogs in mists of green*
> *Preparing for the fray."*

"Be careful," said Velissa, kissing him. "I love you!"

Her caution to him was unnecessary, but he loved hearing her say it. Velissa was his treasure, and he sometimes hated himself for bringing her from one war to another.

"I'll be careful," he said, taking her in his arms.

"When this war is over, if Rensgaard stands
I'll fly you to the other lands:
The world we knew and loved."

They kissed. "Raccoman, I want to go home," she said and dropped into the same affected speech that she had grown to love:

"Once more to look at Quarrystone,
When the candolets are red
And the mountains gleam with snow."

"I know," he said. And kissing her again, he left for the day.

It was the first time that she had heard him confess his homesickness for their other continent, though she had felt it much of late.

It was just after Evensong one night, when Raccoman and Velissa were remembering that summer had now come to the land of the Canbies, that they heard the ring of the great gong that hung from before the portico of the palace. With the Titans, they headed for the palace square. As they walked, they could tell that, in the long night of the preparation for the war, there was singing and dancing in the streets once again. By the time they reached the palace facade, a large crowd of farmers and knights had already assembled.

A low hubbub of conversation ran through the crowd. No one knew for sure why they were assembled, and yet each felt that he or she was about to witness a great event. In but a moment of time, a figure appeared on the balustrade.

The sky drew upward, and a great shout rose from the Titans as the queen appeared carrying her baby.

When the cheers had subsided a bit, a knight in the crowd waved the hubbub to silence. "The queen Izonden has given us joy!" he cried out among the uplifted faces. "Rensgaard, after a thousand years of waiting, has an heir! Noble Titans, I give you Garrod the Second, heir to this land." Raccoman felt stunned. He dropped to his knees and the Titans fell back from him.

All the way from the very balustrade, the crowd divided itself to make way for Izoden and her infant. She walked slowly down the steps, not quite free yet of the pain and trauma of the life and hope she had given her people. Upon the level paving stones of the plaza, she made her way in regal dignity while the crowd gazed at the new baby in her arms.

Raccoman did not dare to lift his eyes. The honor of the announcement hung like a stone of great joy and responsibility from his rounded shoulders. Too soon his downcast eyes saw the queen's feet before him, and he felt her slender hand beneath his chin. She lifted his face so that their eyes met.

"Raccoman," she said, "this is Garrod the Second."

Raccoman had lived as long as the queen had waited for a child. Now his life was rewarded in a special way. Raccoman stood, and the queen gently handed him the bundle in her arms. It was an awkward moment, for Izonden was twice as tall as the Graygill, but the bundle was small even in Raccoman's arms. Velissa, who had been kneeling beside her husband, rose as the queen pulled her upward, and she too peered under the cloth to look at the new heir. She smiled broadly and looked at Raccoman, and his lips also parted and his white teeth beamed from under his gray moustache. At the sight of their smiles, the Titans cheered again.

The tall queen preceeded Raccoman and Velissa, and the trio moved back to the balustrade.

"A song for Garrod the Second, Raccoman!" demanded Hallidan.

Raccoman felt unworthy. His usual egotism seemed to have vanished, and his whole demeanor said that he wished to decline the invitation.

"Please," Izonden entreated, "for your father and our son!"

Raccoman stood still a moment, looked at the baby in his arms, and then looked away. He handed the child upward to the queen, and as he crossed his hands before him, the square grew silent.

"There's a continent under the dreaming skies
Over the grand dividing seas,
Where the starlight falls on the Moonrhyme cliffs
And the sun ignites the ginjon trees.
Garrod the First was a Moonrhyme man
Who, like the sun on the crystal grass,
Warmed the world like the fire that fell
On the sentinels of Demmerron Pass.

The Father left his world of men
And the son he loved in Canby glen,

And disappeared to be born again
In loyalty to Rensgaard."

He stopped his song, then looked up at the queen's child and carefully sang as though he were singing a lullaby to his father's namesake. He sang barely loud enough for the Titans to hear.

"Sleep, child, your father's a Titan king.
And the blood of all his Riders keep
This citadel, so the queen may sing
Her kingdom heir a song of sleep.
Know this, Garrod, child of hope,
You've come to us in a time of war,
But safety shall your cradle keep
One thousand knights shall guard your sleep."

The song was as soft as a lullaby. It was affirmation for the king and queen, now separated for the uncertain future.

It spoke to applause, and one knight in the corner of the plaza began to applaud. But no sooner had he begun than Raccoman said, with a quiet finality, "Please, the baby sleeps. Now is the time for a quiet covenant."

And so the crowd remained still. Raccoman sang quietly, and the melody floated on the warm night air:

"Upon the winds of holocaust
Shall drift a lullaby,
Against a future held in store
Has come an infant's cry.
In love, Izonden holds the prince.
To shield him from this war.
Sleep, Garrod—watchful do the condorgs fly.
For the Titans guard the valleys,
And the Falcon soars the sky."

Saying nothing further, the queen walked back into the palace, and the Titans dispersed in silence.

Distrust the fond year that insists upon having its way,
When the past becomes angry and crowds on the instant and now.
There are demons that feed on those too afraid of the day
And chew on the fingers of hands that won't hold to the plow.

CHAPTER VIII

The Deception

WHILE IT WAS GENERALLY KNOWN
that Rengraaden had defected, Raenna's spirit could hardly have
been more troubled than that of the queen herself. Izonden felt
more insecure than ever, and she called Velissa to her a second
time. As they talked, she nursed the infant prince.

"Velissa, she began, then paused. "I'm terribly troubled."

She needn't have said so, for it was clear that she was, but it did
open the conversation. Velissa wanted to say something to her—
anything that might help the queen to bear more easily the awful
affairs of her kingdom. Still, she knew what Izonden wanted, and
she was determined not to disclose the whereabouts of King Ren.
So rather than say too much, she said nothing, extending a silence
long enough for the queen to begin again.

"Rengraaden is a traitor—a fact that the king does not know,
wherever he is. I am sure that if the king knew this, he would
return to Rensgaard. Do you realize, Velissa, that if the invasion
were to come too suddenly, there would be no monarch or crown
prince to assume command?"

"Yes, but Hallidan is capable."

"Capable, but not king. He does not symbolize his sovereign as
my nephew did. These are times when we must have someone
around by whose sovereign command the citadel might be enjoined
to its own defense."

Izonden's words were not so much an argument as a plea.

"Velissa," she went on, "I know if the king knew of Rengraaden's treachery, he would want to be home—but he does not
know. Velissa, you must disclose the king's whereabouts!"

"Hallidan knows. Ask him."

"I cannot, said the queen. "You know he feels that the security
of the king would be threatened if he were to tell."

"Don't *you* care about his safety, Izonden?"

The question was unfair. Velissa instantly regretted having asked it.

The queen's eyes brimmed with tears. She tried to speak and
couldn't. Velissa felt ashamed.

Velissa studied the queen, a lean and weary mother who was a
symbol for the war-torn kingdom. Neither of them spoke for a
while. And then suddenly Velissa's face lit up.

"Izonden, I see a kind of hope."

The queen waited for her to go on.

"I will go to the king myself."

The queen considered Velissa's words carefully and only gradually did her face show pleasure. "You're not afraid?" she asked, shifting her infant in her arms.

"Yes, I am afraid. I have never been more afraid. Still, there is an absence of peace in the streets and lanes of Rensgaard. I could go alone. . . ," Velissa stopped. "No, I *must* go alone. It may be that only alone would I be undetected by Thanevial's hordes; I cannot handle a condorg. Besides, the beast would draw unnecessary attention." She thought a moment and then said, "Yes, alone is best."

Izonden smiled. Her infant son was sound asleep.

Hallidan thought little of it at the time. Velissa had questioned him about the various landmarks along the trail that they had passed on their passage from Smeade to Rensgaard. Had Hallidan been aware of any specific design to her questions, he would have placed her under the watch of a Guardian Rider to prevent her from making an attempt to reach King Ren alone. The idea was madness.

Velissa carefully noted the landmarks that Hallidan mentioned, memorized them, and then reversed their order in her mind so that the natural markers would direct her from Rensgaard to Smeade.

Velissa became wary lest she probe too directly and arouse the suspicions of Hallidan or her husband. Once she had sufficient, if minimal, information for the trip, she dropped the subject. But the subject was not as easy to leave as she might have wished. The talk of war was the only talk, it seemed, that the citadel knew. Raccoman and Hallidan discussed the main roads that the Drog swarms seemed to be using in their travel in and about the city.

The ominous portent of war was now immediate. There had been three major cave-ins at the Desert of Draymon, and the liquid sand tides were eating into the caladena belts that surrounded the Tower Altar. Thanevial could see that his pyrimid was doomed. The fiery fingers of boiling sand were now lapping the very foundation of his Tower Altar. The molten tides had come to the tower. The liquid breakers roared, and volleys of fire caressed the black shrine.

For reasons of his own, the lord of the Drogs had begun to group the Drogs into three units of two thousand each. Their numbers had begun to diminish. Very few were coming from the forming pits in the Valley of the Changelings. More than fifty Drog scouting parties had been destroyed by the Ally. They disappeared quietly in caves or were found murdered at their campsites. Thanevial himself had gone to inspect one of the decimated campfire sites near the Desert of Draymon. There he found fifty of his beast-warriors lying dead in heaps. During the night, the Ally had torn out their throats.

Raccoman talked to Velissa night after night about the war. He told her of Thanevial's consolidation of his Drogs into units, and of how it looked as though the Drogs meant to charge the citadel from three directions, leaving the thousand Titan knights to stand against his own hordes in defense of the six bridges of the city. Although the knights were well outnumbered, they remained hopeful. The Ally, whoever he was, seemed to be on their side. In the middle of their hope stood the inspiration of Garrod the Second and the vanished king, whom they still believed possessed the treasure of Maldoon.

Velissa knew she must act before the coming of the war. Her husband had warned her repeatedly about leaving the city. She knew she would be in danger once she went beyond the walls, but she was now firmly committed to Queen Izonden and to act as a lone courier in a desperate attempt to find the king in the Caverns of Smeade.

Velissa had always worn blue in the other world, but her resolve led her to fashion a dark brown and maroon cape and dress for herself for hiding in the caladena groves as she traveled alone through the Drog-infested highlands. She crossed the west bridge just after the sentries let it down for the day. One sentry noted that she was leaving the citadel and told her to be careful and not stray far from the city.

She walked the edge of the field and thought of the joy that had characterized her life on Estermann while she enjoyed the summers in the other continent. She remembered how she had often walked in the late summer sun with the serpent Doldeen close at her heels. How Doldeen would slither along in the forest when Velissa took steps that forced the snake to wriggle extra fast, especially if they were moving across bare stone that became too hot on her scaly belly when the sun was high.

It seemed to Velissa, when she closed her eyes, that she could still see the blue observatory where she had lived from her birth to her one hundred and seventy-fifth year. She could remember that her mother had died somewhere in the swimming recollection of her thirty-fifth year. Velissa had been so small then that not much of her mother's memory would surface now. But her father—that was another matter. For she had known and loved her father, and she would never be able to erase his fond memory. And Doldeen had been the best friend she had ever had. There was nothing that she could not have discussed with the serpent. None of Velissa's conversation had ever eluded Doldeen. No secret would ever have been unsafe with the serpent. Velissa felt that the huge diamond that had been Doldeen's one preoccupation had sometimes tied the serpent to its care. Usually Velissa and Doldeen had taken the Singreale with them, even if they were only going to share lunch on the hillside near their home.

Velissa's thoughts wandered. She was careful not to venture too near the edge of the field where the forest began. She took care to stay near the trench that surrounded the castle. There were trees in the chasm at the bars of the citadel, but it was a narrow band of forest, and no Drogs had ever been known to come to the very edge of the city. In a little while, she found herself moving in the purple-red grass at the edge of a field near a grove of the trees that surrounded the northeast wall. For the first time in months, she could not see even the sentry houses that stood over each of the six bridges that guarded the gates and roads that led into the citadel. Soon the citadel itself was left behind.

For some, it might have been a great insecurity not to see anyone who could offer help. But Velissa loved it. She could not even see one single soldier. She had heard too much talk of war. She was tired beyond belief of watching mounted riders and listening to the latest conversation of the positions of the three armies that Thanevial had created.

She walked all day.

Avoiding the main road, she threaded her way through the perimeter of forests that rose toward Mt. Calz. At times, she sat down just to feel the raw earth beneath her and the smiling sun above that warmed her. By late afternoon, she decided to lay down and rest. She looked up into the sky and saw nothing. Once a white camdrake flew across her line of vision, but he was soon gone. It always seemed to her, when she stared at the skies, that the blue would fall to earth and move around her and into her. She knew now why she had always loved blue. But never did she love it more than when it washed her and filled her again and again.

"The sky invades everything on a day like today," she thought. Sky, everything was sky.

Toward evening she passed a large group of Drogs moving toward Rensgaard. Yet she was well concealed, and though their presence terrified her, she was left undetected.

Night fell and the forest was darker than she remembered. She made her way slowly since she traveled through the thickest part of the forest, carefully avoiding the openness of the trails.

On her first night, she could see a distant campfire and hear the raucous laughter of a large group of Changelings. They were a great distance away, and yet, in the stillness of the night, it seemed as though they were very close.

The next morning, she carefully walked under the green mists and felted-moss floor that spread like a brown carpet beneath the huge trees of the Caladena Forests. Staying well off the road, she fared well for three days and nights, drinking the small drafts of water and eating as she would from the dembret nuts that were plentiful in the forest.

On the afternoon of the fourth day, she rested in an open lea in the sunshine.

Fatigued from her travel and warmed by the sun, she fell sound asleep. While she slept, she was transported. She found herself home again, sleeping on the hillsides of Quarrystone Woods. She floated in the blue sky as she laid on her back.

"Quarrystone Woods! I love you. You are blue!" she cried through her sluggish delirium. She heard the gazinger fowls. She cuddled congrels in slow motion as she dreamed. And best of all, she was with Doldeen again.

She and the serpent were talking and waiting dinner and brewing red candolet tea with its green vapors. She saw her father bending over his scope in the blue observatory. Blue swirled through every fissure of her soul. How lovely was the world! Even Singreale was blue as it gleamed from between the graceful fangs of the petulant Doldeen with her knobby silver horns shining in the summer sun. Soon all her images faded into blue consciousness. The heavy blue skies closed her eyes, and she dozed and even napped unobserved.

The warm was upon her and, indeed, at her very side.

The warm blue upon her and at her side . . . yes, at her side. Why at her side? She knew she must wake herself and find out why she felt the warm at her side. At last, she pulled herself out of the delirium and sat up, rubbing all the blue away. She hated to rub the blue away! Instantly, she was terrified.

A long, warm animal lay next to her. What was it? She felt a surge of dread until she realized that she was otherwise quite alone and that the long, warm beast was not a Drog. Besides, the situation had not yet proven itself dangerous.

The form beside her raised its head and said, "Hello, Misssey." It was Doldeen!

Velissa could not believe her eyes. Quarrystone Woods was hers again. It loomed all around her. Blue flooded the entire landscape; washing the world with newness and cleanness. She could do nothing but ask, "Doldeen, is it really you?"

"Yesss, Misssey," replied the serpent.

If this was a dream, it was one from which Velissa wished never to be awakened.

She grabbed the silver horns on Doldeen's head and twisted them with a gentle violence. She had done that so many times in Quarrystone. The two of them rolled in the soft grass until Doldeen's body was completely coiled about her. Velissa laughed and her friend hissed until the two of them were exhausted in their embrace. Soon Doldeen was lying beside her in the sun with her beautiful head upon Velissa's stomach.

"Misssey, remember how father always called me Essssey?" asked Doldeen with an exaggerated movement of her head because her lower jaw was still resting on Velissa's stomach.

"Oh, Doldeen, do *you* remember the afternoon when we rode Collinvar to the western meadows and found the grumblebeak hen with her chicks?"

"Misssey, misssey," she said embarrassed.

"I never will forget how those two chicks perched on the silver balls of your horns and would not let go. Even when you shook your head, they held on and defied you to dislodge them." Velissa smiled at the memories that neither contested.

"I tried to lasssh them with my tail, but they were defiant and would not let go of my sssilver knobs."

They laughed again, and then Velissa mused and lay silently until Doldeen seemed asleep. Suddenly Velissa sat upright, rudely knocking Doldeen's beautiful head to her lap.

"Whatsss the matter, Misssey?" the serpent asked.

"Doldeen, you were dead!" blurted out Velissa.

"Nonssssenssse—when?"

"The night we left the woods for the last time. I saw Raccoman bury you," Velissa insisted.

"Now that's a foolisssh conclusssion. You buried me in the sand a thoussand times and I alwaysss wriggled out when your back wasss turned," reasoned the serpent.

"I know, but this time your body was completely severed just below your head."

Doldeen objected in one word, "Ssevered!"

"Yesss—I mean, yes." Velissa had always found it hard to keep from picking up Doldeen's 'essey' way of speech.

"Velissa, will you look at the ssscar on the ssside of my neck?"

Velissa looked and was horrified. The scar was so big that it did appear as though her head had nearly been cut off.

"Regrettably, Velissa, you thought I wasss dead. And I found it mossst difficult tunneling out of that grave that your Raccoman dug. It left me hisssing and ssspitting dirt for a week. The nexssst time you think I'm dead, will you ask me first pleassse for my own opinion on the sssubject?"

Velissa laughed at her old friend. It was just like her to make light of even the most serious subjects. "But how did you get to this continent?"

"Getting to thisss continent was nothing, Misssey. It was getting out of the grave that wasss the hard part." Doldeen stilll sounded as though she were chiding Velissa for the premature burial. "Oh, I'll admit," Doldeen went on, "that I wasss hurt pretty bad, but I wasssn't dead. And jussst the idea that I had been burried by my bessst friend! It wasss the indignity of the whole thing, Misssey."

"Well, I didn't take time to check you personally, you looked so bad."

"Thankssss!"

Velissa remembered how Doldeen hated to be told that anything was wrong with her personal appearance.

"I mean—your, your—" Velissa stammered, "your head looked loose."

"Thanksss, yesss, thank you very much!" said Doldeen, tilting her silver horns in an arrogant fashion. Velissa realized that it wasn't much of a compliment to tell anyone that her head looked loose. She could see that she was only making things worse by describing for her friend how badly the serpent had looked on the night that Raccoman buried her.

"Raccoman buried you—well, well, because you looked like you should be buried. You usually look nice, but that night you didn't!" said Velissa firmly. "Anyway, how did you get from there to here?"

"I ssswam," she said.

"So that was it . . . but the ocean!"

"What'sss so hard about that?" asked Doldeen.

"With your head cut off—half cut off?" said Velissa doubtfully. She had never known Doldeen to lie, but she had never seen Doldeen do anything tiring for any great length of time either.

Doldeen did not want to be reminded even one more time about her head being cut off. She obviously wished that Velissa would not bring up the whole issue that called attention to her scar, for even though the hideous scar was still there, she didn't like to think of it because it made her feel ugly.

She decided to be remote, and so she slithered from Velissa and turned her face away. With her face toward the forest and away from her mistress, Doldeen no longer felt self-conscious about her scar. Velissa didn't want to doubt her, but somehow she felt Doldeen wasn't being truthful.

"Please, Doldeen, forgive me," begged Velissa.

For a while, Doldeen continued to be remote as though she would never forgive her mistress. At last she blurted out a weak defense, "Well, how far do you think that you could ssswim with your head nearly cut off?"

"Never mind," said Velissa. "Tell me, where have you been staying since you got here?"

"Near Mt. Calz—over there in the grove. There'sss a forester'sss wife that feedsss me fresssh vegetablesss and the eggsss of the camdrakes that nessst at the edge of the field. Would you like to sssee where I have made my little nessst? It'sss not like the quartersss I usssed to have when I lived at the blue obsssservatory, but it is warm, and I've alwaysss plenty to eat. The camdrake eggsss are quite tasssty," she added as an afterthought. She uncoiled and slithered off in the direction of the trees that ringed the wall. "Come, Misssey and sssee my nessst."

Dutifully, Velissa watched her and followed as fast as she could. The serpent had a smooth and gliding pattern, constantly elevating her head and looking right and left and then lowering it and slithering forward again. The ripples in Doldeen's beautiful skin always had intrigued Velissa, and she could not believe that she had the good fortune on such a beautiful and sunny day to find her old friend whom she thought was dead and buried a continent away. She suddenly felt ashamed that she had not personally checked Doldeen to be sure that she was dead before she had permitted Raccoman to bury her. Inwardly she grieved about the abuse as she followed Doldeen's golden and brown form into the trees.

Even though the line of trees was dark, she was amazed at how deep the darkness was. Her eyes had to adjust before she could see her friend.

"Wait, Doldeen! You always did try to out-distance me when we were in the woods." She ran, laughing, and tripped and fell. Her snakey friend rushed up to her and raised her head and coiled, grinning an unusual grin that Velissa had never seen. It was almost as if Doldeen were gloating.

"Wait a minute," Velissa said. "You detest eggs. Why would the forester's wife feed you eggs when you detest them so?" A horrible moment of revelation came upon Velissa and she tried to get up. "You're not Doldeen!"

"That's right, Misssey," replied the serpent, already turning black. The creature coiled itself into a tight knot and sprang, knocking Velissa to the ground. Once more, Velissa tried to get up, but found the horrible blackening thing had already wrapped itself around her legs so tightly that she was powerless to move. The serpent changed to a big, black Drog as three Drogs more stepped out of the trees.

"Gukka! Kalanka bandagmo!" grunted the largest of the four.

"You're a Drog!" gasped Velissa, looking at the monster that had so recently held the beautiful form of her lost friend.

"Yesss, Misssey!" he hissed and then laughed. "Hun, hun, hunga!"

The morning that Velissa left on her secret mission, Raccoman also left, not telling Velissa of a secret project of his own. Raccoman had wanted to surprise her: it was his intention to rescue the Paradise Falcon. He was not exactly sure how he would to this. Like Velissa, however, he was homesick, and it had been nearly a year since he had first revealed his marvelous ship to her in that faraway "other continent."

There were metal smiths in the citadel, but no welders. Raccoman marveled that, while the stone-workers of Rensgaard were much better than those of the other continent, the art of welding had not yet been discovered. His own talent, therefore, seemed all the more remarkable to the Titan metal-workers who had heard of his marvelous craft.

One other reason stopped Raccoman from revealing to Velissa his idea of rescuing the craft. He was not altogether sure that he would be able to retrieve it, nor could he be sure how badly the ship's steering system might have been damaged by its awkward landing in the caladena grove. Raccoman knew that the fingers of liquid sand that were eating into the huge trees would soon destroy that part of the forest where the Paradise Falcon had come to rest after its long and impressive voyage. And, too, there was the possibility that the ship had been damaged by Drogs. Or, even if they had not damaged it, there might be an encampment of the monsters so near the golden glider that it would be dangerous to try and rescue it from its lonely jungle outpost. The Paradise Falcon seemed like a beautiful animal caught in the jaws of some monstrous trap. It was Raccoman's ship—and he felt he must make one last attempt to save it. He knew Velissa would be excited to know of his plan. But he also knew she would be most disappointed if the rescue attempt failed. Therefore it seemed better to the Graygill not to tell his wife.

Besides Merran and Zephrett, Raccoman and Hallidan took two other condorgs that had not been used since their masters had defected to become Drogs. Raccoman decided upon a tactic that would lift the huge, shiny craft vertically out of its forest enclosure. The craft was made of windfoils and was certainly light enough to be hoisted upward by even one strong condorg. Its size, more than its weight, would make it hard to disentangle from the trees.

Raccoman had spent a week weaving a coarse rope out of dembret fibers. The rope was very long and could be attached to the undersaddle girth of the riderless condorgs. Raccoman intended to cut away the branches and entangling vines that held the Paradise Falcon. There was no reason then that the craft could not be lifted vertically from its landing place.

In less than two hours, Raccoman and Hallidan were flying over the area of the jungle where the Paradise Falcon had settled in. The riderless condorgs flew along with them, sometimes straying in the sky but always coming back to accompany them in their soundless flight. In the distance, they could see the Tower Altar. They stayed as far away from it as they possibly could. Raccoman remembered that it was in the very shadow of this altar that the craft had originally settled in.

Hallidan remembered, too. And for this reason, he circled wide to the south and brought his condorgs in as near the top of the treetops as possible so that they could not be seen by anyone who might have been on the long, steep steps that mounted to the top of the hideous black tower. From the distance, they could see that something was hanging in the chains at the top. It appeared to be a Drog who had been killed and left to hang there as a public example for any others who might refuse to fear and obey Thanevial.

They had skimmed the treetops for only a few minutes when Raccoman spotted the bright yellow edge of the sail-plane jutting upright through the purple trees. The forest was so thick that there was no place for the condorgs to land. Condorgs wearied quickly if they tried treading the air in order to stay in flight without moving forward.

Now came the dangerous part, and Raccoman volunteered for it. Beneath the green mist, nothing at all was visible. It was impossible to tell what was on the ground beneath the green mist out of which rose the purple caladena trees. Raccoman dropped a rope from the bottom of his own condorg, and it fell outward into the air. The cord uncoiled and hung limp, disappearing in an instant through the green mist.

It was obvious to Hallidan that Raccoman had practiced this maneuver in some other less risky place. At once, he slipped his hand beneath the upper girth and slid forward and off the left side of his condorg and slipped onto the gently rotating pinion of Merran's wing. Avoiding the wing, he slid in front of it, keeping his hand on the girth and hanging like an insect over the green mist with the purple branches and the sleek hulk of the Paradise Falcon sticking up through the fog. With the rope attached to the condorg's saddle girth, the Graygill moved deftly hand over hand into the mist as a spider travels along a single strand of a thin web in the bright sun. The rope appeared like a filament of gold hanging from the underbelly of his huge mount, and down, down, Raccoman lowered himself into the green mist.

He soon disappeared in the vapor. For a moment, he saw nothing but green and the hulk of the inverted Falcon he hoped to liberate from its snare of branches and purple limbs. Inching down the rope, he broke cautiously through. Then his heart froze. For directly beneath him was a Drog who had seen neither Raccoman nor the rope dangling through the low ceiling of fog.

While the Drog looked away, the Greygill surveyed the situation to be sure that there were no other Drogs. This one seemed to be completely alone, a sentry posted there to guard the ship.

Slowly, Raccoman began to swing on the rope, gradually and silently enlarging the arc until his small body became a pendulum. He intended to land directly on top of the Changeling sentry. His problem was that the condorg hovering silently above the fog was not quite as steady in holding the rope as Raccoman would have liked. Finally, however, the arc of his swing was sufficient.

He reached the zenith of his swing and let go of the rope, drawing the fire-glass and grasping its hilt with both hands. The Drog heard him but too late. He barely had time to turn his ugly head when the fire-glass caught him and the blade, sharp and hot, sliced into his hunched torso, splitting his back open. Raccoman was proud of his work, so efficiently performed that the creature had not even had time to cry out. He was also relieved that his initial assessment turned out to be correct. There were no other Drogs around.

Acrid fumes filled the jungle. The gore that had been the insides of the beast soldier lay smouldering and smoking in brown and black.

Raccoman left the Drog and awkwardly climbed the caladena tree, disappearing into the green ceiling of mist. He worked to determine the nature of the entanglement that held the Paradise Falcon. The glider's stabilizer mechanism appeared to be snagged and snarled in two huge vines that would have to be cut loose.

The real problem, however, was the landing skids. Raccoman wished now that he had not tried to lower them during the flight. The purple tendrils of a huge tree limb jutted through the bracing of the skids. Before the Paradise Falcon could be freed, the limb would have to be cut off. He tied the descent rope securely to the rear of the ship.

His second step was to attach the long rope that now dangled from the riderless condorgs. This rope, he knew, had to be attached to the front stabilizer bar. Then the ship could be pulled through the sky in the direction that it was designed to fly once it was free of the vine. Raccoman knew that the condorgs would have difficulty pulling the ship against the wind if they tried to draw it in the opposite direction from which it was designed to fly. The probability was that erratic sky currents would tear the moorings loose, and the craft would float to the ground once more and be lost.

Even as the Graygill decided on a course of action, he was delighted to realize that nothing on the ship appeared to be badly damaged.

Deliberating no longer, he climbed the rope again. With signals he had prearranged with Hallidan, he asked for help. The knight dropped a second rope. Sliding to his condorg's left pinion, Hallidan grabbed the saddle girth of his own mount and swung outward into space. The muscles of his arms and chest rippled as he dangled free. He was much heavier than Raccoman, and this sudden drop to the underside of his mount seemed to tip the condorg in midair, but the animal righted itself as the knight moved on down the rope, hand over hand. Using the sheer power of his own strong body, he quickly descended. His muscular legs dropped into the green mist, and soon he was gone from sight.

Above the green mist, Raccoman had signaled into position the condorgs trailing the large rope. The hovering beasts dropped to the surface of the fog. The dembret cable was twisted to keep the apex of the rope in a crisp V-shape as it dangled from the underbellies of the two riderless condorgs. Suspended from a single rope beneath the huge wings of his own condorg, Raccoman began again the pendulum action, swinging his body in space until he came within reach of the long, long rope that hung down between the riderless condorgs.

Like an aerialist, the Graygill grasped the strong, double-fiber rope and held to its V. He then dropped the rope that had held him. He had changed supports in space.

The V of the rope where Raccoman held the apex became elongated as the hovering beasts moved slowly together. Once again, Raccoman's feet dangled in the green mist. His yellow boots stirred the stuff as he was lowered into the colorful fog.

This second descent was more difficult. He drew his fire-glass and sliced the purple limbs around him to keep from becoming ensnared in the same branches that held his wondrous craft. Every branch that looked as if it might be in his path, he cut away. Hallidan below was nearly hit by some of the falling branches that Raccoman sliced free.

The condorgs above could not see the Graygill, and they continued to lower him. He hit the ground. The rope piled up. Hallidan, seeing the problem, moved back up his own rope until his head and shoulders appeared above the mist. He motioned for the condorgs to move apart gradually. They did. The V began to widen, and, therefore, shorten once again. From below, Raccoman watched the rope uncoil from the ground and move up. Then, though he hated to do it, he shouted up to Hallidan who was still above the mist.

"Enough!"

Hallidan cringed to hear the welder make such a noise, but he immediately stopped the condorgs. They remained stationary in their hovering.

Raccoman repeated the swinging process. From above, the upper portion of the V began to sway until it reached to a wide arc, stirring the green mist. Then it stopped.

Raccoman found his target. His swinging brought him directly against the nose of the sail-plane, and he quickly attached the connection he had preforged to the stabilizer bar. It was secure.

He smiled.

"Hallidan!" he cried again. He hated himself for breaking the silence a second time. Still, the forest seemed deserted. The near-naked hulk of the Titan Star Rider descended out of the ceiling of the green mist. Raccoman spoke loudly and forcefully.

"Can you tie your rope to the rear of the craft?" It was a whole noisy question.

The knight saw the Graygill's logic and quickly and efficiently obeyed. Now neither of them had a free rope. Raccoman motioned for Hallidan to cut away the heavy branch that protruded through the mist and snarled the landing gear.

This was the test. Hallidan chopped at the huge limb with his searing fire-glass. The two dembret vines snapped and fell free, stirring the mist. The weight of the ship came at once upon the hovering condorgs. The ship dipped a little, then held. Raccoman smiled underneath the mist. Hallidan smiled broadly back. The entire weight of the ship was now on the condorgs.

Raccoman motioned Hallidan across to the huge limb on which he was standing. He leapt out and grabbed the landing skid and swung free in space. The ship was not quite vertical but hung at a steep angle. With effort, Raccoman worked his way, hand over hand, across the stabilizer bar till he reached the strong, outer edge of the ship. He kicked and swung through the green fog until he flipped himself to the upper surface of the Paradise Falcon. "Hah-hoo!" he laughed. The condorgs fluttered uneasily at the Graygill's laughter rolling upward from underneath them.

Hallidan leapt out into space and caught the landing skids. Like Raccoman before him, he dangled over the ground, stirring the fog and moving hand over hand until he reached the edge of the ship, completing the same exaggerated swinging of his body until his whole muscular torso came up over the edge of the ship at such a height that it shocked even Raccoman. He thudded onto the upper surface. He was so much heavier than the Graygill that the ship rocked in the green vapor as the condorgs treaded the air furiously with their wings just to keep the whole thing level.

"Hah-hoo!" laughed Raccoman again.

Hallidan motioned for him to be silent, for although both of them were now in the middle of the green mist, the nose of the ship still dangled downward through the fog.

They climbed into the glider's seats. The seats, tilted forward, were hard to get into. Only by bracing themselves backward from the stabilizer bars could the Titan and the Graygill shove themselves against the backs of their seats and buckle the fiber straps across themselves. Hallidan took Velissa's old seat, which was shallow enough in itself. Velissa was so much smaller than the knight that he scarcely fit into it at all. But it was enough to hold him.

Soon they were both buckled in firmly. Raccoman lifted his head.

"Ho-hay-ho!" cried the Graygill, and then both of them shouted together.

The circling condorgs heard and were grateful for the command. The effort of treading air had wearied them. Steadily the three condorgs moved off and upward together. It was beautiful to see the ship rising out of the green mist, resplendent in the morning sun. Once the condorgs could see the ship and its two riders, they leveled it by adjusting their flying position. The ship rose slowly upward higher and higher.

Raccoman was amazed at how close the Tower Altar really was. It was a miracle to him that they had not been discovered. When they were high in the sky, Raccoman asked Hallidan if the fiber seat strap was secure. Hallidan nodded an assent.

Raccoman checked his own seat strap, then leaned out to the side and took an extra coil of cord and tied it to the hilt of his own sword. The hot blade slid back across the windfoil and the fire-glass glowed red in the shiny yellow metal. A moment later, his sword fell awkwardly against the stabilizer bar and then swung into the single cord at the back of the ship. With one searing touch, the grass cable was cut in two. The sail-plane fell backward and so did Raccoman and Hallidan until they were dangling on the surface of the ship, looking straight upward a long distance to the strands of rope that held them there.

Hallidan commanded his condorg to fly home, and the two beasts that now supported the ship flew higher and faster. As their flight leveled off, their speed increased and the Paradise Falcon, too, leveled off. The fast flight of the condorgs created a powerful, artificial wind that was more than adequate for the short flight.

Raccoman smiled broadly. Hallidan felt exhilarated.

Soon they were going so fast that Raccoman felt confident to do a bold thing. Having drawn his sword back on the cord with which he had lowered it, he repeated the same procedure down the front of the ship. Their riderless condorgs felt the tension ease abruptly as their towing cable was severed by his fire-glass.

Hallidan was surprised that the ship did not even dip. It was flying at a safe speed now, and whatever anxiety Hallidan felt, Raccoman was confident.

"Won't it crash?" asked the Titan.

"Not this time!" replied the Graygill.

"Why not?" asked the knight.

"Because I'm going to be very careful."

"But where will we land?" asked Hallidan.

> "If my glide is right,
> By the edge of night,
> This craft will glisten
> In the palace light!"

They were moving fast, and there was much more of a breeze than there had been on that fateful day when Raccoman and Velissa had fallen into the Caladena Forests.

Hallidan watched as Raccoman stomped the stabilizer bars. The wings of the craft were pulled down and the speed of their flight and the resistance of the upper breeze moved them slowly skyward. Raccoman knew it would not last for long, but he deflected the rudder rod and steered slowly toward Mt. Calz.

Gradually Hallidan left all his insecurities behind.

"This craft is the work of a genius!" cried the knight. Somehow he had started believing in the Graygill. It was nice of him to compliment the Graygill, but it only set the Graygill to complimenting himself.

> "Hallidan,
> As sure as the fire of my sword is most hot
> I'd just as soon tell you—I'd rather than not—
> That I am the best of a marvelous lot."

Hallidan smiled. He ordinarily didn't like arrogance, but it was hard even for the knight to sit on the deck of the Paradise Falcon and be humble. So he said again, as he gazed at the peak of Mt. Calz far below him, "Son of Garrod, you are a genius!"

"Agreed!" said Raccoman, matter of factly.

They passed a flock of camdrakes who skittered before the craft in amazement.

By the middle of the afternoon, Raccoman could tell that the breeze that had been so helpful was subsiding and the sky was becoming still. In the distance, he could see Rensgaard, and he turned his plane in a wide, slow arc. When they were closer, he reversed the stabilizers, and the edge of the ship turned up a little. The sail-plane gradually settled to the north wall of the citadel. Miraculously, Raccoman skimmed the very walls and then pulled up the edge of the ship so swiftly that the glider dropped rapidly, almost as though it were going to crash.

When Raccoman reversed the stabilizer rod, the Paradise Falcon leveled. It was moving awfully fast, and Hallidan felt for a moment that they would crash into the facade at the south end. But the instant the steep skids touched the paving stones, the glider poured forth a double trail of sparks and stopped almost instantly. It tilted forward sharply and then leveled itself and was silent.

"Ho, lay-ho!" shouted Hallidan to other knights in the square. "This Graygill's a genius!" Raccoman added his own nod of assent.

Hallidan's excitement was so great that he had forgotten he was nearly naked. He unloosened the fiber strap, which had held him faithfully, and leapt from the ship. A crowd soon gathered in the square, and there was excitement in the streets as Raccoman climbed out of the plane. He looked around, but the one face that he wanted to see was not there. Where was Velissa? Raccoman had wanted this to be his surprise, and he hated it that she had not been the very first one to see their gleaming ship on the white paving stones of the plaza.

Raccoman swiftly made his way through the streets to their cubicle on the wall. Already it was late evening. No sooner had he burst through his own door than he called out, "Velissa, I have a surprise for you!"

There was no answer.

The apartment was empty, and Raccoman was suddenly afraid.

The original sin is ultimate sin—
Claim thrones and be gods as you may!
And the last pair alive, like the first pair alive,
Would rather have power than obey.

CHAPTER IX

The Miserians

$\bigvee$ELISSA SOON DISCOVERED that,
as clumsy and slow as the hunched Drogs appeared to be, their
scaly forms were twice her size and could move almost twice as
fast. Her hands were bound behind her. She had never realized
that not having them free to swing at her sides was somehow a
terrible impediment to running.

She felt a tremendous wave of bright green guilt. She had deliberately disobeyed the city's logic, knowing it was wrong to leave
Rensgaard. Further, she knew that Raccoman would be devoured
by his concern for her. Her fears for her own life were as great as
the monsters who held her captive. But her concern for her husband surpassed even that. She knew he would grieve her absence
and be driven to bleak despair at the thought of his small bride in
the company of the grunting, vicious Changelings. He would un-
doubtedly be killed in some perilous rescue attempt. For, she didn't
doubt that he would try to save her. Lives would be lost in the
attempt, whenever it came. When she saw the bloodshed that
would come on her behalf, she would suffer in her anguish all over
again.

She found that the Drogs were obscene and mindless things—as
dimwitted as they were cruel. As they marched along, she hated all
over again what Thanevial had done to sire this evil race of bald
and brawling brutes. She thought of the Drog lord's first murders in
the citadel and of his kidnapping of the infant prince. Now Rengraaden himself had become one of these horrible beasts. Their
grunting conversations were as ugly as their naked, leathery appearance.

"Uggun, thisss iss Velissssa!" grunted the blackest of them,
pointing to Velissa and still mimicking Doldeen. His mucous-filled
eyes were too gray of milky slime to sparkle. But as he said the
words, he pointed to Velissa and laughed. The others roared in
laughter, too, in their thick and dull syllables of laughter.

"Hunga, Velissa, Gukka, ssstupid!" laughed another through his
toothy mouth. His receding chin nearly disappeared into his hairy
neck as he laughed, "Hun, hun, hunga!"

"Ssstupid and sssoo sssweet gukka Kalanka," grunted a third.

From the forest where they had captured Velissa, they trekked through the thick trees at the base of the mountains and worked their way forward until they entered the jungles of dembret vines to the west. There they forced their shuffling march on toward the northern slopes of Mt. Calz.

By evening, they had come to the Valley of the Changelings. They decided to make their camp. Whenever the Drogs could, they camped in the Valley of the Changelings. They loved the stench of decay that bubbled from the malformed and unfinished creatures growing in the gory, red fluid of the forming pits.

The knights stayed far away from the place for two reasons. First of all, it was the perfect place for an ambush, since there were always likely to be Changelings in the area. Second, no knight wanted it known that he had been near the place lest the unholy desire fall upon him. Even if a knight was not tempted by Thanevial's darkness, he would never want Ren to suspect his allegiance.

Velissa watched as the Drogs built a fire. She knew they were cannibals, but didn't worry about them eating her. Rengraaden was now a part of this leathery horde, and he would lose no time in making Thanevial's camp aware of Singreale's disappearance and of the three individuals who knew where the king and the diamond were. She, Raccoman, and Hallidan had discussed the fact that they would each be the prey of the army of the Tower Altar.

In the amber flickerings, the Drogs debated over who would furnish supper.

"Ugghun," said the blackest. The firelight was discolored in the gray reflection of his eyes. "Golokanga Hund!"

"Uggun, gukka!" agreed the others.

He walked off. In the distance, Velissa could hear him raking a tree limb through the pits that would by day appear to be filled with a red, thick liquid.

"Hunga," he grumbled when he had searched the first pit and found it empty. A moment later, through the darkness they could hear him stirring the second pit. "Ugghum, ugghum," he grumbled as he went from pit to pit. There was more swishing of the red fluids which in the night had appeared black.

"Choung!" came an exultant cry through the dark.

"Choung! Choung!" the others laughed. "Hun, hun, hunga!"

There was the sound of the first Drog dragging a heavy object through the dry grass. Soon the Changeling came into better view. The fire roared so high that Velissa had no trouble seeing the prize.

By a foot, he dragged a half-formed Changeling. The mass of un-formed being was neither knight nor Drog. It was an ugly delicacy over which the mewling monsters mulled the meal they would make of it. And it was so drenched in the thick, dark red that it was an ugly meal, indeed. Further, the dragging of the malformed beast-knight had caused it to be clotted with dust, mud, and sticks. It was a most unpalatable dinner. Velissa could not stand to look. She felt nauseous.

"Choung!" they cried as they began to tear bits and pieces off of the muddy, malformed monster. They ate loudly, and the dark and pungent fluid rolled down their chins and dripped onto their bris-tled and leathery chests. As they slurped and ripped, the Change-lings wiped their mouths so that dark red fragments of their meal clung to the back's of their hands. In the fire light, Velissa could tell that their bodies were covered with their meal. Their claws dripped with their appetites.

Finally, one by one, they leaned back against the rocks that formed a grisly ring. They grunted in their horrible contentment. They knew that their cracked-face commander would be pleased that they had captured a prize for their lord.

"Ugghum," grunted one, patting his satisfied stomach.

Across the campfire, one of them belched loud and the others laughed and grunted, "Ugghum hunga," in agreement. The crude and huge denizens caused Velissa to turn her head away. One of them saw her disgusted look and said to the others, "Velissa Choung!"

"Gukka!" the others rasped. Their ugly, mucous eyes blinked their approval of the idea. "Velissa choung!"

The largest of them grabbed a bloody bone, brought it to her, and shoved it in her face. "Velissa, choung! Ugghum hunga!" Ve-lissa had never seen such an ugly bone. It still was covered with the red slime. The Drog tried to shove it in her mouth, and she turned her head in terror. "Raccoman, Raccoman," she cried aloud.

The Drogs exploded in laughter. "Hun, hun, hun, hungun!" they bellowed and repeated the procedure. Again and again, they thrust the bone in her face. "Oh, Raccoman, Raccoman," she sobbed.

"Raccoman, Raccoman," mimicked one fo the Drogs. "Oh! Rac-coooohhman, chounga, chounga Raccoman!" And he thrust the bone at her mouth again. Finally Velissa collapsed from her ex-haustion and went unconscious.

"Chounga," cried one of them, smearing her face and arms with the slippery bone.

Velissa seemed to will herself unconscious for the rest of the night. When she woke, even for an instant, she shut her mind against the horror of her captivity. Besides, she was so utterly fatigued that she needed the sleep desperately. Her captors were so huge that she had had to race just to keep up with them as they marched to the valley. She was not used to such strenuous hiking.

The morning came early. She had heard that it was the custom of the Drogs to eat only at night, and so she hoped that she would not have to watch a Drog breakfast. She had awakened earlier than the rest of them, but she kept quiet. In the gray light of morning, she could see their horrible bodies piled up like mounds of black earth. They were heaving in the loud, labored breathing that characterized them whether they were awake or asleep. Their fire had all but gone out, and there was a slight chill in the morning air. The mutilated carcass of their meal was lying cold and foul just to one side of the campfire.

Velissa had no idea what their grunted words and gutturalizing meant. She had figured out, during her ordeal the night before, that "chounga" meant food. "Hunga" was some sort of command word, and the various other grunts were expressions of amusement or unrest or contentment.

Her blood ran cold when she heard one of them say, as he sat up, "Condungra!" it was evidently a morning word. "Condungra! Condungra!" he shouted. They all began to stir. In a while, they had buckled on their swords and were standing. Velissa stood up, too, assuming that they were ready to move on. She had no intention of being jerked to her feet by a cruel Drog.

"Velissa chonga!" laughed one, pointing to the red stains on her face and arms. "Gukka, gukka," cried the others and laughed. "Velissa—drangummi Drog. Hun, hun, hunga!" Velissa could feel the dried liquid on her face and see it on her arms. It was revolting to her, but her hands were still bound, and she was powerless to remove it.

Another picked up the bone with which they had tormented her the night before. He waved the bone in her face and cried, "Raccoooohman chounga." They all laughed. Then he threw the bone away and roughly pushed Velissa out into the forest before them. "Hun, hun, hunga!" they cried and laughed again for no reason that Velissa could see.

Velissa's thoughts moved from Raccoman to Ren, from Doldeen to her childhood, to the other continent again. She thought of the horrible meal that she had watched the Drogs devour. The reddish bones had only an hour before been a knight of Ren. She knew that while she was being tormented, some new wife of a nameless knight had wept. A new Miserian had come to be. Like the others, she would be disconsolate over the defection of her husband. Only her husband never had a chance to show his allegiance to Thanevial. He had been dragged from the forming pits to be devoured at the campfire. "Perhaps it was best," thought Velissa in her disgust.

The day wore on. Velissa could not enjoy the sun, knowing that the night would come again all too soon. They marched in a double file where the forest moved back to permit it. They passed the opening to the Caverns of Smeade just before nightfall. Never stopping, they moved on into the forest where they would make another of their ugly camps at evening. They came to a wide, open area of ground where it was obvious to Velissa that they had obviously built other fires and slept other nights. The trees had been cleared in a perfect circle.

There was to be some sort of rendezvous, for the Drogs built an especially big fire and camped on only one side of the clearing as though they were saving the other side for some other group that would be meeting them. "No chounga, uggum," said the large Drog who appeared to be their leader. He was apparently telling them that they would not eat yet.

The leathery Changelings sat down to watch the fire.

After a while, Velissa heard the trees in the distance splintering and the padding of heavy footfalls that sounded like muted thunder on the earth.

The Drogs all stood. The huge fire was bright enough to display the large form of a sauroid and rider.

Sauroids were cumbersome beasts. Though they were horrendous to behold, they moved slowly, for their heavy, clawed feet were set too close to their sagging abdomens to permit them to move very fast. Their wide, scaly necks provided a natural saddle for the Drogs, but the tangle of dembret vines and the thick Caladena Forests made them almost useless once they left the trails. Their green, slitted eyes were protected by an outcropping of jagged bones that further flattened the appearance of their ugly heads. Their tails were nearly as long as their flat, dragonish bodies.

There was only one sauroid with his rider, and Velissa was thankful that this lone rider was not the army of Drogs that he first sounded like.

The tall Drog dismounted from the sauroid.

"Drograaden, bandagmo, Velisssa," said the leader of the drogs who had captured her, pointing to her.

At the sound of her name being pronounced as Doldeen would have said it, there was more Drog laughter.

"Hunga!" commanded the rider. "Caldranga!"

"Hun, hun, hun, hungun," they laughed in their breathy, coarse humor.

They brought her forward, and the sauroid rider rasped, "Velissa, Cummundh Drograaden." Velissa wondered at his name.

"Crundammi Rengraaden!" he croaked, as if he had read her mind.

Velissa gasped. She understood enough to know this was Ren's nephew!

"Cummundh hongunri Thanevial." Velissa felt she knew what he had in mind.

Velissa looked into his ugly face. It was hard for her to believe that this was what was left of Raenna's handsome husband. It was difficult for her to think that once he had been the crown prince of Rensgaard. She mused within herself how fate could be comic horror. Once this ugly Changeling had been an infant rescued by Garrod so that he might one day rule as the lord of knights.

"Rengraaden—I mean, Drograaden—Raenna grieves your defection." It was so pointless to say anything. But at her words, the Drog threw back his ugly bald head and laughed, "Hun, hun, hunga." He took his scaly claw and scratched her face. His breath was foul, and he said only, "Raenna chounga!" Velissa could see enough in his milk-white eyes to know that he meant it. Now his wife was only meant for the eating.

At the mention of "chounga," the other Drogs realized how hungry they were. They eyed the sauroid greedily. "Sauroid, chounga!" suggested one of the ugly Drogs. Drograaden quickly dispelled the idea. He designated an alternative in a dramatic way. He drew his sword, swung it, and cut into the Drog who had suggested eating his sauroid. The other Changelings laughed to see that Drograaden had so quickly put an end to the hunger of the Drog who had been so brazen as to suggest that they eat his master's mount. Soon they were devouring the dead Drog, muttering "Ugghum," and belching in contentment.

They had tied Velissa to a tree while they fed their night fire until it became a roaring inferno that bathed the forest in a bold, amber light. As Velissa listened to their conversation, she found she could make out enough of their words to tell that Thanevial did, indeed, plan a siege of all six bridges of Rensgaard at once.

They seemed to have forgotten about their captive. Then suddenly one of them turned and looked at Velissa. His too-steady gaze made her feel uncomfortable. Then his dull eyes, reflecting the campfire in their milk-white surfaces, brightened a little. He was remembering the merriment that they had devised the night before by trying to get Velissa to gnaw on one of the bloody bones. The bones seemed to the Changelings an incentive to their brand of humor.

Leaping from the circle of firelight, one of the large Drogs grabbed a bone and thrust it into her face and once again cried, "Chounga, Racooohman!"

"Hun, hun, hunga!" roared the others. And Drograaden laughed loudest of all.

Again and again, the Drog thrust the bone into Velissa's face. Again and again, she turned away from the Changeling's bloody claw. The bone with which he menaced her was tinged with the sulfur stench that characterized all dead Drogs.

Velissa's tormentor at last grabbed her chin with his claw and tried to force her mouth open to receive the bone. He was laughing even as he savagely held her jaw. But his laughter softened and quickly died. Behind the tree to which she was tied, the dead forest had responded to Velissa's need. A single light blinked on in the darkness.

"Hunga!" he cried, dropping the bone and pointing. Two or three of the other Drogs stood up and stared at the single light burning among the dark trees. Then all of them stood, including Drograaden.

"Hunga!" commanded the arch Drog.

The Drogs drew back as if they were afraid.

"Hunga!" commanded Drograaden, drawing his sword. It was clear that the Drog who had been commanded to go and kill the light must choose either to be killed by Drograaden or to take his chance with the light.

In the distance came the haunting taunt as the light blinked off and on.

*"Lissa Nissa, chon, chon, chon, chon nie
Drograaden's Droggynoggen, ugly-killee die.*

> *Hah hah Droggynoggens bringem ringem bone.*
> *Lissa, Nissa, chon, chon, leavie, leavie lone."*

So much talk had circulated about this funny voice and its songs and so many campfires had been decimated that none of the Drogs now laughed.

The Drog who had been ordered to kill the light drew his sword and advanced into the darkness. He never came back. The other eight Drogs quailed when they heard his quick and final scream.

"Hunga!" cried Drograaden a second time. He designated a second Drog, and with his invisible sword point, he nudged him toward the forest.

The Drog under orders refused to budge. The other Drogs drew him to his feet and shoved him to the edge of the campfire's circle of light.

"Hunga!" All of the others echoed Drograaden's command. Reluctantly the Changeling waited for the light to come on. Two lights blinked on side by side.

"Groatee throatee Droggynoggens hie-yie-hie," the voice began.

The other Drogs shoved their reluctant comrade into the thicket of trees behind which the little yellow lights were shining. They could hear him crunching on through the thicket as the voice continued and the lights went off:

> *"Biggee biggee chon chon taken en em tree.*
> *Hairee hairee, biggee biggee Droggynoggen see*
> *Groatee throatee, oh! oh! notta gonna bee."*

One by one, the Drogs were ordered into the darkness. When there were only two left, Drograaden took his sword and cut the ropes that bound Velissa to the tree. He grabbed her and slung her small form over his leathery shoulder. He crossed the clearing to his mount.

"Condungra, sauroid!" he shouted to his beast.

The sauroid got up.

Velissa looked so small slumped across the Changeling's chest and shoulder. Drograaden was as tall as he had been when he was Rengraaden. In either form, he was twice Velissa's size. Rengraaden had once frightened her; now Drograaden terrified her completely. Still carrying her, he mounted and commanded the sauroid into the darkness. The last two Changelings begged him not to leave them with the lights and the darkness. But he ignored them and disappeared into the utter black of the jungle.

Fortunately for Drograaden, sauroids have eyes that make the darkness theirs for travel. Thus Drograaden and Velissa escaped. But the last two Changelings found themselves alone. They stayed as close to the fire as possible. The two lights that had been some distance away in the forest were moving closer to the edge of the camp. The Drogs knew that it would be only a matter of time before the fire would burn down and they would have to go for more wood to keep it going. Like all the other Drogs in recent weeks, they were loathe to face a foe that they had never seen nor any Drog had ever survived to describe.

For an hour, there were no lights, and the fire grew dark. In another hour, the campsite was frozen into darkness. The Drogs remained paralyzed with fear. But since they had seen nothing in the forest for two hours, they dared to wait for the still-distant morning, grateful to have been left unharmed in the dark forest.

Suddenly the lights blinked on.

"Droggynoggens too-too, too-hoo-chun
 Droggynoggens too kommen Droggynoggen one."

The lights blinked off. The night closed in. Nothing remained in the morning.

Besides Raccoman and Hallidan, the women of the citadel were most moved by Velissa's capture.

Raenna hurried across the central plaza. A crowd of more than half a thousand had gathered there, and all were women. Izonden at last disclosed the reason for Velissa's disappearance. The report was confirmed by a Star Rider who had seen Velissa on the back of a sauroid moving swiftly toward the Tower Altar. All the women gathered were wives of defectors. Each of them had known their hours of grief and a life of disconsolate shame for what their husbands had done in disallegiance to the crown.

Raenna had come to perceive herself in a new way since the defection of Rengraaden. She was a woman who had lost everything and, thus, had nothing more to lose. It was typical of all those who had once been the wives of Changelings that they should cling to each other in a kind of hungry need to understand and be understood. Some of the disconsolate had grieved on for nearly a thousand years. They felt a kind of shame they had freely adopted, for no one forced it upon them. If anything, everyone understood, and these women had never become objects of scorn in the citadel. But still they felt shame. The consolation that they allowed themselves only further marked them as a people whose degraded status existed only within their minds.

None had ever done what Raenna was about to challenge them to do. When the crowd in the square was quiet, Raenna called out to the women and asked them all to be seated and to make themselves as comfortable as they could.

"Miserians!" she cried. "Some of you have grieved for nearly a thousand years. I have found my shame very recently. But I have asked myself if we must simply live out our misery or is there to be some use for us, some means of redemption?

"Velissa is stolen. We cannot know what awaits her. Whatever her fate, ours will be as bad or worse. For the husbands who once loved us now despise us. Those who were our husbands can never be our husbands again. We have no husbands nor will we ever have."

The women listened. There was a new kind of militancy in Raenna's voice which frightened some of the women and intrigued others.

"Some of you have children and secondary reasons to live. Most of you have neither children nor any real reason to go on with your lives. I have been to the queen and told her of my plan. I want to train myself in the art of war."

The idea was so novel and so unheard of or unthought of that the other women sat stunned. Raenna waited a moment before she went on.

"I do not ask you to join me unless you feel that it would be a valuable use of your life. The times are serious, and I believe that we could turn our self-pity into something strong and usable for the defense of the citadel. The queen has given her consent, and Hallidan has assigned several of the knights for our training. Already I can fly a condorg, and I am learning to handle fire-glass."

Some of the women gasped at the idea. Others leaned forward.

"I intend to make myself useful, even if it means I must give up my life. I have no good reason for saving it, and if my life can be of use, then it is well to so use it. There are hundreds of condorgs all trained for battle. They are the ones our husbands used to fly. There is enough equipment in the armory to outfit a thousand of us, and there are less than half that many gathered here. I am ready to stand with the knights in anyway I can. I hope to bring this horrible struggle with Thanevial to an end."

"Is that all?" asked a tall woman, horrified by the idea of women in combat.

"Yes, yes it is," concluded Raenna, lowering her head.

The horrified woman walked away, and gradually most of the others got up and followed her. But fully two hundred women stayed. When Raenna looked at their faces, she could see that her logic was theirs. They, like her, had grown weary of self-pity and the consolation of the good citizens of the citadel whose condolences had marked their lives year after year. Now they were ready to wear a new mark. Their meaning would compensate for whatever disrespect the other women of the citadel might give them. Doubtless, there would be those who would scoff at their militancy, but perhaps even those who scoffed would envy their meaning.

Within a week, the armory at the north end of the citadel was alive with women. Each was retailoring old mail and armor. There were some bad strains and many injuries as the women learned to handle the fire-glass. Yet it was amazing to most of the knights who served as their trainers that they had such an agility and grace in the saddle on the condorgs.

It was inevitable that Raenna would soon become their leader. She had offered the initial challenge, and she mastered the military arts with a great deal of agility and speed. She was lighter than her husband had been, and although she picked his very mount, she found that the condorg could fly higher and faster with her on its back than it had bearing Rengraaden. At least, that is what the other knights told her. One thing was sure, with her lighter weight, it could fly without tiring for longer periods of time.

On the fourth day of training, one of the Miserians fell from her mount and was killed. The fault lay in a girth strap that had not been properly tightened. The tragedy came so early in the women's training that the other women of Ren castigated Raenna's efforts and tried to call the training program to a halt.

All the women in training grieved her death, but none of them wanted to stop the program.

"She was a Miserian! Her husband died in the forming pits six hundred years ago. When he changed, her life was over. She was dead anyway," said Raenna. "Where was her life going? We grieve the loss of our sister. Yet for the first time, we, too, have a future that is worthy and a dream that makes our own lives worth living. She was the first to die, but she will not be the last. For in our efforts to stem the war for our king and queen, many of us will be forfeited, just as she was. But death is not the great curse. Life without meaning is the great curse."

The women of the Miserian cause understood. The other women did not. But nothing daunted the urgency they gave to their training. Some of them could swing the fire-glass with an astounding swiftness that amazed all who saw it. And within two weeks, Raenna was ready to take the best trainees on a surveillance flight to the perimeter of the north shores and their first view of the Desert of Draymon and the Tower Altar. The knight who had trained them told them that they would be safe as long as they kept high in the sky. In their perception of the scope of the Drog war, they would know the size of the horrible ordeal that awaited the future of Rensland.

Ten women flew out into the morning sun. At night, all ten returned. Their flight had done nothing but survey the lands west of Mt. Calz, but it excited in all of the others a hunger to see the countryside as well. On successive days, most of the two hundred women trained on the condorgs had circled the high skies west of Mt. Calz.

Now it was difficult to tell, when one saw flying riders overhead, whether they were knights or Miserians. Raenna was proud of the progress that the women had made, but she was still not satisfied. Their proof would come when they joined the men in the defense of the citadel on the wall of Rensgaard. She knew that the king and queen, as protectors of Garrod the Second, would never be content until all danger was purged from the land. The knights pledged themselves to such a hope. Certainly that was Raenna's dream, too.

She had one other goal. She desired to learn the art of flying long distances at night. She yearned, like the brave knights of Ren, to be able to cross the seas—high in the upper skies—on a condorg that glowed with the heat of its own inner light. She hungered to be a part of what those in the other land had called "moving starfields." She desired this with such an intensity that she could be quiet no longer. At last, she blurted out her desire to Hallidan.

"Hallidan," she said "I want to be a Star Rider."

The knight looked down in disbelief. Yet something warm in Hallidan approved.

Hallidan thought of the two of them soaring together on fiery steeds, wing to wing in the lonely sky.

The stars seemed to settle about them as they walked home from the armory. The gentle hues of evening illuminated Raenna's eyes. Hallidan grew hungry in the starlight that set him deeply in need of the Miserian. He wanted Raenna in a storm of desire that shouted all around him. He was afraid the night would give way to a stronger light that would expose him.

"Could I?" Raenna pressed, startling Hallidan out of his reverie. He couldn't remember what she had asked him.

"Could you what?"

"Could I be a Star Rider?" she repeated.

It was a mundane question compared to all that the handsome Titan had been considering. So he ignored her question and moved to that which was more immediately on his mind.

"Raenna, I love you!" he blurted out.

They both stopped. She touched his broad forearm in the soft darkness. His face bent toward hers. Their lips all but met.

Then she turned away.

"Please, I have a husband!" she said.

"You are married to a Drog," he replied, "and, therefore, not married at all."

She brusquely brought the conversation back to the issue at hand. "Can I be a Star Rider or not?"

"Your dream to defend the citadel is one thing," said Hallidan. "But to be a Star Rider is an occasion of glory that can only be achieved once the war is over."

His logic was sound. Raenna knew that Hallidan was taken with her. And even though she was married to a monstrous creature, still she was married. She had no right to the handsome Hallidan. Yet she was very much afraid she loved him.

She put the matter forcibly from her mind.

Raenna realized that her reputation as a Miserian had been built upon her ability to fly and her willingness to train and lead her sisters into the war. They were lovely as they flew, mounted upon the great condorgs, with their capes trailing behind them and their proud, regal looks as they entered into the war. At the same time, Raenna knew in her heart that no war could really be called a war without conflict. It was a bloody business, and Raenna had never seen blood nor wielded the fire-glass against another living creature.

She had felt pain on the day that her sister's saddle girth had come loose, and the woman had plunged to her death. Raenna would never forget the anguish of holding the bruised head of the dead Miserian and the sense of burden that she had felt for her.

But those days were left behind, and she knew that the time had come to prove to the knights that the women could be a formidable force. It was no secret now that Thanevial was planning to lay siege to the city. This the knights realized from watching the movement of the Drogs into select camps north and south of Mt. Calz. The only question was when.

Raenna and a fourth of the war-trained Miserians flew past Mt. Calz and then doubled over the entire area, but they were unable to locate any activity east of the Caverns of Smeade. In an entire morning of flying, they had seen only a few encampments, one of which was still cluttered at the Tower Altar. Another of the encampments was north of Mt. Calz as though it would move to the north bridge of Ren, and the third was out of the Caverns of Smeade as though it would move on the west bridge of the city. Nothing had changed in a week.

Raenna knew it would be folly to attack any of these three encampments, and the Ally, whoever he was, had frightened all the isolated movements of Drogs into the main encampments.

In the early afternoon, Raenna decided to circle east of the citadel so that she might view the sea from the sky. It was not a direction in which the knights usually flew since the greatest part of the Drog strength was expected to come from the environs of the Tower Altar. Raenna's immediate attention was drawn by a sauroid with his head lowered into the water at the edge of the sea. When she flew down over the animal, he was startled and fled directly into the trees only a short distance from the shore. Across the trees to the east, Raenna could see the white stone of the citadel rising proudly in the afternoon sun.

Raenna flew out over the sea, then turned and headed for the short beach area. There she and the other women landed and reined their condorgs to the ground.

They all peered into the trees where the sauroid had disappeared. Beyond the narrow strip of forest were the fields and then the citadel itself. Raenna was amazed to have seen a sauroid in this part of the forest. There was no room for the condorgs in the forest, so she decided to walk into the woods. She could not escape the feeling that she was being watched.

"Miserians!" she called. "Move close together and come with me." The women dropped the reins of their beasts and moved in close, and all began to walk into the forest together. They had not gone very far into the trees when they were set upon instantly by a core of fifty Drogs. The surprise could not have been more unexpected, since even the knights had not known that there were Drogs in the narrow necks of woods east of the citadel. They had obviously traveled in the thin woods by night, completely unobserved by sentries or Star Riders.

One of the women, seeing the size of the Drog encampment, retreated quickly to her condorg and remounted to return to the citadel and inform the knights of the encampment. She knew that if the women were overpowered, they would need the knights to finish their work.

Inside the woods, the women fought valiantly. The Drogs outdid them in terms of sheer weight and their ability to swing their huge, invisible blades. But the women were light on their feet and could maneuver the thin fire-blades with great agility. None of the women had ever killed before, but now they entered into the fury of all that they were obligated to do.

Several Drogs were slain, and for a while it seemed that the women would be victorious, but the number of ugly Changelings in the encampment was too much for them. Gradually the Drogs formed a circle around them in the trees and then the ugly beasts began to close in. It appeared that all of the women would soon be killed. Back to back, the women lashed out with swift parries of fire-glass. The heavy, invisible blades came closer. One of the women was decapitated. New determination rose in the others. They fought valiantly. For a while, they pushed the ring of Drogs back toward the edge of the thin forest. At last, however, the women began to tire, and the ring closed again. There seemed little hope.

Suddenly condorg wings whirred overhead. And a few moments later, a ring of knights surrounded the Drogs who were closing in upon the women. As the Drogs turned toward the knights, the women struck them from behind. Soon, all of the Drogs were dead.

Raenna caught sight of the tallest of the Drogs escaping to the edge of the forest. With her blade drawn, she ran after him. She saw him leap to the back of a sauroid. The beast wheeled and turned toward the heavier forests that joined the caladena groves north of Mt. Calz.

Raenna ran to her condorg and mounted. She flew directly into the path of the escaping Drog and sauroid. Her mount felt the pain of the Drog's sword. His blade cut a huge streak into the condorg's white side. Blood gushed out. Raenna could see that her steed was too wounded to fly much further. Still, she was determined. She wheeled it in midair and crossed again into the path of the fleeing sauroid. But her condorg fell too quickly from the sky, tumbled into the earth, and sent Raenna sprawling on the ground.

Miraculously her beast had, in its untimely death, fallen across the sauroid's path. The sauroid stumbled and fell heavily on the path. Without hesitation, Raenna plunged her sword into the animal's neck. The beast never rose from its knees. It rolled over on its side, and its rider tumbled onto the ground.

The Drog grabbed the hilt of his weapon and swung his invisible sword at Raenna. A huge tree trunk beside her was severed. She knew she must carefully avoid a blade that was not only invisible but also infinitely dangerous. She decided to fight the Drog in the open if she could. She was not able to maneuver him to the seaside of the narrow woods, but soon they were facing each other in a little clearing among the trees.

Now there was only Raenna and the Drog. But the Drog knew that the rest of the knights would shortly be moving out to this part of the woods, and then he would be outnumbered. He tried to retreat, realizing that even if he escaped the woman's sword, the other knights would kill him. He moved back, but with each step he took, Raenna advanced.

"Raenna," he rasped, "Drograaden!"

Raenna said nothing. She continued to advance.

"Drograaden!" he croaked again, "Crundammi Rengraaden!"

Raenna stopped at the word.

"My husband?" she asked, looking directly into the milky-white eyes.

"Ughum hunga!" he said. His words were meaningless to her. But it seemed that he wanted her to stop her advance and let him escape.

"Raenna! Ughum hunga! Crundammi Rengraaden." He spoke slowly now as though his thick tongue could no longer easily manage the speech he had once loved. "Ughum. I loved you! Gukka!" he rasped.

"You should have loved Ren!" said Raenna, standing firmly in his path.

Raenna was still a woman. She thought of the handsome prince she had married. It was hard for her to believe that this heavily breathing monster before her had once been the light of Rensgaard.

Drograaden could see that her will was weakening. He knew that Raenna could not kill the man who, for so many centuries, had been her husband. She stopped, and he turned to run into the forest. Raenna was paralyzed by the thing before her. Even as he fled, she wondered if she would ever be able to kill him. Before he disappeared into the woods, he turned, threw back his head, and laughed at her, "Hun, hun, hun, hungum!" His strange laughter croaked, "Raenna chounga, hun, hun, hun, hungum!" It was then that she knew he would easily kill her. When he was gone, her resolve was strengthened in a new way.

Several knights came running into the clearing. They searched thoroughly, but did not find the arch Drog.

Raenna sat in the center of the clearing and looked vacantly away. Someday, she knew, her husband would be back, and she knew that when that time came, she must answer him with force. Rengraaden and Drograaden were not the same man. Rengraaden had perished in the forming pits and was gone. The monster that occupied his former place was not her husband—or was he? She knew she must believe that Drograaden was not Rengraaden, because until she believed, she would have little chance of survival when next they met.

Even as she stared at the wall of foliage into which the Changeling disappeared, she prayed that she would never have to face him again.

Drograaden's image loomed above her. At the same time, so did the handsome Hallidan. The knight's very image stopped her heart in joy. She prayed that she would never have to face him again either.

Life may be traded for life,
  And bargains be bartered in blood.
And kings, for the lives of their sons
  Will stomp their crown jewels into mud.

CHAPTER X

The Descent

VELISSA WAS TIED TO the top of the Tower Altar. This report had been confirmed by a half-dozen flying knights. Raccoman was destroyed with grief and mad in his desire to rescue her. The largest of the three Drog encampments was still the one at the base of the Tower Altar. The size of the tower army made any attempt at rescue look impossible. Raccoman knew it would be foolhardy to risk the lives of the knights in a daring but hopeless foray.

The motive for Velissa's detainment did not become apparent for several weeks. Those who observed her on the surveillance flights could only guess at the reason. It appeared that she was still alive, but that mistreatment and exposure to the elements was devouring her strength.

At last, three weeks before the Festival of Light, Thanevial demanded a ransom. On the morning of that fateful day, a company of Drogs in the western woods set themselves to a plan. They held a sauroid and tortured it with their swords and claws until the creature was driven mad to escape. The tormented beast was so desperate with pain that, when it was finally released, it drove insanely toward Rensgaard and took the southwest bridge into the city for sanctuary.

The knights inside the citadel struggled to capture the beast. By the time they had finally chained it, the sauroid lay exhausted, bleeding and groaning from the ordeal of its torture and crazed with pain. Several of the Miserians gathered around it and, with soothing reassurance, were able to give it some water and treat its gaping wounds.

Tied to the neck of the maddened beast, they found a note. Its message was addressed to Hallidan and read simply: "Velissa for Singreale."

Thanevial was making his bid not for Rensgaard as a whole, but to the only two living men who knew where the treasure was hidden. Either Hallidan or Raccoman must reply within ten days or Velissa would be destroyed. Everyone within the citadel knew that even Raccoman would be loath to bargain with Thanevial. It was impossible to reason with the demon-beasts. But the treacherous note brought a new determination to the heart of Raccoman Dakktare. He would deliver his wife—or die in the attempt.

"No!" said Hallidan as they talked about it for the third time in two days. "It is madness. It's far too risky. If either of us were to be lost, the morale of the rest of the knights would suffer greatly. The queen loves you. You are the symbol of your father Garrod. I tell you, the kingdom cannot live without you. I, too, must stay alive to coordinate all the facets of our defense, for the siege is sure to come. And our city's friends are well outnumbered by our foes."

"But what of Velissa?" Raccoman's voice grew thin. "I cannot let her die. Whatever Izonden thinks, or even if I must do it alone, I will do it."

"No, Graygill, you will not do it. I will not let you."

The two men had never countered each other so strongly.

"I will find the Singreale and fly to Thanevial. I will meet the Drog's demand. We can win the war without Singreale. Oh, Velissa, Velissa," lamented Raccoman, burying his head in his sleeve.

"We cannot win without Singreale. Besides, Thanevial is the great deceiver. He would not give you Velissa. The moment you produced the Singreale, he would kill both you and your wife," said Hallidan.

"At least we would die together," said Raccoman without looking up.

"No, no, no!" The knight spoke with finality. "I'll hear no more of this; the rescue is impossible."

Raccoman said nothing. He turned away and stood for a moment. Hallidan could see that the Graygill's shoulders were trembling. Raccoman was in agony. Hallidan walked to him and touched his back, then turned him around. Raccoman's eyes were washed with his desire. The tears streaked his face and collected in his gray gills. The tall knight knelt and looked directly into Raccoman's eyes.

"Hallidan, my Velissa, my Velissa!" he wept as the two of them embraced.

Hallidan could not stand to see him so brokenhearted.

"All right! All right!" Hallidan cried, breaking under the strain he saw in the soul of his little friend. "We'll go by night. Just the two of us. I won't risk the lives of the others. We'll settle close above the altar and come directly down. But we must be prepared to fight. Perhaps there's a slim chance. The top of the Tower Altar is not wide and we'll have the advantage, if we can hold it. If they should swarm up the steps of the altar like insects, they will push us quickly aside. Our condorgs might bolt and fly without us. It is most risky."

"Let me go with some other knight. Izonden needs you," Raccoman replied, seeming to change his mind. As though he knew that the mission was already doomed, he felt suddenly ashamed that he had been willing to waste the best military mind in Rensgaard.

"No, we will go together; at night and by ourselves," said Hallidan with finality. "That way we can best avoid detection and have the best chance of making it. We'll both fly on your condorg, Merran."

"When?" asked the Graygill eagerly.

"Tomorrow night," said the Titan.

Raccoman was delirious with joy. He was also frightened.

The next day, Raenna and several of the Miserians discovered that there had been a major cave-in on the eastern edge of Draymon. A jagged fingerlet of molten sand had ripped its way through the jungle and was lapping at the very base of the Tower Altar. Some of the black foundation stones of the outer perimeter of the Tower Altar had been dissolved in the intense heat of the lava. For some reason, the tides of molten sand were higher than they had ever been seen to be before. Unless they receded, the Tower Altar would be unsafe within the week.

The knights knew that, when it crumbled, Thanevial would have to move his monstrous troops. Probably they would move them directly against the city. Thanevial's weapons foundry was at the base of the Tower Altar. When that was destroyed, his undiscovered means of forging the invisible swords and spears and arrows would be gone.

Raccoman greeted the news with heaviness. Because of the erosion of the molten seas, there was not much time left to rescue Velissa. The attempt that they had secretly planned for that very evening would have to work. Raenna had reported the encroaching sand tides, but she had no idea that the brave knight and the impetuous Graygill intended to try a rescue.

On the same afternoon of Raenna's report to Hallidan, Thanevial climbed the long, long flight of stairs to the top of the tower. The lava sea scorched Velissa's hopes of ever being free. When the breezes blew in from across the molten sand, they carried unbearable hot drafts. These scorching winds were a horrible portent of the fiery finale of Lord Thanevial's tower. The lava that now washed the bottom of the tower had melted only some of the foundation stones. Even the black stones of the upper tower were growing unpleasantly hot.

The arch Drog approached Velissa. He raked his claw across her cheek. She was not even half the size of the monster who had ascended through the burning, searing gales to torment her. Yet her size in no way evoked pity from the evil Drog lord. "Gukka, ughum. Can you see the molten tides?" he grunted. Though his speech was not as animalistic as that which most of his underlings spoke, it repelled Velissa.

She said nothing.

A sudden hot breeze blew in from the molten sea, and she turned her face to avoid its chafing. Her weeks of exposure to the weather had roughened her complexion, and her wrists were raw from the metal bands that fettered her arms to the upright stone pinions that crowned the black tower.

She not only remained silent in the Drog's presence but refused to look at him.

"Some of our Drogs killed Raccoman yesterday," he told her. His milk-white eyes bulged outward. He laughed the same guttural syllables of the monsters who served him. Velissa started against the chain, then relaxed.

Velissa felt he was lying. Her husband would have been even a better prize than herself to barter for Singreale. Even though she knew what he said was a lie, Raccoman's name and welfare came immediately to her mind and inwardly she shuddered.

"You don't love your husband anymore?" he asked her.

"Ughum, galanka, Singreale," he went on, dropping into the coarse speech unintelligible to Velissa. "Gukka," he croaked. "Mugranga hund, Velissa!" When Thanevial realized that Velissa could not understand, he began again slowly, croaking out his cruel proposition, in the language of the knights. "You can be queen, my dear, of all the meat eaters. In time, we could feed you your own husband, and you would enjoy the meal."

Velissa was powerless to stop her ears against his wicked talk.

"Look, my dear, food! It is a hand off of your enemy."

Velissa looked at the dark claw severed from an ugly arm. She turned away. Thanevial threw the claw at her feet.

Again the hot winds from the molten tides scorched the air. She could hear the giant waves crashing against the stones below. Each time the lava sea assailed the base of the tower, its molten appetite gnawed away a little more of the black stones of the foundation.

Velissa had not eaten in a week. The Drogs brought only enough vegetables and tepid water to keep her alive, knowing she would not eat the meat they fed upon. Her stamina was gone. She was glad that Raccoman could not see her now. She was emaciated and her hair was fused to her face and neck with the perspiration in which she constantly sweltered on top of Thanevial's tower.

Thanevial knew she could not live much longer. Yet he knew that once she died, he would have little hope of finding the Singreale before he began his siege of the citadel. Mercifully for her, the heat of the sun plus the heat of the molten tides were more than the Drog lord could stand for very long. He left, his long, black cape trailing after him on the dark steps of the tower as he descended. Velissa loathed him. She was glad his domain was dying. The arch Drog knew his altar was doomed by the molten oceans. And Velissa knew that, within the week, his armies would have to leave as well. Then they would move against the citadel, knowing that only the lofty eastern highlands were safe from the encroaching molten seas that daily widened the Desert of Draymon.

A sentry Drog was always stationed on the top of the tower to prevent any attempted rescue. When one Drog left, another came. Velissa was grateful when the days cooled into night. The glass tides ebbed at evening, and in the darkness the horrible heat subsided.

Velissa sweltered and sometimes fainted in the hot gales. Again and again, she thought of the fresh meadows of Canby and the clean snows of her winter highlands on the other continent. She remembered the summer fields that she and Raccoman had loved. She thought of the oval barn where he had created the Paradise Falcon and of their wondrous flight that had sliced the upper skies and brought them to their current time of woe. A hot blast of searing winds choked her reverie.

A tear crossed her cheek. She looked at the back of the Drog who sat on the top of the Tower Altar. She was not given easily to despair, but now her courage flagged. She watched the skies in a wild hope of rescue, and yet she knew that she would never see Raccoman again.

"Oh, Raccoman," she cried softly. "Raccoman, Raccoman, Raccoman." The heat from the blasting winds left her so exhausted that she fell asleep and dreamed of snowfields and of the husband who had made her unafraid of the sky.

She was awakened at midnight by the quick flash of fire-glass. The Drog who had been guarding her gasped and fell without a scream.

"Hallidan!" she cried in joy and, in greater joy, "Raccoman!"

Merran, the condorg, waited behind them on the tower. They had a swift instant to complete the rescue. The Drog who had slumped, wounded by the fire-glass, suddenly stirred and rose and turned and screamed a blood-freezing yell. Far below on the ground, a flow of Drogs started up the long steps. Raccoman swung his own sword and cut the single Drog from the top of the tower. He fell a hundred feet. His black body thumped against the side of the tower as he tumbled down, rolling over again and again until the ugly hulk tumbled at last into the hot, molten sand that was threatening the west side of the altar.

Hallidan turned to cut the rope that held Velissa's right hand with a forceful blow. But he did not complete the action. He felt a sharp pain in his arm and saw that his sleeve had been sliced by an invisible arrow. Red gushed from his arm. He couldn't find the strength in his wounded arm to cut Velissa free.

Three Drogs swarmed over the top of the tower. A second invisible arrow caught Raccoman's leg.

"Flee, Raccoman and Hallidan!" she cried.

In an instant of decision, Hallidan knew this would be their best course of action. Now fifteen Drogs had reached the top of the tower. A shower of arrows cut the air all around them. The condorg spurted blood from half a dozen wounds. Raccoman and Hallidan had no choice but to retreat. They leapt to the saddle of the condorg and shot skyward. Raccoman called down, "We will be back, Velissa. I love you!"

Miraculously, the shower of arrows had not touched her. But she felt wounded by the sight of her husband and Hallidan in pain.

Merran had not gone far when Hallidan realized that he was too severely wounded to travel any further. In the heavy forest east of the Tower Altar, they settled into darkness. Their great mount stumbled on the black earth, crashed into a tree, and spilled them onto the ground. The condorg shuddered and then lay still in the inky night. It was dead, its long wings snarled in the dark and tangled thicket.

"Oh, Hallidan, Velissa, this is my fault!" lamented the Graygill.

He fell upon the wide neck of the dead condorg and wept. "Merran, Merran."

"Come, friend," said Hallidan. "Merran is dead! We must deal quickly with our own needs." Hallidan felt for the shaft of the invisible arrow that had pierced the Graygill's small leg. "This will be painful, my friend," he said. With one broad hand, he held the surface of the Graygill's leg, and with the other hand, he drew out the invisible dart.

To say it did not hurt would be a lie, but Raccoman's guilt and shock over the failure of their rescue attempt plunged him into such a numbed state of mind that he did not feel the open anguish that he would otherwise have felt.

"Raccoman, now you must remove this arrow from my arm."

Dutifully, the Graygill responded. Placing his hand around the wound, he found the invisible shaft and grasped it. Steadily, he drew the arrow out. The forest was so dark that he could not see Hallidan wince in pain. Raccoman threw the dart aside.

"Now, apply the fire-glass," said the knight. Raccoman drew his blade. The red light from the fire-glass glowed on their faces. Raccoman touched the flat side of the blade to his leg. The bleeding stopped. Hallidan carefully took the hilt of the hot fire-glass, seared his arm, and then sheathed the sword again.

The pain was excruciating. Neither of them cried out, but anguish raked their torn bodies.

The wounded knight embraced his small, bloody friend.

"Our condorg is dead, but we are alive," said Hallidan.

"But where are we?"

"In the morning, we must identify our position and try to work our way around the Drog encampments. Within a couple of days we should be able to find some place to hide while we regain our strength. Then we can make our way back to Rensgaard." Inwardly, they both despaired, for they knew that by day the woods would be infested with Drogs, and their wounds were too severe to allow them to fight for long. Yet they still had their fire-glass, and neither was willing to abandon all hope without the best possible struggle.

The forest around them was quiet, and they lay down to rest only a few feet from the silent torso of the great Merran.

They slept for a couple of hours. It was still a long time till morning. After only two hours, Raccoman found that his wounded leg had grown too stiff for walking, but after exercising it a little, he felt that, though the pain persisted, he could manage.

Suddenly he knew he had to wake Hallidan.

"What's that?" he cried, pointing into the black, inky forest ahead. The forest was so dark that Hallidan did not even know that Raccoman was pointing.

Ahead of them were two small, bright lights. The knight and the Graygill stood with hope in the thick gloom.

The day dawned. The sand tides rose again and battered the bottom of the tower with fury.

The time had come, and Thanevial commanded the Drogs to move at last from the base of the Tower Altar. There were thousands, it seemed. All day long, the ugly monsters moved in a single gray-black file eastward into the jungles. Thanevial came in the afternoon to tell Velissa that they would all be on the Tower Altar for another night. Tomorrow he would take her on his sauroid to the second Drog encampment not far from the Caverns of Smeade. As was her custom, she said nothing to her monstrous captor.

Drograaden led the file of Changelings on a ten-day walk that would bring them at last to the security of the upper highlands.

When night fell, there were fewer Drogs clustered at the base of the altar than Velissa had ever seen during her captivity. No more than a half-dozen campfires were visible. Velissa was so emaciated that she could not stand for long. So she leaned heavily against the tower and was grateful that the cool night had brought another reprieve from the horrible heat. She fell asleep and began the hum that the Drogs had gotten use to. Of course, she herself never heard it.

When she awoke at midnight, she was startled to see that the Drog sentry was lying prone and still at the edge of the tower. In the starlight, she could see that he was dead. However it had happened, she realized that the Drog had been slain so silently and so swiftly that she had not even been aware of it. She saw that his throat had been torn out. And she saw a something short crouching against the post. The creature was half as tall as she, and even in the darkness, she could tell that it's body was nearly covered by the hair that shagged out from the top of its head. She looked over again at the dead Drog and felt secure in the presence of the thing now crouched silently against one of the supports to which she was bound.

Then suddenly she realized that she was not bound. Someone or something—perhaps the little creature, for reasons of its own—had set her free. She found that she could move her hands freely for the first time in weeks. She looked down at the encampment. No one stirred. No one was aware that she had been set free. She turned again to the short, dark form.

"Who are you?" she called softly. She spoke so softly that her voice could hardly be heard above the sand tides far below.

"Velissa, missa chon chon Droggynoggen lie
Uglee-killee, uglee-killee Droggynoggen die."

She meditated on the riddle for only a moment to see what the creature meant. Then she went to the dead Drog. The Drog's body was huge, but, she realized, it would have to be propped upright so that anyone looking up from the ground would think him still alive and on duty. Velissa struggled to push his ugly body up again. The wound at his neck was horrendous, but his head, lifeless and ugly as it was, was still attached.

After a great deal of effort, Velissa managed to set the Drog upright. Then, in her weakness, she took his cape and twisted it and tied it into the ropes from which her riddle-making savior had set her free. From the ground, the cape gave the appearance that she was still bound at the top of the altar between the uprights.

The short figure turned its face away from the Drog camp. Velissa saw it's eyes open, and they shone in the night as if they had been lit from within. It had come for her, and whatever it was, she was most willing to follow.

Quietly it said:

"Raccoman is safen taken em Smeade
Taken en em chon-chon, taken en em neede
Lissa-Nissa foll-foll, Grendlynden Frend of Ren-den leade."

The short form disappeared over the side of the altar toward the molten sea, the only side they could descend. It was impossible for them to be seen by the Drogs below, for the lava seas stretched like an ocean always beneath them. On the other side of the Tower Altar, the monsters were camped at the base. As Velissa and the creature descended toward the lava sea, the temperature rose unbearably. Finally the heat became so intense that they could descend no further. They moved to the north steps of the tower, knowing that they would now be visible as they hurried into the night.

There were many Drogs camped on that side, but none of them seemed to be looking. Velissa and Grendelynden slipped to the base of the tower unnoticed. When they were safely off the tower, the strange little creature hid Velissa among the bushes and said,

"Retzie—retzie, Lissa Nissa."

It was a crazy command. Velissa had been immobile on the tower top for so long that she could not have gone a step further. She rubbed her legs that were painfully rebelling against the flight they were going to have to make. Still, she felt insecure when she thought of her tiny deliverer leaving her if only for a moment.

"Where are you going, Grendelynden, Friend of Renden?" she whispered. She hated to call him by such a name, but these were the only words she had heard from her short savior which could, in any sense, be called a name.

"Lissa Nissa, retzie retzie
Grendelynden Frendorenden chony chonny hie
Uglee-killee, uglee-killee Droggynoggen die."

So saying, he slipped off into the shrubs and everything remained quiet. Velissa stretched her legs and tried to massage some life back into them. As soon as her darksome, short friend returned, they slipped quietly into the forest. Velissa suspected that there were at least two or three less "Droggynoggens" than there had been when he left her for the silent moment.

They entered the forest north of the tower. It was so dark that she could see nothing. But she knew that Grendelynden could see. He reached up his hand and she reached down. Now she knew how the Titans must have felt whenever they were around the Graygills. For as they were twice her size, she was twice Grendelynden's size. Yet he walked surprisingly fast, and she found herself having to stop and rest too often as they hurried along. Velissa was too weak to move quickly.

Several times they stopped and rested during the night. She ate greedily of the dembret nuts and gulped water from a small stream. Once Grendelynden allowed Velissa to sleep for an hour. Then he woke her gently, saying nothing, and they moved on. Velissa could neither see where they were going nor where they had been. It was a relationship of trust.

Toward morning, as streaks of light began to appear in the sky and the long night's had begun to tell on Velissa, her small guide turned to her and said,

"Caven en em Caladena taken en em tree."

They were standing next to a stone ledge when he uttered the strange statement. Grendelynden pulled back the orange vines that covered a small opening.

"Caven en em Caladena, taken en em tree,"

he repeated.

The opening was wide enough for Grendelynden to enter easily, but Velissa had to bend and stoop to follow him through the niche in the stone. Inside the little opening was a wider room with a thatched pallet upon the ground. The walls were dry. The cavern was pitch dark, but Velissa continued to trust her guide as she had throughout the long night. Then, all at once, light flooded out of the little creature's round, yellow eyes, filling the tiny cavern with a bright incandescence. Now Velissa could see him well. She loved the little creature and the bright light he brought to end the fearful hours of darkness they had crossed.

Grendelynden made the longest statement he had spoken throughout the night:

"Lissa Nissa, retzie heer, retzie en em cave.
Chon, chon, retzie seepie-seepie, retzie day!
Droggynoggens not em taken, not em taken cave.
Lissa Nissa retzie safee—nottem, nottem, nottem,
*   nottem leevee cave!"*

Velissa knew she was being ordered not to leave the cave and being reassured that the Drogs could not enter the opening even if they knew of it, for it was too small.

How well her small redeemer had provided for her! At daybreak, the Drogs would be coming through the forest, looking for her, but this tiny dry chamber with its small opening completely covered by vines would go undetected. Meanwhile, her efforts to analyze Grendelynden's language never stopped his curious speech. The problem was that by the time she decoded one statement, he was already on to some other cryptic conversation.

"Toonie eveee Grendelynden commen backee cave.
Blackie, blackie, Grendel backee—Lissa Nissa.
Chon, chon takee Lissa, takee chonnie-chonnie,
Nother cavee chon-chon, Grendelynden chonnie,
Hidee takem Hallidanee, takem Racconmonnie."

"Oh, then he's alive!" cried Velissa.

The yellow eyes blinked bright and wide. The small creature could see how pleased Velissa was.

"Raccomonnie chon-chon safen en em cave.
Toonie-evee Lissa Nissa, chon em taken chonnie,
Takee Lissa-Nissa, toonie eevee, too em Raccomonnie."

Velissa was so excited at his words that she nearly bowled him over. She grabbed him up and hugged him. His big, yellow eyes expressed embarrassment, but she kissed him anyway in her delight. The light he cast was now so bright that she could see how her kiss had caused his brown skin to redden. Suddenly Velissa realized that this was the Ally. This was he who stalked the lonely forest destroying evil. And his tiny hands knew such strength that they destroyed whole camps of Drogs. How could she help but love him? she thought, and she kissed him again before setting him down.

"Lissa Nissa, chon chon takem en em hugg
Huggen Grendelynden, huggen, huggen—hugg hugg hugg!"

Velissa could not believe it. He raised his thin, strong arms that for good reason of their own were set against evil. He wanted to be embraced again. She picked him up and hugged him with all her remaining strength. A tear fell from one of his bright, yellow eyes, and she wiped it away with her finger. She kissed him again.

"Thank you for saving my life," she said.

They hugged again, and she set him down. He walked awkwardly to the opening of the cavern and turned back to her just before he left.

"Grendelynden chon hugg-huggie Lissa hie!
Lissa Nissa, kissa Grendel, Grendelynden flie!"

He said this with excitement, then jumped up and landed again on the cave floor, his strong, naked feet clapping the earth. His unusual way of showing excitement amused Velissa and made her love him all the more. His heavy thatch of hair seemed to shake and shimmer even after he had ceased his antics of jubilation.

"Lissa retzie, Grendolynden taken en em stone
Gettee-killee Droggynoggens killee all alone."

He turned and went out into the early morning shadows. No sooner had he left her than her little enclosure went dark.

Velissa was tired and needed the rest. Still, she could not help but muse over her strange rescuer. He lived alone and was at once full of life and yet deadly. How long he had lived in the caves of these forests she could only guess. How he had learned to speak his riddlesome speech or had developed such strength and quiet efficiency against evil perhaps no one knew. Still, she loved him. And she would carefully obey him and not leave the tiny opening through which she had squeezed for a day of rest and security in this land of war. One of his lines kept coming back to her again and again, and as she thought of the sweetness of Grendelynden's promise, she found it easy to fall asleep.

"Raccomonnie chon-chon safen em en cave," she quoted aloud and drifted off to humming slumber in delight of the evening yet to come.

"Do you think the defection is over?" asked Raccoman, rubbing the wounded muscles of his upper leg.

"It is at last!" said the Titan.

Another day had passed.

The cave where Grendelynden had hidden the two of them from the Drogs was rather like the one in which he had hidden Velissa. They, too, had been instructed to rest in the tiny enclosure until he returned. It was a bright day and light from the outside flooded through the opening of the cavern so that they could see while they talked.

"When the war is over, I want to supervise the filling in of the forming pits. There will be no more disallegiance."

"All of them must die—the Drogs?" asked Raccoman, rather scrambling his question.

"All!"

"I hope that I personally get to deal with Thanevial," said Raccoman with disconsolation. "He killed my father and tortured my wife on the tower. Oh, Hallidan—my wife, Velissa!"

The Graygill turned his face to the wall.

"There is still hope. Thanevial will not kill her so long as there's still a chance to trade her for the Singreale," Hallidan reassured him.

"When her life is over, mine will be over also," said Raccoman, passing his thick hand across the crown of his bald head.

"You are small of stature. I will kill him," said Hallidan in an effort to turn Raccoman's attention from his concern over the unknown estate of his wife. "Yes, I will kill him. Thanevial is my brother and my enemy."

"Your brother!" Raccoman blurted out.

"Yes."

"But I have never heard the other knights mention this," objected Raccoman.

"They are kind not to speak of it. We were twin boys, identical," the knight shrugged.

"But he's so ugly!"

"He was fair once, a handsome and gifted Star Rider."

"Thanevial was a Star Rider?" Raccoman seemed stricken.

"Until the murder of Rengraaden's parents."

Hallidan looked away as though he were trying either to forget or to recall something. Raccoman reflected upon the strange course that the twins had taken. One lived to destroy the citadel, the other to defend it. Somehow Raccoman knew that if they ever were released from their place of hiding, it could well be that the twins would meet a final time upon the bridges. Oh, how the Graygill was weary of war. And yet the war had to be acted out, and each man had to play his part in this deadly charade begun and continued by the Drog lord who now held Raccoman's wife as a hostage between dread foes.

Hallidan's mention of Rengraaden had set Raccoman to reflection. The Titan at last broke the silence.

"I am impressed with Raenna!" exclaimed Hallidan all at once, working to massage some feeling into his wounded arm.

"Impressed?" asked Raccoman.

"Impressed," said Hallidan, and he looked away again staring fixedly at nothing. Raccoman observed him carefully.

"I am impressed with all the Miserians, especially those who fight," replied Raccoman.

"But Raenna is different."

"I never noticed that," said Raccoman, then wished he had not. For he could see that the Titan, pale from the loss of blood, colored a little at his remark. And, he could see, there was a gleam in Hallidan's eye.

Thanevial awoke suddenly with a feeling that things were not right. The sand tides had grown boisterous during the night, and the smoking lava was now smashing in molten waves against the

(175)

lower steps of the towering pyramid. Thanevial ordered his Drogs to break camp and begin their pilgrimage east to the place where they would join the second camp and combine forces against the six bridges of Rensgaard.

He started up the tower to cut Velissa from her lofty imprisonment. On the second step, he turned and looked out over the giant tides of lava that were smashing against the west side of the Tower Altar. The altar could not last the week. Above him, he saw the immobile Drog sitting on top of the tower and staring at the camp below. Velissa was slumped against the west pinion stone. He prided himself that Raccoman's rescue attempt had been repulsed and that both the Graygill and Ren's best knight were probably mortally wounded, if not already dead.

He called to the Drog sentry, "Condungra! Hunga!" The command to rise had no effect. The Drog did not move. Thanevial hated insubordination. He set his black boots on a swift course and bolted the steps to the exalted top. His labored breathing sounded even more hideous in the exertion required to climb to the pinnacle of the towering black altar.

When he reached the Drog, he realized instantly why he had been disobeyed. Thanevial was stunned that the little creature who so hated Drogs had possessed the courage to come to the Tower Altar.

"Singreale be damned!" he shouted and swung his sword through the already dead Drog as though he could somehow kill him a second time. The sentry's lifeless head tumbled down the side of the tower, bouncing off the risers and disappearing far below in the rising smoke of the molten lava.

With even greater hostility, Thanevial cut through the cleverly tied cape. How he raged, realizing that he had been tricked by a creature only one quarter his size! Again and again, he swung his sword through the shredded cape. He cut away the pinions, raving in fury as his blade sliced through the stone and steel. At last he ceased his roaring and raised his sword hilt high.

"Death to Rensgaard!" he cried with his arms stretched upward in vengeance. Below him, the swelling molten surf crashed against his altar. As deadly as his own hatred, the lava smoke swirled about him and rose into the heavens.

The siege machines rolled to the wall.
The city was wounded and bled.
The mothers drank small sips of water,
While children shed tears on their bread.

CHAPTER XI

The Edge of War

R ENSGAARD WAS CAUGHT in fear and grief.

By the end of the week, most of the Titans no longer believed that Raccoman and Hallidan were alive. The Drog troops were on the move. The disappearance of the Titan and the son of Garrod was keenly felt by all the inhabitants of the citadel. But it was Raenna who seemed to be most visibly moved about their loss. Her feelings for Hallidan had enlarged somehow from the small base upon which they began. Hallidan had trained her in the arts of war. He had been reluctant at first to attempt the training, for he had never viewed war as the work of women. Yet he had been impressed with Raenna's determination, and he soon admired her for her dedication to the proposition that no life should hold for its only course the condolences that others offered. He understood that she needed other reasons for existence.

Still, something in Raenna quickened when she saw the tall knight flying the night course of the Star Riders. Technically, Raenna had no right to love Hallidan, for he was a Star Rider and she a Miserian. She still had a husband who, though totally changed, was not yet dead. Further, she knew that her husband was committed more to her death than she was to his. As horrendous as she had found the brutish Drograaden to be, she had been unable to kill him. Even so, there was little doubt in her mind that she would have been slain by her ugly husband had he not feared so for his own life. That fear had driven him quickly into the woods to save his monstrous life.

Even before Rengraaden had defected, Hallidan knew he had feelings toward Raenna he should not have permitted himself. Now that Rengraaden was a Changeling, Hallidan was becoming bolder in his pursuit of the Changeling's abandoned wife. Following her discovery of the Drog colony east of the citadel, Hallidan had met her at the east bridge as she returned to the city. He had congratulated her, using the characteristic armlock that he would have used for such an expression to any of the knights. But in the armlock, his forearm had brushed her hair and he had pulled her face to his. In the closeness of the moment, he awkwardly forgot to congratulate her. Their eyes held each other overlong. Their faces flushed. And while he had done nothing out of the way, he apologized, then reddened again. Raenna knew that his apology did not come from anything he had done. He felt that he had been too forward with the Miserian.

For Hallidan, the emotion was new.

Raenna felt unworthy. For her, the emotion was not new. She had once been married to the prince of Rensgaard. She knew what it meant to love and be loved. She knew the pride of seeing her husband in the gold boots, cape, and mail of a crown prince. She had never seen him at the Festival of Light but that she fell in love with him all over again. For centuries, she had felt secure in Rengraaden's love. In their moments alone, she had once felt that she had all that she would ever need. Now she was married to a Changeling. Still, she felt that the love she had once known for the handsome Rengraaden banned her from looking at Hallidan as she did. She dared not think that the yet-unmarried knight could ever desire her. For half a millennium, she had been married to a traitor who had at last left her and his king for the forming pits in the Valley of the Changelings.

Perhaps the long look Raenna and Hallidan had shared on the east bridge came out of a dreadful sense of mutual loss. For Hallidan's twin was Thanevial, the Drog lord now bent on his destruction, while Raenna's husband was now the arch Drog, Drograaden, who would slay and devour her if he could.

The number of bachelors was no longer great among the knights. Bachelors more often had been the first to defect to the forming pits. The married knights better fought the temptation to defect because they knew they were loved by women who would be left to loneliness if they entered the Valley of the Changelings. The desire for home and family seemed to strengthen them and enable them to defy the ever-pressing lure—whatever it was—that seemed to draw Rensgaard's brightest and best to the forming pits.

It was no secret to Raenna and the Miserians, nor any of the others, that they were about to experience the pain of siege. Every surveillance flight brought back more information that the three divisions were marching—if the slumping, shuffling evil beasts could be said to march—to the bridges of the city.

Against this eventuality, the city had long prepared. The farmers had stacked the community larders with ample provisions of fresh and preserved fruits and vegetables. They were aware that the fresh fruits would all be gone in a little while and that the dried and preserved foods would become their sustenance against what could be a siege of long endurance.

Ironically, the Festival of Light would come in only one week, and it was certain that in less than that time the city would find its bridges drawn and its walls encircled by Drogs. The third army of Thanevial had already arrived at the northwest wall of the citadel. All of the bridges were drawn. By the afternoon of the same day, the other two armies of Thanevial came within sight of the west gate. Gradually, the gray hordes surrounded the citadel. The city was officially closed, and those on the inside braced themselves at every cranny of the walls. From the sentry houses above the bridges, the Titans watched the movements of the Drogs, especially at night.

The Miserians had discovered an ingenious way to carry molten sand from the growing ocean that devoured the Desert of Draymon as well as the western caladena groves and the Tower Altar. They found that lava dipped into metal containers would quickly harden into a thin shell of glass. The thin glass containers could then be filled with the molten sand, and the sand would reamin as hot as it did in the core of the fire-glass swords. The Titans carried great quantities of sand in large containers from the molten sea to the citadel. It was hot work, but it was to become one of the chief strategies of the war, for it could be dropped on any Drogs who attempted to climb the walls on scaling ladders.

The knights and Miserian warriors knew that the Drogs had only one tactic and that was numbers. They further knew that the monstrous hordes would rush the city in a flood of terror—a wave of hideous monsters—designed to overwhelm them.

The Festival of Light was cancelled as far as all festivities were concerned. The queen walked through the plaza with her little Garrod in her arms during the afternoon of the first two days that the citadel was encircled with Drogs. It was her hope to communicate determination to the defenders of Rensgaard. The knights now stood shoulder to shoulder at the wall.

For the first three days, the Changelings did nothing. But the surveillance of those on the wall was constant. Hourly, the condorgs flew. Each knight and Miserian wielded a sword. And they intended to use their shields to push back the Drogs over the walls as well as to physically engage the Changelings in hand-to-hand combat.

At solid intervals and very close together were placed the containers of hot glass that would be poured on the beast-warriors. The hot glass was an effective and deadly weapon, but a dangerous one to keep upon the walls because it could destroy a knight's hand or foot if it were accidentally jarred or spilled from its containers.

The Miserians had planned their own battle tactics. Once any wave of attack began, they would try to fly across the battle ranks and drop fire-glass on those who were on the scaling lattices.

Finally the sky-riders would drag hooks from the air across the ranks of Drogs in an effort to snag the Drogs and pull them to their death. The hooks would also be used to pull the lattices from the wall.

It was important for the Miserians, knights, and Star Riders to keep their proper places in the defense tactics. The Miserians could destroy their own knights by improperly handling the hot glass or by flying too close to the walls.

For the first week, the Drogs held the peace. The hot glass had to be replenished constantly so it would be ready when the Drog warriors came. And nobody doubted they would come.

Velissa had awakened from her deep fatigue. A gray webbing snarled her thoughts, but cleared as she perceived the golden sunlight filtering in on the floor of her little cave. She felt better that afternoon than she had felt in many weeks. The chamber where she rested was quite tall enough for her to stand in spite of the small orifice through which she had entered. She forced herself to stand up and walk around the enclosure. She constantly exercised and massaged her unused legs to get them ready for the night's trek ahead.

She could see the vines hanging over the enclosure through which she had entered, and yet she could see nothing beyond them except more vines and foliage. She wanted so to go outside. But she had learned a valuable lesson on the day she was captured. She intended to obey Grendelynden. His quaint edict, she knew, could well be her creed of life, *"Nottem, nottem, nottem leevee cave!"* Whatever curiosity she had in knowing what was going on outside, it was more than offset by the caution she knew she must exercise in a world she barely understood and a war she knew she could do little about.

After a while, she forced herself to lie down again. She was not as sleepy or fatigued as she would have liked to have been. But as the night would require the utmost exertion, so must the day be spent in complete rest. She tried so hard to rest that she couldn't rest at all. She dozed only intermittently. The sun spot on the cave floor began to darken at last. The jinnidrinnins started singing. Night came on, no longer terrifying her, but wrapping all her dreams in hope.

When it was quite dark, a small hand pulled the vines aside and entered the cavern. The friendly lights blinked on and followed the hand inside.

"Chon chon Lissa Nissa starvie hunggie hoo
Drinkee drinkee Lissa Nissa eatee eatee too."

Grendelynden had brought fruit and water, and Velissa ate ravenously. When she remembered the crude gluttony of the Drogs, she felt ashamed and slowed her eating to a speed appropriate to her own dignity. The food was good and the water was cool as the night. She drank and remembered the tepid water, warmed by the lava fires, that had been her only refreshment on the high tower.

That night Velissa found herself once again following her trusted deliverer.

"Nottem nottem taukee not—waukee, taukee not
Droggynoggens uglee uglee—many uglee, lott."

She knew that there were large-scale movements of the Changelings, and she was frightened yet content to follow Grendelynden through the jungles. One line moved her on:

"Raccomonnie taken en em cave."

Again, she had to stop and rest many times, though not so often as during the previous night. Her day of rest in the little cave had served her well. Her feet flew through the dark forest. Blinded by the night, she could only trust her guide. Her need to rest was shortened by her dream of seeing Raccoman.

It had been so long since they had been together, and except for his brief attempt to rescue her, she had not seen him in weeks. As she carefully followed Grendelynden, her mind flew above the darkness to lighter moments in her past. She and Raccoman were laying in their warm clothes in the snowy meadow before the old barn. The sunlight dazzled the fields and danced the colored dwellings of Canby to life. She thought of how good the red candolet tea, with its enticing green vapors, had always tasted on a cold morning.

She thought of the night that she had first seen the "hall of Dakktare" and of the pride she had felt when she became Raccoman's bride. She remembered her excitement at seeing the Paradise Falcon for the first time. And she remembered with delight the night that the giant Rexel had lowered her on his great talon until she slipped into the seat beside her beloved husband. She remembered all of Raccoman's songs and dances. Her mind raced with their wondrous flight and to their friendship with Hallidan. On the tower, she had despaired of ever seeing her husband again. Now she knew that her assumption had been false. She would see him again, and before this night was over. She took Grendelynden's thin hand, for the area of the forest they were crossing was dark, but she walked in darkness and trusted.

Raccoman and Hallidan had never been able to sleep during the day. Almost three whole days had passed since they had last seen Grendelynden. He had left them plenty of food and water, and that was well because neither of them were in any shape to travel far. However, their injuries were healing, and on their third day in the cave, they managed to get up and walk around. The small cavern was tall enough so that Raccoman could stand easily, but the Titan found that he had to stoop to accommodate the low ceiling in most sections of the cavern. Still, Hallidan knew that it was imperative that he continue to exercise his legs. He dreamed only of escaping and fighting again, if indeed the escape could be managed.

Hallidan was almost certain that, before their escape could be arranged, they would have to deal with the movement of the Drog hordes who were already, he was sure, beginning to assemble for their siege of the citadel. The bridges, he knew, would be drawn, and the only way that the city could be entered would be on the back's of condorgs flying high above the enemy lines. But getting into the city would be an easy matter compared with signalling to be rescued in the dark forests. To stand out in the open long enough to be discovered by possible rescuers would also make them vulnerable to their enemies as well.

Though both of them were healing well, they felt it would be at least a week more before they would be able to leave the cave. Then they would have to decide how to get past the Drog forces and enter the citadel.

"I believe that most everyone in the citadel now believes we are dead—killed in the rescue attempt," said Hallidan.

Raccoman did not acknowledge the remark immediately. Evening was coming on, and his mind had been faraway. The jinnidrinnins were already singing. Raccoman summoned his mind to return to the present. His mind had stepped to the jinnidrinnin's music till it waltzed the northern skies. Like Velissa, he was in a distant land where the tilt winds had already begun to blow.

Raccoman almost resented Hallidan's statement, for it called him back to a war and a continent where there were no tilt winds. This world had threatened him with death and had taken from him his beloved Velissa, and she was even now being tormented by the very lord who had killed his father, Garrod. He reluctantly left his homesick dreams and joined the knight in spirit, even though his spirit was weak.

"Hallidan, the rescue was my finest hour,
Strong intent but weak in power.
I wish I'd died upon the tower.
Oh, Velissa . . . ."

His voice trailed off.

"Come now, Raccoman," begged the Titan. "We did all that we could. Don't give up hope. The first thing that we shall do when we are well enough is try somehow to get back within the citadel. From there, we'll locate where the Drogs are holding Velissa, and then in spite of the state of the siege, we'll make another effort to rescue her."

Raccoman's last words had been a disconsolate rhyme. He had rhymed less lately than ever in his entire life, but the times had stolen the merriment from him, and his affected way of speaking fit better into better days.

"What?" asked Raccoman, coming out of his stupor.

"I said, when we're back in the citadel, we'll try again to rescue Velissa," the knight repeated.

"Hallidan, do you mean it?"

It was obvious that he did.

"We'll take more men, surprise the Drogs at night, distract them with liquid glass, or I—I don't know what we'll do, but we won't give up."

Raccoman smiled in the growing dimness of the cave. In a little while, it would be completely dark outside. As on previous nights, their conversation thinned, but did not stop.

They talked on for many hours. When it was almost too late for conversation, Raccoman asked a question so serious that Hallidan had to pull himself out of a near-slumber to gather the necessary wisdom and attention to answer it. Raccoman's voice echoed off the soft stone ceiling of the cavern. He was now lying across the cave from the knight, so he spoke with some volume.

"Hallidan, how did you feel the night you learned that your own brother had murdered the royal family?" he asked.

"There's the atrocity that is hard to measure, friend Raccoman. I loved Thanevial—we were twins—alike in everything including our daydreams and our love for each other. When we were boys, we used to dream of being Star Riders together. We talked of our love for Ren and nothing else. We flew the night skies. Already I rode Zephrett, and Thanevial rode your beast. On sunny afternoons, we would take our winged steeds to the west slopes of Mt. Calz, and the beasts would graze while we spoke of nothing but learning the night skies and serving the king. Thanevial loved Ren and wrote songs to his honor. Some of these songs he sang in the festival square."

Raccoman looked into the darkness and saw nothing but night. Hallidan's words seemed oblique, as though they were reluctant to travel through the blackness.

"Thanevial wrote songs to the king—festival anthems?" asked the Graygill in disbelief.

Hallidan did not answer Raccoman's question directly. He simply began to sing:

"O come to the monarch whose splendor is white,
   Whose glorious being is day,
Whose city of bridges is quarried in light,
   Where dark is forbidden to stay.

Truth, peace, and justice are ever his seal—
   Honor his substance of might.
He is friend to the falcon and Lord of Singreale
   His reign is as condorgs in flight.

Bring every knight and stand them as men,
   Sing honor to Rensgaard and Ren."

Hallidan ceased his song. His voice was strong and deep. His haunting recall of his brother's ballad spoke both of his pride in the past and his agony with the present. It was incredible to Raccoman that the composer of what Hallidan had just sung was now trying to annihilate the same king he had once heralded with joy.

"Would he destroy Ren now if he could?" asked Raccoman, knowing the answer before he posed the question.

"He hates all that he once loved and loves all that he once hated," said Hallidan.

"The land I once loved is in turmoil; there is war there, too," said Raccoman, staring vacantly into the dark that he now felt had come inside him. "I had a friend—a Blackgill—he loved me once, but not now. If he could have, he would have slain me." Raccoman paused. The conversation would not serve his logic as well as a song. "Every world knows treachery," said the Graygill. "Our land, like yours, was one bright with hope. My uncle, the Moonrhyme, destroyed himself with his new appetite for power. He killed and then killed again and then joined the dark soul of my best friend. All that is an ocean away, but distant treachery makes the same kind of noise.

> *"There are worlds unspoiled in the deepening sky,*
> *Where the riders of night have not flown.*
> *But here there is red where the animals bled,*
> *And tastes, once forbidden, are known.*
>
> *There is fire in the village and blood on the plains.*
> *We fed our best souls to the foe.*
> *Come all you lost men to life once again*
> *Ho lolly, ho lolly, ho lo!"*

Neither the Titan nor the Graygill replied to the requiem. Requiems know no reply. Raccoman's land was a continent on which Hallidan had never set foot, yet their lands were much alike.

A kind of melancholy settled into the blackness. It was well past the middle of the night. In the cave, they had become used to darkness and it didn't trouble them. They talked, ate, laughed, and exercised, all without the blessing of direct light. It was always so dark at night that Raccoman could never tell when his eyes were open. That made sleeping easy. He was nearly asleep when it seemed that he heard a distant voice. But when he called himself back to wakefulness, he realized that the voice belonged to Hallidan. He shook off his near-sleep to listen to his friend.

"Raccoman, is it proper to love a married woman?" asked the knight.

"Not proper!" Raccoman answered in two words and then tried

to decide whether he should extend the conversation or go back to sleep. He did not want to appear disinterested in Hallidan's query, so he forced his mind to concentrate through its fatigue.

> "No, it is not proper at all, not proper I say.
> If a woman is married, there's a man in the way."

The rhyme was weak, but Raccoman was tired and his wounded leg was giving him some pain. It was always harder to rhyme things with a wounded leg and a mind clouded by sleep.

Hallidan went on as though he hadn't heard.

"I think I love Raenna," he said.

> "Please, Hallidan—oh, Raenna. It's all right, yes, fine.
> The Miserian—please, Hallidan, my mind's in a fog.
> It's all right to love someone whose husband's a Drog."

Raccoman's verse was becoming webbed in his attempted replies. His jingles were jangled. The jinnidrinnins were singing monotonously, and soon his mind was no longer able to think about Hallidan and Raenna.

"Hallidan," he said dreamily to the accompaniment of the jinnidrinnins,

> "Hallidan, could you give my groggy logic a jog
> Hallidan, why would a good woman marry a Drog?"

"He wasn't a Drog when he married her," said Hallidan.

"He wasn't," said Raccoman. "Hmmm." Hallidan knew that once the humming took over, Raccoman was sound asleep. But Hallidan went on thinking of Raenna, and he sang a deep-throated tribute to his own inner feelings. The melody was for the darkness and himself:

> "Raenna, my love, when the fighting is done,
>   We'll saddle our condorgs and fly.
> We'll sail past the seasons and circle the sun
>   And skim the dim reaches of sky.
> We'll reign our bright steeds to some cosmic spire,
>   Embrace on dim planets flung far,
> And lie our communion in warm stellar fire
>   And purchase our own private star."

Hallidan wondered if Raenna would have approved, or if she too much feared his love. He decided to sleep for the night, hoping that one day he could sing the song to the Miserian who, more than all else, would have loved the song had she known of it. Tonight no one knew of it. Raccoman was humming in a sound sleep, and the jinnidrinnins paid no attention.

Velissa had walked most of the long Estermann night in anticipation. She was tired and yet would not complain of her fatigue. Twice she and Grendelynden had passed small Drog encampments. Once a group of Drogs had heard them, but nothing came of it. Grendelynden had but to stay in the trees and flash his eyes. Then the Drogs quailed and refused—and sensibly so—to investigate the lights in the darkness.

When the morning came, Grendelynden moved quietly along a stone ledge directly west of Mt. Calz and north of the Caverns of Smeade. They had walked along the same stone ridge for some time when they came at last to a mossy stone shelf. Grendelynden did not have to stoop to go beneath it, but Velissa did. Grendelynden pulled back the vines and said out loud, *"Raccomonnie taken en em cave."* Velissa crawled into the darkness out of the bright morning. Her eyes did not adjust immediately to the dim light, and she tripped over a huge hulk in the cave and fell stumbling.

"What is this?" said Hallidan when Velissa tripped over him and fell ingloriously in the darkness.

Velissa cried in joy, "Hallidan, you're alive!"

At the sound of her voice, there was another voice that thrilled her.

"Ha hoo! She is here, Hallidan!
  Life is good!
Velissa, my bride of Quarrystone Wood!
  Ha hoo! I love you!"

At once, Raccoman and Velissa found each other in an embrace. Their world closed in to themselves so tightly that the universe itself slipped away. In their ardent celebration of joy, they shut out Hallidan and Grendelynden altogether.

"Raccoman, I thought you were mortally wounded!" cried Velissa. Then cold fear came over her and she recoiled. "You're not a Drog?" she asked and drew away.

Raccoman was offended. But Velissa had not forgotten how the horrible monsters had twice before deceived her, once as her father and again as Doldeen. Now she suspected Raccoman.

He laughed and drew her back again.

"Nonsense," he said and put an end to her fear by holding his face against hers in a long embrace.

"My darling," she said softly. But his exultation was so great that he could not speak softly as yet. Instead, he shouted to the top of the cave,

> *"Ha hoo, I'm alive—while Estermann shall spin.*
> *Tell every knight in the army of Ren*
> *The Graygill is healed and living again!"*

He spoke so loudly in his joy that Grendelynden became afraid and spoke up to caution him.

> *"Notten tauken, notten tauken, tuaken en em cave*
> *Uglie-killee Droggynoggen, making cavee, grave."*

Raccoman stopped his boisterous laughter with the riddle's logic.

"Grendelynden, is Rensgaard under seige?" asked Hallidan.

> *"Toonie evee, Grendelynden findee outee war.*
> *Notten nowee, retzie, retzie moren moren more!"*

The Titan and Graygill had already slept a full night, but Velissa needed no further coaxing. She lay her head in Raccoman's lap and soon was humming in pleasant slumber. Having traveled all night, she was so exhausted that she slept through the rest of the day until the jinnidrinnins began their evening songs.

Monsters never can be cherubs—
  Contentment never sleeps with dread—
The Siamese that kills his twin,
  Finds his alter ego dead.

CHAPTER XII

The Siege of the
Six Bridges

O N THE FIRST DAY of the Festival
of Light, a distant roar shook Rensgaard. The crash that shook the
citadel was a seven-day journey away by foot. Still, the ground
trembled and quaked for several minutes. All knew the tremor's
source. Far away, the evil Tower Altar that had seemed as high as
Mt. Calz had at last fallen in the molten sea. The Desert of Draymon had conquered Thanevial, and the Drog lord's throne was
gone. Although Rensgaard could have no festival celebration, there
arose a great shout at the shock waves that rippled gently underneath the citadel.

Outside the walls of the city, Thanevial knew that the siege must
work. His altar was lost, his kingdom gone. The homeless Drog lord
now gloated across the walls of the gleaming citadel with longing.
He needed a new throne and meant to seize the alabaster city.

Izonden knew the first assault on Rensgaard would come soon.
She no longer dared to walk through the city with the infant prince.

"The invisible arrows fly far," a Rider had warned her. "Stay
behind the palace facade. If you would watch the war, watch from
your chamber."

The queen bowed to his logic. Several times Izonden met with
the Riders. The walls bore a tension that always steeled itself, for
they felt that when the Drogs came, they would swarm in tides that
would require a herculean effort to turn.

It was near noon on the second day of the festival without festivities that the unseen arrows began to rain from the sky. The Star
Riders and Miserians leapt to their mounts. Waves of Drogs came
up the long lattices that were many yards wide and gently sloped
against the wall. The lattices were so gently inclined that the Drogs
began to wash up them and spill onto the wall. So rapid was their
advance that they managed to take the wall before the Miserians
were over their position. The strong knights held back the tide with
their fire-glass swords. Ghastly sulphur fumes rose as headless torsos fell back to the lattice. The knights kept close together and
swung their searing blades.

One knight screamed when he stepped back too quickly and
accidentally tripped over a container of molten glass. The glass

destroyed his foot, and he toppled backwards into the citadel. But the molten glass also ran across the feet of a dozen Changelings, and they also fell, some facedown into the searing, instant death below.

Knights saw and felt wounds suddenly open in their bodies from the invisible arrows shot by the Drog archers far below. These invisible darts were hard to reckon with. At last, the Miserians came. They poured their liquid glass in faint trickles that spilled and thinned in the bright air, looking as though they were showering the Drogs with cascades of diamonds. But each of the diamonds was a drop of molten death that split the armor and leathery skin of the Changelings. Fifty of them died on the first pass of the Miserians. Where the molten drops fell, fires sprang up and the sulphur eruptions from the dying Drogs shot volleys of yellowish fumes into the morning air.

The stench of the wounded and dying Drogs nearly gagged the knights who wielded their strong swords against the invisible blades. The siege continued with a second and third wave of Drogs trying to move up the lattice work that was becoming riddled with fires as the liquid glass ignited the frameworks and burned holes in the scaling lattices. The Miserians returned and circled again and again. More than two hundred of the flying riders brought volleys of death that rained a sparkling shower of hot glass on the Drog hordes.

One of the Miserians' condorgs was struck in the eye by an invisible arrow. It was blinded and fell until it crashed into the wall. A beautiful Miserian fell beneath her mount, and the hot glass flew in a burning arc across a half-dozen Drogs. The entire lattice where the Miserian accident occurred caught fire and pitched the Miserian and fifteen or twenty Drogs to a fiery death.

In half an hour of bitter fighting, knights died frequently along the wall. Scores of Drogs were also killed. Still the grey hordes came. As many as a thousand died in the first assault. Finally, in desperation, the Drogs drew back, and in trying to retreat, they moved down the unsure burning lattices and fell through. They retreated rapidly to a distance safe from the wall.

The first assault had failed. The citadel had held. The Titans were joyous.

The walls were cleaned. The wounded knights were taken to the shade of the citadel facade to be treated. The dead knights were taken to the center of the city till arrangements could be made for their burial. The dead Drogs were burned in an open field just inside the north bridge where the condorgs usually were kept.

It was decided that, since the Drogs would not attack at night, evening would be the best time for the Miserians to go to the Desert of Draymon to gather more of the molten sand. They flew as soon as it was dark to retrieve more of the liquid glass. Thanevial noted their leaving.

Near midnight, while they were gone, the Drogs made a rush on the northern wall and attempted to set fire to the bridges that were drawn into their ramparts of stone. The knights found it impossible to see the gray forms at night. Their fire-glass blades glowed brightly, but they did not emanate enough light to see that the Drogs were swarming on the dark lattices. The Changelings gained the wall before they could be repelled. The invisible arrows rained. A third of the knights on the north wall were killed. The Titans fought valiantly in the dark, but Drogs leapt through the lines where knights had fallen.

The fighting was fierce and continued for more than two hours. Word came to the palace that there were Drogs in the streets. The queen moved to the tower and locked the gate behind herself and the little prince. She hid as far within the inner recesses of the royal residence as she could.

Other knights from the west defenses joined those on the northern wall. At last the holes in the weakened defense were filled. The northern wall was sealed. Once again, the Drogs broke through, but the valiant Titans triumphed. It was a costly night of fighting and would have been lost except for the tireless efforts of the Miserians.

The Miserians at last returned to the city and drew near enough to see that it was in the midst of another siege. Even though they were returning from a long and arduous trip, they flew at once into the thick of the battle. In the darkness, their molten death fell and sparkled fiery flakes of snow. They flew across the Drog armies that were still swarming up the walls. Once more, death rained upon the Changelings.

The ugly Drogs cried out in agony. The knights, seeing the Miserians, took heart and fought on. Again they closed the gaps on the wall. For an hour, liquid death rained upon the Drogs. Again the lattices were burned, and Drogs fell in flames and sulphur smoke. In the small hours of morning, the entire lattice caught fire and Drogs were burned by the hundreds. The knights cheered when they heard the cries of the Changelings from the east wall. In strength, Thanevial left the north defense and mounted a new assault upon the east wall.

The Miserians fled and from their condorgs, rained fire for an hour upon the new assault. The Drog hordes moved tide after tide against Raenna's section of the wall. The entire detachment of knights was inspired by the beautiful warrior whose blade cut a fiery swath of wrath through the night.

The women had proven themselves supple in their use of the sword and the glass. Now they discovered an efficient tactic. They dipped their swords in the molten glass on the inner side of the wall and flayed their foes as Drogs climbed up the ladders. Their blades dripped with hot liquid glass that murdered as it fell. With their light and quick steps, the Miserians were as effective as the Star Riders. Many of the women died—but never did they abandon the fight. Drogs caught fire and fell in flames against the waves of Changelings. The Miserians on the wall had held the last defenses. The lattices were now aflame, and scores of Drogs perished in yellow fumes and grunting wails.

The night siege ended. Both the east and north walls had been secured.

The flying Miserians had run out of glass. They knew they had no choice but to return to the Desert of Draymon in a forced flight. Their condorgs were exhausted, but the Miserians knew they could return and be ready for the day if they left at once. Off they flew into the black night.

When the Drogs had been repelled from the east wall, those knights who could be spared entered the city. Within an hour, most of the Drogs who had spilled over into the citadel when the north wall gave way had been located and killed.

Yet one escaped detection. It was Drograaden, Raenna's monstrous husband. In stealth, he slipped from the shaded land to the darkest niche. He made his way through the streets to the very cubicle that he and Raenna had once inhabited. There he hid and waited for his wife to return. The room seemed unchanged since those days when he had been heir to the crown. Two things he wanted to destroy—one was his wife and the other was the queen's child. After he had killed his wife, he planned to move on to the palace nursery.

Hallidan and the Graygills felt the earth tremble when the Tower

Altar collapsed into the boiling sea of glass. They knew that the eroded desert had swallowed up much of the western caladena groves. The purple trees always burst into flames as they fell into the molten glass. Still, they had no idea how Rensgaard had fared in the siege. Nor did anyone in the citadel suspect that the trio was still alive.

On the third morning of Rensgaard's Festival of Light, their small friend, Grendelynden, went blind. His huge, yellow eyes dulled to a dead, graying black. He sat silent and unblinking in the little cavern where the Titan and the Graygills waited for the day, disconsolate in their ignorance about the security of Rensgaard. Though Grendelynden was not dead, he sat immobile, as though his inner light had been stolen.

"Your eyes won't serve you, friend," Raccoman told the small creature.

"*Grendelynden chonnie-chon, lie-tee, sie-tee chon*
Falcon steelie lightee now, Singreale gone."

Grendelynden spoke as though he were in a coma. The words came slowly and so softly that the trio had to listen very carefully. They tried hard to make something out of what they had heard.

The near-blind Grendelynden stumbled toward the rear of the cavern until he found a small opening in the stone. That part of the cave was very dark. Hallidan intended to help the little creature, but he stood up too quickly and bumped his head on the low ceiling. By the time he reached the opening to the inner cave, his friend was gone, almost as though he had been absorbed into the black stone.

"He's gone!" Hallidan called back to the Graygills.

"Gone?" asked Velissa.

Hallidan fumbled in the darkness and then turned to make his way back to the outer part of the cave. As he groped his way forward, he tripped over an unseen form. He lurched forward, then felt around for the soft object over which he had fallen.

"There's a body here!" shouted Hallidan.

"Is it a Drog?" asked Velissa.

Hallidan touched the dark form. The skin was soft and warm.

"No," concluded Hallidan, "It feels more like a Star Rider."

"Unconscious or dead?" asked Raccoman moving in the darkness toward the sound of Hallidan's voice.

Hallidan placed his hand upon the chest of the large man. It was moving up and down.

"He's alive," the knight answered.

A moment later, Raccoman, who had been moving too rapidly into the dark, ran into the knight with such force that he was knocked backward. But he soon oriented himself to the positions of both Hallidan and the prone form. The Rider and the Graygill took hold of the heavy, unconscious man and dragged him to the lighter part of the cave.

Velissa looked away. The man was naked.

"Ren!" exulted Hallidan.

"Ren?" Velissa cried in disbelief.

The king's eyes blinked open.

"Rexel will come soon," said Ren, not speaking any specific word of greeting. His voice was a little more than a whisper. Then he asked in a stronger voice, "Hallidan, are you well enough to return to the city?" He turned as though he would speak to the Graygills. He had addressed Hallidan without any greeting as though he had been in their presence all the time. And before he could say anything to the Graygills, Hallidan said, "My Lord, the King, where have you been?"

"I was born again," said the still-naked monarch rising to his knees.

Hallidan, sensing Ren's discomfort, removed his cape and threw it around the shoulders of the sovereign.

"Born again?" he asked. "As what?"

"Grendelynden chonnie chon chonie born again,
Grendelynden taken cave Grendelenden Ren."

There was silence in the cave. The truth was as glorious as the Singreale itself. For the king had been the Ally who had shed the trappings of his monarchy to wander naked in the forest and destroy the Drogs with a mighty hand.

"But when we saw you last, you had the Singreale!" Hallidan blurted out.

The king nodded. "I carried the great diamond into the cavern of Smeade and there I experienced the great power of the Singreale. I laid the point of the diamond over my breast and pressed it with my bare hands until it passed into my own being and flooded every window of my soul. Then my form dwindled and became that of the naked ally whose treasure was an inner light. It was by the inner light that I was able to save all those who had not sold themselves to Thanevial."

"But where is the diamond now?" asked Velissa.

"Soon you will see that the light still is an inward light. What were the last words you heard the Ally speak?" asked Ren.

All three fell silent, trying to recall the Ally's last words to them.

"*Falcon steelie lightee now, Singreale gone!*" cried Velissa.

"Yes, that was it! But what do you make of it, Lissa Nissa—I mean, Velissa?" asked Hallidan.

"I don't know," said Velissa slowly and then repeated, "'Falcon steelie lightee now, Singreale gone.'" She pondered the riddle until she was touched by a moment of rare insight.

"Raccoman, maybe it doesn't mean anything, but when was the only other time that we've seen eyes that seem to be lit from within?" she asked.

He thought for only a moment before he exclaimed, "Rexel—when Singreale was inside of him!" too excited to think of rhyming.

"Do you suppose the falcon now has those backlighted eyes that Grendelynden had?"

"I don't know," replied Raccoman. "Maybe—yes, yes, that has to be it. Ha hoo! That's it, Velissa! 'Falcon Steelie lightee now, Singreale gone.'"

Ren smiled. At last they had perceived the inner glory of the Singreale.

"Unless I miss my guess, Hallidan," Velissa told the confused Star Rider, "we are about to be rescued by a falcon, the size of which you have never seen before. And not only will he be the biggest falcon you may imagine, but his eyes will be filled with a gleaming light exactly like that which we saw so often in Grendelynden's eyes."

Ren stood up, a naked but powerful monarch, and walked out of the cave. The rest followed.

Within the hour, they heard the roar of giant wings.

"Rexel!" exclaimed Velissa. The great bird settled in splendor before them. And his eyes were, indeed, glowing with inner light.

"Come! The desire of Ren decrees it!" declared the booming voice of Rexel.

"I must return first," the king said. He climbed on the wing of the great falcon, and the others knelt in his presence. Rexel bolted to the sky. Hallidan and the Graygills were struck with the splendor of his flight as the falcon soared into the ether of lofty Mt. Calz. Hallidan's cape fluttered behind the monarch. They could only imagine the reception he would receive in the war-torn citadel.

Raenna paused while pouring a cylinder of hot glass because she heard another of the Miserians cry, "The desire of Ren!" She looked up and saw, boldly silhouetted against the bright sky, a new image of life. Even from a distance, she realized that this growing vision was not a condorg. It was a bird, a falcon—indeed, a giant falcon. It was Rexel! All heads turned to watch the great bird winging its way toward the citadel. And Rexel was ridden by a warrior—a great Star Rider! Raenna stared at the man who clung to Rexel's neck. And then she realized—it was His Courage, the king!

It is Ren! The word traveled along the walls. Weary Star Warriors and tired Miserians, sooted with the grime of liquid glass, began a low chant, "Ren, Ren, Ren, Ren, Ren, Ren."

Raenna carefully set down the hot cylinder of molten glass.

"Ren, Ren, Ren, Ren," continued the chanting.

Raenna noticed the roughness of her hands, calloused by the meaning she had found in life since she had learned the art of war. Her face was smudged. She removed her helmet and used her roughened hands to brush her hair away from her face. Her eyes drank in the vision before her. There was hope!

"Ren, Ren, Ren, Ren!" The chanting grew in volume. The roar of the new moment set the war to the hopeful side of the weary battlement. The chanting swelled until it reached the ears of the inner palace. Izonden had been playing with the king's son. She had just taken him from his bath, and now she held his chubby, naked body in her arms. She lifted the little prince and said to him, "Too much you hear the noise of war and once again the chants of death come, sweet Garrod!"

"Ren, Ren, Ren, Ren!"

"It is all a roar. But listen, Garrod." The infant prince could not understand the strange hope that flooded Izonden's face. Her eyes drew wide and they sparkled. "Listen, Garrod—they cry your father's name!"

"Ren! Ren! Ren! Ren! Ren! Ren! Ren! Ren!"

She grabbed up her little one and ran outside to the balustrade. The vision had stopped the city. Tears flooded every eye. The king had come home. The great falcon descended before the balustrade, fluttered to the plaza, and folded his wings. The king dismounted from Rexel's proud neck. He ran up the steps, to the side of the facade, grabbed his queen and embraced her. Between them, they pressed his infant son. At the sight of their embrace, the citadel roared with cheers. The great Ren turned to his people and raised his hand to the new skies. The great falcon rose and winged off again in the direction of Mt. Calz.

While the royal family stood in the center of the city's esteem, the Matin broke in the lusty morning of hope:

"This is the land
  where honor reigns.
This is the land
  where truth is king.
Here is the kingdom
  void of change,
Where men live free forever!"

Drograaden had waited through the night in Raenna's cubicle. Even into morning had he waited. She did not return. While his dark desire was to kill his wife first, it became clear to him that this was not the best approach. So he decided instead to try to reach the royal residence, kill the infant Garrod, and then return here for Raenna.

To remain unseen in the light of day was no mean feat. He remembered the city well, for it had been less than a year ago that he had walked in the bright gold trappings of his royal office. He moved silently from shaded passageway to shaded passageway, hiding in door frames and stooping so that his head never crossed directly before any open window.

Most of the city was so occupied with the war that the streets were not guarded. The Titans felt sure that those Drogs who had broken through the wall on the north had all been killed and their bodies added to the huge pile that was to be burned. Drograaden slipped beneath the shaded eaves that hid the sidewalks from the bright morning sun. Finally, in his stealth, he found a secure hiding place under the small shrubs that flanked the portico beside the royal residence. A couple of knights were crossing the plaza from the south, walking back toward the center of the city. Drograaden's milk-white eyes mirrored them as he gloated in hatred upon them.

Then he looked up and saw a great condorg settling into the level and elevated part of the plaza right before the facade of the fortress. When the steed had landed, he realized, to his amazement, that its rider was Raenna. Her mount folded its wings, stared at the bushes that concealed the arch Drog, then snorted and reared back. Raenna noticed this action, but felt that the condorg had behaved strangely only because it had been pushed to the limits of its endurance. With the war on, most of the condorgs had taken to snorting at every potential enemy. Raenna's mount shied at every bush and tree beyond the walls of Rensgaard where death might be waiting.

The King's return had turned the city to hope. When the joy of his return had settled, the king commanded every loyal rider and Miserian to the walls to watch the camps of the Changelings.

"The rejoicing will come later," he said. But for the queen, the rejoicing was now.

"Dear Garrod," she told her baby, "now your father is home. Ren is in the citadel, my son. Now, at last, the desire of Ren will triumph!" In her joy, she kissed her son and flew through the palace with a new lightness of soul.

Raenna came to report to Ren that the Drogs were building up across from the eastern bridge in great numbers once again. But not knowing that the king was already back on the wall, She went on into the castle.

Drograaden realized that the castle was largely unprotected, since most of the knights were now on the walls. As he watched, the queen and Raenna appeared on the outer balustrade. They were talking quietly not far from where he was hidden. It was the most choice of opportunities. The queen was holding the infant Garrod and caressing his back gently as she talked to Raenna. Drograaden's hatred swelled in blood lust.

"The king is on the west wall now," he heard the queen tell the Miserian, "but he should be back before long." Izonden paused, held her baby close, and looked across the dwelling of the knights inside the citadel. Raenna, in her fatigue, well understood when the queen said, "He needs so badly to rest." But she put aside both her own fatigue and that of the king and stated the business for which she had come.

"Please tell the king that the Drogs are gathering an unusually large number of troops across from the east bridge. I will need more reinforcements to hold the wall," said the Miserian.

"I will tell him," replied Izonden. And then, as one woman to another, she cried plaintively, "Oh, Raenna, when will this dreadful siege be over and my Garrod be safe again?"

While they talked, Drograaden had climbed up the rough masonry and slid along the upper ledge of the castle until he was directly behind the jutting stone that hid him from the two women.

"Who can say?" Raenna answered the queen. "The Drogs have suffered severe losses. It will not be a long siege either way. But if they ever break through our ranks in significant numbers, the citadel will be lost. On the other hand, if the Drogs continue to die at their current rate, the city will be free in less than a week, perhaps two days."

"Oh, my child," said the queen to her infant Garrod, "it is a dreadful time, and yet I'll not despair."

Raenna bent and kissed Izonden's hand. "I must go back to the gate," she said. "Singreale save you and Prince Garrod the Second!"

But as she turned to leave, the air between them was blotted out by a monstrous form. Drograaden had swung his evil form over the balustrade and directly into the royal residence.

Izonden drew back in horror.

"Rengraaden!" gasped the Miserian.

"Hun, hunga, your husband, gukka!" rasped the hunched Changeling. "Gukka, hunga! Bandagmo, Garrod!" he said, breathing heavily.

"Stand back, Drograaden!" cried Raenna, drawing her fire-glass.

"Hund," grunted Drograaden. "Galanka, Raenna, I am your husband. You could not kill me before and you cannot kill me now. Gukka hunga!"

The queen gasped. "Rengraaden!" she exclaimed, unable to believe that the sinister and ugly form that stood before was her nephew and one-time heir to the citadel.

The Drog reached out to snatch Izonden's baby. Raenna's fire-glass fell in a swift arc, and Drograaden's severed claw fell with a soft thump onto the marble floor.

Again the queen gasped as sulphur fumes poured from the amputated limb of the ugly Changeling. Drograaden forgot about the child for a moment and turned toward his wife.

"I only need one hand to kill you, my wife," he said, advancing toward Raenna. She looked steadily at the evil thing before her.

Then he said, "I'm going to kill you as I killed Hallidan on the Tower Altar, my ugly wife."

Suddenly Raenna tightened inside. If only he had mentioned another knight, she could have stood it. But now that the arch Drog stood before her with a hilt that held a blade she could not see, she knew she must act and she must win for the honor of the man Drograaden had killed—a man she loved without any real hope or reason. She hated him all the more as the image of handsome Hallidan crossed her inner vision.

She retreated a step. Drograaden swung his sword and missed. She backed up again and thought of Hallidan and of how their eyes had met that day on the east bridge. She had no right to love him, but she knew she did.

Her heart took on a new determination to kill the evil thing before her.

Drograaden swung again. Deftly she sidestepped the invisible blade. The queen backed away in wide-eyed fear.

"Ughum," grunted the Changeling. "I ate the handsome face of the prince of the Star Riders. Chounga! Chounga! Hallidan bled in this mouth," Drograaden told her. "And today I shall eat the crown prince. Bandagmo caladranga, chounga Garrod! Hun, hun, hun!" he laughed and spat in Raenna's face.

With his every taunt, something inside Raenna grew stronger. She knew that even if the evil thing before had once been her husband, his hideous form and monstrous talk were now more than she could stand. In a fury that was more than human, she swung her fire-glass. Her searing blade cut a red arc in the air, and Drograaden backed up several steps. Again and again, she sliced the air, and at last her hot blade rang out against the invisible sword of her Drog husband. They finally traversed the floor where his severed hand still lay. Drograaden shuddered when he saw the severed hand. In an act of daring, Raenna reached down, picked up the claw, and threw it in his face. His own foul claw punctured one of his large, white eyes, and purple fluid ran out.

Furious in his pain, he lurched toward Raenna. She retreated a few paces. Then she thought of how the ugly form before her had fed upon Hallidan. She advanced again. With one daring swing of her fiery blade, she cut his sword from his uninjured hand. Both his claw and the blade it held clattered loudly as they fell to the palace floor. Yellow fumes gushed out of his second empty wrist. The handless Drog stood with his back to the balcony. Behind him was a beautiful day. He had retreated as far as he could go.

"Raenna, ughum—hund! My wife!" he reasoned, then pleaded, "No, Raenna!"

His uninjured eye saw a great red arc coming out of the dark of the inner castle. He tried to throw his hands up in front of him for protection, but his hands were gone. A moment later, his head fell oddly backwards and tumbled to the pavement below. It thumped in yellow fumes down the palace steps, startling Raenna's condorg.

Raenna watched his ugly body smouldering with the odd fumes that emanated now from the stumps of his neck and arms. The lifeless Changeling collapsed on the floor before her. She made no effort to remove the corpse—there wasn't time. She had been gone from her post too long as it was.

Once more, she bowed to Izonden and turned toward the stairs to leave. Then she heard Garrod behind her. He was crying, and it was a welcome sound. She advanced toward the queen, bowed again, and with tears in her eyes, said, "Please go to the tower and lock yourself in and nurse your child. There may be other Changelings in the city."

The queen glanced at the smouldering Changeling on the castle floor. She kissed Raenna and embraced her. "I love you," she said simply before she walked away, holding her infant close.

In the distance, the Miserian heard a welcome shout, "Hallidan lives!" Then Raenna saw the huge falcon Rexel settling once again, this time in the open plaza before the west gate.

"Drograaden lied—he's alive," she shouted. "Hallidan lives!" Something sang in Raenna as she left the castle and hurried joyfully to the falcon and to the man whose face she had last seen in studied intrigue on the east bridge some weeks before.

It was the east bridge that presented the most formidable challenge of all to the Drogs. Their assault was the heaviest of the three that they had attempted their first two days of fighting. But Thanevial had made a terrible mistake in his reckoning. He delayed the assault for a whole day while they repaired the lattices that had been thrown up against the west and north walls. He had ordered this done as a devious tactic to give the Titans the impression that he intended to attack from three directions at once.

The delay in the third assault came on the third night of the festival, and the interim had given all of Ren's defenders a chance to rest and the Miserians a chance to return from Draymon with a heavy store of molten glass.

The Drogs' assault on the east wall was doomed, for it cost Thanevial a third of his remaining Changelings. Raenna's prowess was second only to that of Hallidan himself, and through the long night, the Titan Star Rider and the Miserian fought tirelessly.

In the middle hours of the night, the lattice collapsed entirely, and the Drogs plunged to their death in the ravine far below the citadel's foundations. By daybreak, Rexel took the Singreale back to the inner castle, for his unfailing light during the siege had illuminated the victory of the knights and the dwindling hopes of the Drogs.

There was silence for two more days, and the sixth day of the Festival of Light saw one final siege around the entire city. The lattices lay burned and partially in ruins. The fire-glass of the Miserians had completely destroyed most of them. Thanevial could see his cause was failing, but still he ordered his defecting Drogs, on the pain of death, to stay and fight. One after another, they disappeared into the woods.

A great tumult rose from the citadel, and the Titans all stood with one voice to cry, "The desire of Ren!" The bridges were lowered. At last, the knights began a long and dangerous search of the woods, determined that none of the Changelings should escape.

Hallidan made his way to the wall over the north bridge where Ren, smudged with perspiration and the soot of the last seige, was talking with the knights.

"My Lord," said Hallidan, "I'm going after Thanevial!"

Ren had taken the Singreale from Rexel shortly after the great bird had brought the knight and the Graygills back to the city. In response to Hallidan's statement, the king reached inside his open tunic and took out a small leather pouch that swung from a leather thong tied at the back of his broad neck.

"Thanevial is no ordinary Changeling—you will need this!" said Ren as he slipped the thong from over his own head and placed it around Hallidan's neck. Without opening the pouch, Hallidan knew that the king had given him the treasure of the city, the treasure that would be his best possible defense against the Drog lord.

"Thank you, my king," said Hallidan. He turned and made his way to the armory just beneath the high north towers.

The knight saddled his condorg, Zephrett, and went to search for the arch Drog. He had no way of knowing exactly where Thanevial would be, but he suspected that the Drog lord would go as fast as he could to the Caverns of Smeade. There was a universal report that Thanevial had mounted a sauroid and was headed south and west of Mt. Calz. Hallidan flew swiftly, surveying the upper trails, and overtook him before the Drog had traveled very far from the southwest gate of the citadel.

Hallidan dismounted in the middle of the trail and waited. Soon he heard the black sauroid moving through the forest. Hallidan stepped back into the trees, and when the running sauroid was almost directly before him, he leapt into the trail and drove the fire-glass into the beast's chest. The black lizard-like body stumbled forward. Thanevial tumbled headlong over the sauroid's left shoulder. But he quickly jumped to his feet and drew his sword. And when he whirled around, he found himself facing his twin brother, separate in both heart and appearance.

"Hallidan—ughum, I have lost the citadel, but I will have your life." He swung his invisible blade. The leathery chest of the Changeling heaved with heavy breathing as it rippled in brutish musculature.

"The war is not over, brother," said the Drog.

"Not as yet," replied Hallidan, "but we will find each of the escapees.

"Fool," cried the Drog. "A thousand of them left for the other continent last night!"

"The Drogs cannot fly, but they do lie," said Hallidan. The Titan swung his sword in a heavy red arc, and the flesh of the Drog's shoulder gaped and spewed sulphur smoke.

Hallidan was about to swing his fire-glass again in a fatal and final arc when he was jumped from behind by two other Drogs. He felt his helmet split away. Then everything went black. When he awoke, his neck was covered with blood and he lay alone in the sun. He was glad to be alive until he felt his neck and then his chest. The Singreale was gone.

In the weeks that followed, the city was cleared of the wreckage of the siege lattices. Many Drogs were located and killed. Some were killed in groups and others were killed alone, but, one by one, they were hunted down. Gradually the city was cleaned up. Night after night, the funeral pyres of the dead Drogs consumed the ugly remains of the rebellion. Life in the city continued on a high plane of rejoicing. And yet Hallidan and the king remained disconsolate. No trace had been found of either Thanevial or the Singreale.

Hallidan and Raenna were invited to the royal residence for a victory celebration. So were Raccoman and Velissa. When dinner was finished and the table cleared, Hallidan openly lamented that the arch Drog had never been found. He blamed himself for the loss of Singreale.

"Thanevial could be dead," suggested Raccoman. "You did wound him mortally."

"Yes, he could be," agreed Izonden. "And we may yet find Singreale."

"Or," said Velissa, "he might be very much alive. Do you think there will be other defectors?"

"Next week we are going to the Valley of the Changelings and fill in the forming pits with liquid sand. There will be no more Changelings," Hallidan replied.

"Raccoman," said the king, "I must tell you that I admire the marvelous sail-plane that you welded. Could you weld with glass as our welders and glass-workers do?"

"Perhaps I could. Yes, I think I could," Growing confident, he stated the truth as he believed it to be.

"I am a fine welder, I know I could,
But, honestly, I doubt I should."

"But we don't weld metal here, so how shall you work now that the fighting is over?"

"Velissa and I would like to go home," the Graygill told the king.

"Home?" said Raenna. "This is home."

"Not our home," said Velissa. "Our home is troubled by war, but it is still our home."

"You see," said Raccoman, "we miss the snows and the Moonrhymes and all the people we left, but we are afraid, yes, very much afraid that the Moonrhymes themselves may be under a siege like the one that threatened this city."

"Garrod the Second will grow up in a secure land, while our people are captive to a lord not so ugly as Thanevial but just as despotic," said Velissa.

"But then it would be better to live in Rensgaard, now that there is peace," reasoned the queen.

"Perhaps," said Velissa, staring vacantly into space at things long remembered.

For a while, the dinner guests fell to silence.

"Raccoman," said the king at last. "I must tell you this. Our lands are not as separate as you think. Your father came to this world from the grand caverns of the Moonrhymes to emerge from the Caverns of Smeade."

"Do you mean they are connected?" asked Raccoman gleefully.

"There is a long cave; a tunnel connects our worlds. It took your father nearly a year to make the journey. Tunnel number four—that's the one from which Garrod emerged. And as far as I know," said Ren, "I am the only Titan to which Garrod ever disclosed his secret. Tunnel four! The long and unlit burrow travels its inky course beneath the mountains and plains and oceans that divorce our worlds."

Hallidan grew pale. The king noticed his demeanor.

"What the specter do you see that still is invisible to us?" asked Ren.

"It's probably nothing, but I suddenly recall something that Thanevial said to me after I wounded him."

"Yes?" asked the king.

"He said that a thousand of his Drogs had already left for the other continent."

"And?" The king faltered.

"Could he know about this passageway? Could he know that tunnel number four offered a pathway between the worlds?" asked Hallidan.

"I don't think so—unless he forced Garrod the First to tell him before he killed him," said the king, suddenly sensitive that they were talking about Raccoman's father.

"What did you say when he told you that a thousand Drogs were enroute to the other land?" asked Velissa.

"I told him knights fly, but Drogs lie," repeated Hallidan.

"And it probably was a lie," said Ren.

"It probably was," said Hallidan. "But what if it was not?"

"What if these huge beasts in a year or less should suddenly show up in the Grand Caverns of the Moonrhymes?" asked Velissa.

"Let us remember two things," counseled the king. "First of all, Drogs are notorious liars, preferring falsehoods to the truth. Second, there are numerous tunnels in the great domed room of the Caverns of Smeade. It is unlikely that Thanevial has any knowledge of the destiny or importance of tunnel number four. So the chances of them becoming lost in a long, blind alley are quite good."

"Still," reasoned Hallidan, "what if Garrod told the ugly Changeling of the tunnel?"

"Grendelynden would get them," shouted Velissa, suddenly remembering the Ally.

"No," replied Ren. "Remember, Grendelynden was only the expression of Singreale." He walked to the pedestal where Rexel was perched. The diamond was gone. "Unfortunately, the Singreale will work as well to Thanevial's evil purpose as to our own. If the Drog lives and if he has the diamond, he will have its light to guide him all the way to the other world."

"What if?" asked Raccoman.

"What if?" echoed Velissa.

"But surely Thanevial is dead!" declared the king. "And surely we will find the lost diamond!"

"Yes, but, what if?" asked Raccoman again.

There are errors that bludgeon perfection.
There are doubts that blemish our peace.
There are demons who court insurrection,
And devil's whom angels must tease.

CHAPTER XIII

Smeade

𝒯HERE WAS LITTLE surprise when Raenna and Hallidan at last announced their coming marriage. The siege had been over for three months, and Hallidan and several of the other knights had filled the forming pits with liquid glass. Some of the knights, in the wake of a permanent peace after a thousand years of war, turned to farming. The Star Riders had cut their nightly flights in number as well as in length.

From week to week, there were tales of Drogs who survived the siege. Each report was checked, and the isolated Changelings were found and destroyed. But three months after the siege, the children were allowed to play in the eastern fields outside the citadel, and the king believed that the day was not too far distant when the gates of Rensgaard could be left open during the night.

The glass-workers had decided to build a towering crystal fountain at the southern end of the citadel plaza. It would be a hot tower of white light whose inner structure would gleam with imprisoned fire-glass, but the water that filled it would flow from the main aqueduct that came from the upper snows of Mt. Calz. The fountain would commemorate the city's victory over the forces of Thanevial and would take nearly a year to build. It was to be finished by the next Festival of Light.

Raccoman and Velissa went every day to walk the eastern fields. They talked almost daily now of home. Home for them was that "other continent," where Parsky now reigned unchallenged. At least, they imagined that to be the case. Raccoman still wore his fire-glass sword in case they should happen upon a Drog—or in case one should happen upon them.

"There's a certain intrigue in war," admitted Velissa as they lay one early afternoon in the red grass that bordered the eastern fields. She looked into the blue sky and spoke gently. Her words floated on the careless day to Raccoman who chewed a tender stalk of grass and answered her with a stem dangling from between his teeth.

"It's odd that what we fear the most
Is that which sets us free—
We killed the Drogs by horde and host,

Experienced triumph and yet,
When you kill a fiend and slay a ghoul,
What's left?
Your world is bored, without intrigue.
You've lost the mystery.
And those who fought are all forgot,
Tamed Titans drinking tea
Sit cursing their dull luck and lot
And boring liberty."

Philosophically, Velissa understood. When the demons are all gone, so is the mystery.

"How long can the knights go on contentedly with so much tea? For a thousand years now, they have had an enemy. As long as they have lived, they have had to fight to live. Now their enemy is gone, and they have taken to farming and building memorials."

They both lay quietly in the sun for a moment. Then Raccoman rolled over and wrapped his arms around Velissa. He kissed her.

"How different were we? Remember
We sang on the ridges while Collinvar played.
Our constant obsession
Was waiting for wind and dreaming of flight."

Velissa kissed back. How right he was. When their own lives had been in great danger, Raccoman and Velissa had worked without taking time to doubt themselves. They had loved more intensely then and lived more intensely. But now that the war was over and the Drogs were dead, they looked upon the snows of the northern continent with an appreciation that neither of them had ever gained in the southern land.

"Oh, Raccoman, I want to walk in the snow again.
To kick the white, powdery frost,
And fly on the shadows of Quarrystone glen,
To surf the wild joys we have lost."

Velissa had picked up her husband's affected rhyming. She had been answering his rhymes so long now that she rarely noticed that she had acquired the habit. She was homesick for a land that Raccoman also desired. He looked far across the field and thought first of Rensland and then again of the other continent. He was homesick, too. In his mind, he kicked the white snow with his yellow boots and cuddled congrels in his arms. When he closed his eyes tight, he could see flocks of migrating grumblebeaks. He said nothing, but Velissa spoke again.

"Raccoman, I want to go home," she said simply.

"We can't go home. We'd be captured and killed.
Parsky would be merciless!"

Though his second line did not go far enough to make a rhyme, Velissa nodded.

"Still," she insisted, "there must be a way."

"There are ways as there are seasons;
What we need, my dear, are reasons."

He didn't doubt that their homesickness was a reason to go back. But it seemed to him too short a motive to enable them to face what would likely be certain death. And he did not wish to return to life under threat. His liberty might be boring, but it was liberty.

"That's the problem. Here we're free, but bored.
There we'd be endangered, but alive.
Here we are too bored to really live.
And there we'd be too endangered to survive."

Velissa considered this and fell asleep in the warm sun. She, like Raccoman, dreamed of things long ago and faraway.

She awoke before him. When she awoke she realized that a huge shadow had fallen over them in the field. She had not been so terrified since she had been a captive on the Tower Altar.

"Raccoman, wake up, it's a Drog!" she cried with a second glance.

At the horror of the word, her poetic husband staggered upward out of his sleep and drew his sword.

"Back, Drog!" he shouted, swaggering in the sun.

It was Hallidan.

"Oh, Hallidan, you frightened us terribly," admitted Velissa, feeling sheepish at her groggy accusation of the Star Rider.

Raccoman seemed disappointed that their friend was not some enemy he could cut up for excitement. It was a plain peace.

Hallidan smiled, for he understood.

"Let's go look for Drogs. Surely there must be one somewhere," lamented Raccoman.

"There are none—they are all gone," replied Hallidan. "But if I had been a Drog, I might have killed you."

"Or I might have killed you!" boasted Raccoman.

"Ughum, hunga!" mocked Hallidan, slumping and walking a few steps like one of the ugly monsters that now were all but extinct in Rensland.

Hallidan sat down with them. They talked about nothing important and were forced to admit that nothing was important anymore.

"Raccoman, do you know that in three months no one has turned up a trace of Thanevial?" said the Titan.

"He must be dead," said Raccoman.

"He must be," agreed Hallidan. "But how do we know? It's a month until my wedding. I think I'll fly tomorrow to the Caverns of Smeade and see if I can find any evidence to the contrary in the fourth tunnel. I'll take some torches and explore a bit. Would you be willing to go with me?"

Raccoman's eyes lit up. "What time?" he asked.

"Early in the morning," replied the Titan.

The two agreed. The morrow held some little prospect of excitement.

"If there's only one Drog, I get him," said the bored knight.

"Not if I get to him first," said the bored Graygill.

In the afternoon, Velissa went to the Paradise Falcon, which was still sitting in gleaming yellow on the west side of the central plaza. It had been a project of hers over the last few weeks to keep it clean and to repair the seats that had cracked in the hot, southern sun. She had made new seat straps by carefully straightening and braiding tiny strands of dembret fibers, which she had discovered were much stronger than the candolet fibers Raccoman had used for the original straps.

And she had discovered a kind of cleaning oil that the Titan women used on their primitive furniture and glass implements. This Velissa had applied, with painstaking care every day, to every square inch of the sail-plane. It gleamed, a thing of rare beauty in the afternoon sun, and she was proud of it. She wondered if she would ever fly in it again. Hallidan had been the last to sit in her seat on the day that Raccoman and he had rescued the glider from the jungle where it had been snared in the trees.

There was little point in keeping the Falcon quite so well polished except that this activity filled Velissa's afternoon hours and helped her to get through each day. She was very much afraid that Ren would demand that it be taken from the plaza. Though she knew it would be safe outside the city, she couldn't bear to think of herself inside the walls while the wonderful sail-plane sat outside.

She was polishing it one afternoon, when she was summoned to the castle facade by Ren. She greeted Izonden and was surprised to see how much the infant Garrod had grown in three months.

"You were faithful in preserving Singreale," said Ren when they were seated. "Because you brought it here—because of the Ally—Rensgaard is saved."

They all wondered about the loss of the diamond. They wondered, but said nothing.

"You are homesick for the land of the Graygills?" asked Ren. His statement and his question did not seem to fit together. Velissa nodded and waited.

"Are you a Moonrhyme?" asked the king. It was another question that seemed disconnected from what he had said before.

"No," replied Velissa, "I am not a Moonrhyme." She thought of telling him about her Graygill ancestry and as much as she knew of her father and grandfather, but decided to answer the king without elaboration.

"I cannot believe it is fair for the Moonrhymes to suffer Parsky's domination while we enjoy the freedom of our own land," he said. Velissa wanted to tell the king that she didn't find her own irresponsible freedom all that enjoyable, but she held her tongue and the king went on.

"I am thinking of sending the Star Riders to see how they fare and if anything can be done to assist the Moonrhymes."

"I hope the widows of Canby made it across the snowy ledges to a Moonrhyme sanctuary," said Velissa, casually interrupting the king. Ren could not be distracted by her concern for the widows. He continued.

"I owe the Moonrhymes much," he said. "If Parsky has managed to enter their cliff dwellings, they might be faring very badly." Then he abruptly changed the subject. "I have seen you working on the sail-plane almost every day."

"I am homesick, my lord," said Velissa.

"If the land were free . . ." the king began. But he did not have time to finish the question for Velissa interrupted.

"Oh, if only the land were free."

Raccoman and Hallidan entered the Caverns of Smeade and turned slightly to the right in the opening vault from which split a great many tunnels. The Titan and the Graygill counted the fourth one from the vault entrance and started toward the passageway. They lit a torch and continued on into the cave. They walked for nearly two hours until they had left any hint of natural light far behind them.

After a while longer, they came to a section of the tunnel where the floor was covered with several inches of light sand. The sand made walking difficult, and Raccoman, being the shorter of the pair, was the first to complain.

"I hope we come back to a stone floor before long," he said. He was looking down and kicking at the loose floor when suddenly he stopped, fell to his knees, and called for a light. The knight knelt down beside him, and the amber flickering of the torch they carried lit up both their faces with an orange glow.

"What do you make of this?" asked the Graygill, blinking into the orange light and studying the knight's face while Hallidan surveyed the floor.

It was obvious that the floor had been crossed by a large cart or sled, for the sand floor was deeply grooved. And there were numerous, shapeless depressions in the sand as might have been made by large people walking along.

"Do you think this groove was cut into the sand recently?" asked the Graygill.

"Who's to say?" replied Hallidan.

This cave has been here for years—centuries, even thousands of years. The evidences of this drayage sled could have been left before Rensgaard was built."

"And could it have been a cart drawn by fleeing Drogs?"

"Perhaps, perhaps," agreed the knight.

They both rose to proceed on down the tunnel. They had not gone far when the knight stopped and held his torch close to the wall of the cave.

In the Moonrhyme characters was written a single word, "Garrod."

"So this is, indeed, the very tunnel that my father used almost a thousand years ago," Raccoman said.

Raccoman thought about his father and about the year it had taken him to travel through the dark tube. For a year, he had never seen the sun. For a year, he had lived in darkness and walked. It was likely there was water in the cave at places, and he had carried some preserved foods with him. "Still, it is a marvel that he survived the trip at all," he thought.

When they had walked another hour, they began to catch traces of an odor. The further they walked, the more prominent the odor became. Both of them had known enough of the stench of the battlefield to know that the smell was that of a dead Drog who flavored the air with his own heavy repugnance. When they came at last to a pile of bones, they knew that it was a Drog—the first to have been eaten on the long pilgrimage his companions were undergoing.

"How long dead?" Raccoman summed up his question in three words.

"Three months!" Hallidan answered.

"Then our worst suspicions are confirmed!" Raccoman cried, wincing at the thought.

"In nine months, Thanevial and the last of his renegade Drogs will arrive at the Cavern of the Moonrhymes."

"By Singreale!" exclaimed Raccoman. "These who have for years feared terrors beyond their high-cliff caves will face a thousand enemies from within their own system of caves. They may feel secure from Parsky and never know that they are about to be set upon by the cannibal monsters from another world."

"Oh, Hallidan,
It's not enough that Ren is free
While noble Moonrhymes die
Beyond the separating sea."

Hallidan said nothing. They both knew they had gone far enough and must return with the sad report that the Drogs, somewhere in the heart of the earth, were making their way toward an imperiled people. The Moonrhymes, who had given Garrod to Rensland, must now face an army of Changelings. The foe was not beyond their ancient cliffs, but deep within the heart of their own tunneled security.

Raccoman knew he must return to his own continent. The only thing that could prevent the massacre of the Moonrhymes would be his own timely word.

"I'm going home," said Raccoman with determination.

"Before the wedding?" asked Hallidan.

"I'm afraid I must," Raccoman replied. "If I leave now, I can take advantage of the mountain breezes to push the glider, and I might be lucky enough to ride the high winds to reach the other continent."

Neither of them said anything more. They walked back in silence. It was late when they reached the grand vault and stepped into the afternoon sunshine. They mounted their condorgs and flew home with what they knew would be an unwelcome word. Thanevial was not dead! The Moonrhymes would have to reckon with an enemy they could not imagine.

Hallidan and Raenna decided to be married immediately and to fly north with the Graygills. The Star Riders' wedding ceremony was always an inspiring event for both the other knights and the farmers. The ceremony was held at night. Fiery light issued from the flying condorgs, and the knights settled into a vanguard formation and raised their glowing fire-glass swords. Hallidan and Raenna flew side by side to the castle facade. Their huge beasts landed together and folded their wings almost at the same time.

Hallidan dismounted first. He was dressed handsomely in glistening gold. His chest was naked, crossed only by silver straps. Following tradition, his bride was dressed in silver cloth that glistened in the amber torchlight. As the couple approached the balustrade, a double column of knights created an archway of fire-glass with their swords, and through this the Titan and his bride passed. Raenna's hair fell free upon her shoulders, and her face glowed with happiness.

The Miserians formed long, outer, triple columns that stretched all the way around the ceremonial area. The king and queen came out upon the balustrade and then descended by the stone side-stairs to stand before the couple.

"Is there honor in your promise?" asked the king.

"There is honor in our promise," replied the tall groom and his beautiful bride.

"Will you defend Rensgaard as one?" asked Ren.

"Forever!" they replied.

"What is the great ground of our lives?" asked the king.

"The desire of Ren."

"Are you one?"

They embraced. Then, according to custom, Raenna faced Hallidan and kneeled. He took his fire-glass sword and extended the hilt to her. She carefully received the glowing weapon. From her kneeling position, she lifted his blade skyward and said, "My life for the defense of Hallidan." Then she stood and he kneeled. With equal care, he took the hilt of his sword and cried upward into the stars,

"My life for the defense of Raenna." He stood, sheathed the fire-glass, and they faced each other once more.

In tender symbolism, he took his cape from his own shoulders and laid it across hers. He walked around her three times. His first circle symbolized that his past was gone. His second circle said that now was the moment for his love. His third circle signified that the future held his unending promise of love.

She did the same. And when she had finished, he took his cloak back and refastened it to the silver straps across his chest. Then she drew her own sword and held it vertically before her. Both raised their searing, glowing blades and crossed themselves in a fiery X, and repeated the words, "For your defense forever! By the desire of Ren, we are one."

They sheathed their swords and embraced.

After the ceremony, Raccoman danced and sang ballads. There was much food and many warm exchanges. It was Hallidan's wedding, but toward midnight he asked that the great palace gong be struck, and he called the musicians and the festivities to an end.

"Tomorrow the son of Garrod leaves," said Hallidan.

"No!" protested the guests. "Never!"

Velissa was standing near Hallidan, and she spoke when the cries subsided.

"Raccoman and I are going home," she said. "Home to Canby. As you love this land, so we love our own. We love you, and you have cared for us and protected us." Velissa was becoming emotional. "I cannot—I cannot tell you —how I love you. But I was born in a beautiful land, a land I cannot push from my memory. It calls to me, and I must go."

The strong tie she felt with these beautiful people who listened made it all the more difficult for her to go on. Tears choked her words to silence. Raccoman took over.

"The enemy you feared for a thousand years is now deep within the heart of the earth and traveling to the land of my fathers. They are a handsome people, but they are small and no match for the cruelty of Thanevial and the Drogs he even now directs on a mission of death."

"We must get to the Grand Caverns of the Moonrhymes before Thanevial does, or our people will be destroyed. We must go now for the winds are favorable, and Raenna and Hallidan will fly with us."

"Not just you and Raenna and Hallidan," said the king, "but all our hope for the force of truth on Estermann will go with you."

Izonden looked at Raenna with deep affection. The Miserian had saved her child in a splendid act of courage against Drograaden. A tear crossed the queen's cheek when she thought of Raenna's departure.

"To the Moonrhymes and the Graygills, our friends beyond the sea!" cried Izonden, though her throat was tight with emotion.

"To the Titans," called Velissa and Raccoman. "For all the love that they have given us!"

"To Singreale, and the hope of life and peace in the other land!" exclaimed Ren.

There was a moment of quiet, and Velissa felt impelled to sing the song she had long ago heard Orkkan singing with the widows of Canby. In rapt attention, the entire wedding crowd listened, and Velissa sang, quickly joined by Raccoman:

"Once more we go to the land of Garrod Dakktare,
Where a people of peace breathe the stifling air
Of a war that claims them and will destroy
The land, the Land, The Land.
We will sing at the base of the ginjon tree,
For Canby's fields are the fields of the free,
And beasts and men are timeless friends
In the ageless land of Estermann."

"Home!" declared Velissa, and as she leaned against Raccoman and kissed him, she was bright with hope.

Raenna and Hallidan mounted their condorgs and lifted the Paradise Falcon skyward. The Graygills exulted! The knights marveled at how light the large sail-plane was, and Hallidan and Raenna had no trouble maneuvering the craft. They gained speed as the glider began to fin even the still air and right itself into an increasingly level position. At last Hallidan and Raenna were drawing it at a rapid pace. They turned south and towed the craft into faster and faster flight. The glider was trailing straight and level behind them as they circled back over the castle grounds.

Below them, they could hear the knights singing the anthem of Ren. Hallidan and Raenna turned upward. They flew higher and higher into the sky until they seemed little more than a dark blip on the blue sky.

Soon they had traveled so high that Raccoman and Velissa in the glider began to feel the tug of the upper breezes. Hallidan and Raenna flew on. The breeze became stronger. They had reached the upper zephyrs. Raccoman knew that the wind would throw them even higher.

Hallidan could see the condorgs were tiring, but he did not want to cut the towline until they had reached the highest altitude that the beasts could endure. The Graygills had worn the same yellow and blue clothes in which they had made their first crossing. They knew that they would have to be dressed warmly for their nights in the lofty skies. They knew also that the flight would grow colder as they advanced across the ocean that was so far below them now they could not see it.

The condorgs could scarcely gain wing leaverage in the thin, upper gales. They were exhausted, and Raccoman felt that the glider would need no more help to make the return trip. He pulled the little cord he had tied around the rudder control rod, and the cord cut the front assembly free. Hallidan and Raenna felt relieved.

No sooner was the paradise Falcon detached from the condorgs than it slowed some and rose skyward. It was on its own. The glider dropped behind the condorgs, but continued to gain altitude. Raccoman realized that Raenna and Hallidan would have trouble keeping their altitude, while he and Velissa would have difficulty maintaining the speed of the free-flying condorgs.

Still, it was exhilarating!

In the late afternoon, they sighted a dark spot in the sky above them. The spot gradually came toward them.

"Rexel!" cried Velissa.

The falcon soared and glided to the surface of the ship, then lit on the rudder rod between the Graygills, pushing it down a little as he landed, causing the direction of the ship to deflect some.

"If you don't mind," said the Graygill, clearing his throat.

"If you'll get off this upright shaft,
I'd really rather steer my craft."

He and Velissa laughed. But Rexel had already flown higher than he was used to and he was consequently out of breath.

"I'm going with you," said Rexel.

Raccoman and Velissa were both glad.

"How can we lose?
This is wonderful news!"

said the metal-worker.

"I have some more news," Velissa said. Raccoman turned to her and waited.

"I am with child," she told him quietly.

"With child! Ha hoo!" he cried.

The moment was worth a little loss of altitude. Raccoman pushed the stabilizer bar, and the ship nosed downward at such speed that Velissa gasped. Then he drew the bar back again, and the fast-moving sail-plane shot skyward and flew a loop that spilled the bewildered falcon into space. Rexel did not think Raccoman's antics were very funny at all for it took him quite a while to get enough of the thin air beneath his broad wings to catch up to the glider again. Hallidan and Raenna thought the ship had malfunctioned, and they hurried toward the ship as it returned to a more level flight. They arrived to hear Velissa complaining,

> *"Please don't throw me against the trace.*
> *I sicken upside down in space."*

But the Graygill only laughed once again so loudly that Hallidan and Raenna could guess at the secret that had sent the Paradise Falcon into an excited, looping flight.

> *"Hah hoo! Hah hoo! At one thousand years,*
> *I'm a daddy at last.*
> *Velissa the queen of the Estermann sky*
> *Shall give to Dakktare a child.*
> *Oh, may he be handsome, emboldened to fly,*
> *As clever and wise and as brilliant as I."*

But no one believed that it could happen twice in the same universe.